AMERICAN MAGIC

— A THRILLER —

ZACH FEHST

EMILY BESTLER BOOKS

ATRIA

New York   London   Toronto   Sydney   New Delhi

An Imprint of Simon & Schuster, Inc.
1230 Avenue of the Americas
New York, NY 10020

First Emily Bestler Books/Atria Books hardcover edition August 2019

EMILY BESTLER BOOKS / ATRIA BOOKS and colophon are trademarks of Simon & Schuster, Inc.

For information about special discounts for bulk purchases, please contact Simon & Schuster Special Sales at 1-866-506-1949 or business@simonandschuster.com.

The Simon & Schuster Speakers Bureau can bring authors to your live event. For more information or to book an event, contact the Simon & Schuster Speakers Bureau at 1-866-248-3049 or visit our website at www.simonspeakers.com.

Design by Jill Putorti

Manufactured in the United States of America

10 9 8 7 6 5 4 3 2 1

Library of Congress Cataloging-in-Publication Data
Names: Fehst, Zach, author.
Title: American magic : a thriller / by Zach Fehst.
Description: First Emily Bestler Books/Atria Books hardcover edition. | New York : Emily Bestler Books/Atria, 2019.
Identifiers: LCCN 2018055031 (print) | LCCN 2018059183 (ebook) | ISBN 9781501168628 (Ebook) | ISBN 9781501168611 (hardcover) | ISBN 9781982121105 (trade pbk.)
Subjects: | GSAFD: Occult fiction. Classification: LCC PS3606.E3643 (ebook) | LCC PS3606.E3643 A68 2019 (print) | DDC 813/.6—dc23
LC record available at https://lccn.loc.gov/2018055031.

ISBN 978-1-5011-6861-1
ISBN 978-1-5011-6862-8 (ebook)

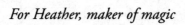

For Heather, maker of magic

PROLOGUE

The evening's two Thai coffees, thick with condensed milk and vaporous with rum, swirled around in the soon-to-be-traitor's stomach. He pushed himself out of the hotel lobby bar and into the neon night, unsure if the jitters he felt were from the industrial-strength caffeine, the syrupy sweetener, or because of the magnitude of what he was about to do.

In any case, the rum helped. The alcohol buzz lent the Bangkok street scene a kind of gentle unreality, and the traitor was carried along among the sights, sounds, and smells as though swept up in some baffling parade.

The man patted his front pocket again, for maybe the fiftieth time since he'd dressed that morning. If he lost the thumb drive, the whole trip would prove a waste. Worse than a waste; a man would have died for no reason. Not that anyone like him was worth shedding a tear for.

As the traitor dodged the handful of people queued up for a street vendor who was hawking something sweet smelling and fried, he realized that the agitation in his stomach wasn't from caffeine, or anxiety, or uncertainty at all. The electric feeling warming his belly was excitement, pure and simple.

This was the night, now was the time, that he'd spent years dreaming about and months planning for. No one suspected him. There was no one to stop him. The only person who'd known his intentions was no longer in a position to tell anyone—except perhaps the demons of hell.

The traitor had been told that he could no longer be trusted with certain great and lofty secrets—so he'd prove his detractors right. He'd betray every goddamned one of them. He'd tear their world down.

What was about to happen, what *he* was about to do, would alter the globe so completely that in a matter of days the planet would be rendered unrecognizable. Governments would topple, that much was assured; part of the fun would be seeing which ones, and how. Categories like rich and poor would quickly become meaningless. The existing structures of power would be dismantled completely.

People claimed to want freedom? The traitor would give them as much freedom as they could take. And then some.

The man reached the next block and crossed the street, narrowly avoiding being run down by a motorbike that zipped by, inches from his feet, leaving him coughing in a cloud of exhaust.

He passed by the internet café that he'd identified earlier, then slipped around the corner into the dingy alley behind it.

No one was watching, so no one saw him disappear. Even if they had, they'd have blinked it away as a momentary trick of the eye. People saw—or, more often, didn't see—only what they wanted to. The traitor knew that better than anyone.

He slipped into the café's rear door using the key he'd lifted easily from the boy that minded the shop during the day. He sat down at a terminal near the back and booted up the computer. He pulled the thumb drive from his pocket and slid it into the USB port.

His face broke out in a broad smile. He was about to change everything.

1

Ben Zolstra gripped the hammer in his fist, then drove the nail home in two hard, sure swings. He repeated the action at the other end of the board, stopping to wipe the sweat from his eyes before lining up the next plank.

The thunderstorm had been bad. Not the worst Ben had ever dealt with, but severe. When he'd made his survey that morning, the lawn and the fields that made up the modest few acres of the Zolstra family farm were littered with fallen branches, and the long dirt driveway that led out to the main road was clogged with broken-off limbs from the surrounding woods. Ben had been busy with the chain saw since dawn.

As the hot day wore on and he'd cleared the road, Ben moved to the barn, which had taken some damage. Could have been worse. The toppling yellow birch had only clipped the corner of the roof. A direct hit might have meant rebuilding the thing from the ground up, a prospect Ben didn't exactly relish. Though he certainly had the time.

Ben steadied himself on the ladder again, then reached up and held the next board into place across the hole in the barn. He hefted the hammer, ready to swing, but something stayed his hand. Ben squinted in the sunshine at a fine haze of dust that had begun rising over the woods. A car was coming up the driveway. No, not one. From the size of the cloud, it had to be at least two. Likely big vehicles.

The squeak of an opening screen door drew Ben's attention to the small clapboard house that stood a hundred feet off from the barn. Mary Zolstra stepped out onto the covered porch.

"Expecting company?" she asked.

"I was going to ask you the same thing," Ben called, descending the ladder and walking toward the little house.

Some dormant part of Ben thought first of defense. The 7 mm Remington Mag hunting rifle in the hall closet. Or the pistol stashed in the duffel under his bed. His mother wasn't a half-bad shot with her police-issue .40 caliber, either.

He pushed the thought from his mind. This was Vermont, not the Middle East. He wasn't liable to be the target of a raid here.

Ben mounted the steps, and he and his mother watched from the porch as two large black SUVs burst from the shadow of the woods and angled toward the house. No sooner had they jolted to a halt than two of the farm dogs emerged from behind the house and began circling and barking at the vehicles.

The back door of one of the SUVs opened, and a man in a black suit stepped out. He immediately jumped back in surprise as one of the dogs snapped his jaws at him.

"Christ," the man said, "you wanna call off your guard dogs?"

Ben leaned forward onto the porch's wooden railing. "I'm not sure yet."

The guy was a few years younger than Ben, late twenties probably. Asian. The German shepherd snarled at him again.

"Please."

"Wait a sec," Ben said, as though putting it together, "you're with the Agency, aren't you?"

"Yes, I am." The man looked relieved. "Thank you."

"Hmm." Ben and his mother shared a look. "*Get him, Shadow!*" Ben shouted to the dog.

The young agent screamed as the dog reared up on his hind legs . . . then rested his large paws on the man's shoulders and started licking his face. Ben and Mary burst out laughing.

The rear door of the other SUV shot open, and a white man in a dark suit leaped out.

"Oh, for God's sake," the older man said, "quit fucking with Agent Wei, will you?"

Ben almost did a double take. He recognized the man at once, but he could hardly believe Jeffrey Novak would show up unannounced at his home.

"Zolstra, you're really off the grid," Novak said.

The man had enough gray in his hair to look distinguished, but he was still in fighting trim, and his strides were long and fast as he made his way up to the porch. Wei managed to untangle himself from Shadow's affections and trailed somewhat sheepishly behind the older man.

"That's kind of the point," Ben answered.

Novak and Wei reached the bottom of the steps leading up to the house. Novak made a show of looking around at the lawn, the fields, the barn.

"What are you, playing farmer now?" he asked.

"I'm not playing at anything."

Ben looked at his former boss and took a moment to assess the situation.

Jeffrey Novak was standing in front of him. The deputy director of the Central Intelligence Agency. In person. In a place that was, if not exactly the *middle* of nowhere, then close enough. Something big had happened. And if they were here for Ben's help, then it had to be real fucking big.

"Where are my manners? This is your mother, Mary, isn't it?" Novak said, looking up at her and smiling. "I understand you retired last year. What a career. Was it thirty-four years on the force?"

"Thirty-six," Mary said, "and I don't find you charming, so don't bullshit me."

Novak eyed Ben. "I see where you get your sparkling personality."

Now it was Ben's turn to smile. "So what's with the social call?"

"We need to bring you in on something."

"What?"

Novak held his arms out. "Do I have to stand out here all day, or can we go in and have a seat?"

Ben said nothing. Mary lowered herself into a rocking chair and settled in. Novak sighed as Wei shifted uncomfortably next to him.

"Look," Novak began, "we got a situation."

"There's always a situation."

"Not like this. This is, uh . . ." Novak shook his head, at a loss. "This is new."

Ben swatted at a fly that buzzed around his face. "Well I don't know about anything new. I've been off the board for, what, two years?"

He feigned indifference, but Ben knew exactly how long it had been. He'd thought about the Agency every day of the seventeen months since he gave his notice to Director Harris. Chopping wood, pulling weeds, changing the spark plugs on the tractor—nothing he did could make him forget what he'd lost when he turned his back on the CIA. But he sure as hell wasn't about to let Novak know that.

"Who asked for me?" Ben said. "I know it wasn't Harris."

After the way Ben had left, he'd half-wondered if the director had a mind to take him out. Maybe that was just the paranoia of spending ten years as a field agent tracking some of the nastiest pieces of shit the world had to offer, but there it was.

"It was my idea to come get you," Novak said. "The director only approved it because I insisted."

That was a surprise. On their past operations together, Novak had, at best, only tolerated Ben.

"Listen," Novak said, "everything unraveled so fast after you returned from Belarus that I . . . I never got to say how truly sorry I was. About your brother." He looked over to Mary. "About your son. He was a fine Marine. He served honorably in Afghanistan."

Ben twisted John's Annapolis class ring, which hadn't left his pinky since it had come into his possession two years before.

Mary nodded. "I thank you for that."

But Ben felt his blood rise. "What does the Agency know about honor?"

"Benjamin." Mary's hand clasped around Ben's wrist. "Let the men come inside."

Ben gave a reluctant nod. He turned and stalked into the house, the screen door slamming in its frame behind him.

"Well?" he called to the agents from inside.

Novak and Wei mounted the steps and entered the house, following Ben to a rough-hewn wooden table pushed against the wall of the tiny kitchen. They sat down. Ben stared at Novak across the table.

"You're trying to bring me in for this . . . whatever this is," Ben said. "Why?"

"You're the best," Novak said simply, "and we need the best right now."

Ben might have been flattered if he hadn't known from experience that the word of a CIA agent wasn't worth much.

"So are you going to tell me what this is about or do I need to read your mind?"

"It's better you see it for yourself," Novak said. "We're here to bring you to a briefing, if you agree to come with us."

"Where?"

"Washington."

Ben had always loathed the capital's swampy air and reek of hypocrisy.

"How about we save the trouble and you just tell me now?"

Novak smirked, but his eyes were tired. "You wouldn't believe me if I did."

"So what makes you think I'm going to pick up and leave with you, if you won't tell me why?"

Wei scowled at him, and Novak's placid facade finally cracked in frustration.

"How about the fact that I dragged my ass all the way out here, *personally*, to come find you? When I tell you we need you, I mean it, dammit. I want you to take the lead on this, if you're willing."

Ben leaned back in his chair and folded his hands behind his head. He was going with them. He couldn't pretend he hadn't known it from the second they'd rolled up.

"If I come and see what this is about, it's not going to be like before," Ben said. "If I don't like what I hear or see, I walk."

"That's fair."

"And if I'm the lead on something, it means I'm the lead. Agreed?"

Novak nodded his head, tracking with Ben. "You'll be free of the usual red tape."

"What about Harris?"

"You let me worry about him. I'll keep him out of your way, you have my word."

His word again. Ben met Novak's eyes across the table, and the man didn't flinch.

"Fine," Ben said. He was only agreeing to a meeting, after all. "But don't tell me we're driving there."

"The chopper's not far. I didn't want to land on your front lawn." Novak stood. "We should move, if we're going to make it. You still keep a go bag?"

Ben nodded once.

Novak grinned. "Figured as much."

"Old habits," Ben allowed.

His duffel was packed and ready, gathering dust under his bed. It contained what it always had: a few changes of clothes, three passports in different names, roughly two thousand in cash, a pair of burner cell phones, a tactical folding knife, and a loaded SIG Sauer P229 with two extra magazines.

"Grab it," Novak said, turning toward the door. "We'll meet you in the car."

Novak motioned to his junior associate and left the room. Wei narrowed his eyes at Ben before following his boss.

Two minutes later, Ben was shouldering his duffel bag as he pushed through the screen door out onto the front porch.

Mary rose from her seat. "Come back in one piece, you hear me?"

They embraced. Ben descended the steps and walked to the open door of one of the waiting SUVs. He tossed the duffel inside. With one hand on the door, he took a last look around him at the little patch of Eden where he'd been raised, and where he'd spent the last year and a half. Whatever was waiting for him down in Washington, was it worth leaving all this again and jumping back into the fray?

There was only one way to find out.

Ben got into the vehicle and closed the door. As the SUVs barreled down the long rutted driveway toward the main road, he didn't look back.

2

The sudden lift of a helicopter, the swooping pitch and yaw, the chop of the blades felt as a fluttering in the solar plexus—Ben was in his element again. The big difference was the terrain below. It wasn't the familiar sun-bleached clay of Helmand Province, or the yellow rubble of Ramadi. Instead, Ben stared down at the reflection of the late morning sun bouncing off the dark ribbon of the Potomac a thousand feet beneath him.

On the seat opposite Ben, facing him, sat Novak and Wei. Novak addressed Ben through the noise-dampening headset he wore.

"Whatever you're thinking this is about," Novak said, "I can tell you you're wrong."

Ben shrugged, but the question ate at him: What was important enough to track him down at his mom's place in Vermont? And why did it have to be *him,* specifically? Sure, Ben had distinguished himself in the field, but he'd also proven to be a thorn in the side of every higher-up who'd ever had the displeasure of trying to manage him. Novak included.

"Whatever it is," Ben said, "I'm confident the CIA will find a way to make it worse."

Wei glared at Ben. "You know, everything I've heard out of you this morning tells me that the director is right. A man like you doesn't belong here."

Ben felt the warm flush of adrenaline. "A man like me?"

"A traitor to the Agency," Wei said.

Novak shot his underling a look. "That's enough."

Ben leaned toward Wei. "Now would be a good time to stop talking about topics you don't know anything about," he said. "I'd hate to get blood on that nice white shirt of yours."

Ben wasn't bluffing; he had nothing to lose. Wei held Ben's gaze for a few seconds, then snorted and looked away. Ben sat back in his seat.

They began to lose altitude. The helicopter made a broad bank to the right, revealing the long, clogged avenues of Washington, D.C. Their destination came into view: the White House.

During his decade with the Agency, Ben had never set foot in the building where his orders ultimately issued from. Now, descending on the place from above, it appeared almost comically small on its patch of grass, its flagpoles like toothpicks. Ben bristled at the thought that a single resident of one little house controlled so many lives across vast swaths of the world. Such a concentration of power, Ben had learned the hard way, was how monsters were made.

No one said another word as they descended to the ground, no comment about how exceptional it was to have permission to land here. The skids of the helicopter touched down on the grass, and a huddle of Secret Service members, suited and wearing their telltale coiled earpieces, rushed to slide open the side hatch. The humid late-July heat poured into the cool cabin.

Ben leaped out of the chopper. Above him, the rotors cut the air with deafening thunder. Ben smiled to himself as he watched Wei jog from the chopper in a rookie crouch, though the Huey's blades were nearly fifteen feet off the ground. As Ben and Novak walked away from the aircraft, Ben took in his surroundings. On the ground, it was hard not to be at least a little impressed to be standing on the famous

South Lawn, steps from the Rose Garden and the White House's southern colonnade.

Two high-ranking officers stood a ways off from the landing pad, a black woman and a white man, both in green and khaki, festooned with pins, ribbons, and medals. Powerful Marines with chest candy galore.

The officers exchanged nods with Novak. The woman gave Ben a grim smile and held out her hand. She called out over the whir of the chopper blades, "Mr. Zolstra, I'm Lieutenant General Moore."

They shook hands as Ben wished her a good morning.

Ben didn't need an introduction to the distinguished-looking man at Moore's side. He recognized the bushy, gray eyebrows, with the gray mustache to match. The reputation of this old-guard walrus of a man preceded him.

"General Walsh," Ben said, extending a hand. "I've been an admirer of your approach with the Kurds. That's the kind of smart power the military needs more of."

The general trained his gaze on Ben, looked him up and down, turned to Moore, and said, "Let's hope this wasn't a mistake."

Walsh pivoted on his heels and started walking up the gravel path that led to the West Wing. Moore motioned for Ben to follow her, then did the same. Wei, too junior for the meeting, remained outside.

Ben followed as the uniformed brass led him past the outside of the Oval Office—curtains drawn tight—and through a side door. They moved down a series of identical beige corridors. Depictions of the building from movies and TV had prepared Ben for halls crowded with young interns, their eyes sunken with exhaustion, sleeves rolled up, hands filled with manila folders. But the place was eerily empty.

They rounded a final corner and came to a door flanked by two stone-faced Secret Service agents. The agents stepped aside, and Ben followed his welcome party into a dark and windowless room. As his eyes adjusted, he saw that a long table took up most of the space.

Around it sat a sober array of men and women in dress uniforms and dark suits, all of whom turned to see who had arrived. Ben thought what an alien figure he must make to be entering this place in his beat-up boots, grass-stained jeans, and loose, untucked shirt.

Three hours ago I was patching up a barn, Ben thought, *and now I'm in the White House Situation Room, surrounded by some of the most powerful decision makers in the country.* It wasn't what he'd bargained for over his morning coffee.

"Take a seat, Mr. Zolstra," said a man in a charcoal suit, with a thin comb-over.

Novak had already sat, and Ben lowered himself into the leather chair next to him, scanning the faces of the assembled group for some small clue as to what the hell he was doing there. What he saw on the expressions of those around him was not encouraging. These people, for all their rank and their toughness, looked terrified.

The same man cleared his throat and spoke again. "Now that we're all present . . . welcome, ladies and gentlemen." His voice was hoarse, tired. "I think there are enough of us from different departments that quick introductions might be in order. I'm George Torozian, the president's national security advisor."

He turned to the white-haired woman in the burgundy blazer next to him. "Meg Byrne," she said with a curt nod. "Director of the National Security Agency."

As the other introductions were made, the full magnitude of Ben's position sank in. He was in the fucking White House, and the country's entire security apparatus was shitting its pants. What in God's name was going on? For the first time, Ben felt the cold finger of fear run up his spine. Not debilitating fear, but the kind that sharpens the senses and prompts a person into action; the kind that demands to be conquered.

A man who had been lingering in the shadows stepped toward the table and into the light. His eyes were black pinpricks behind his wire frame glasses. He had the satisfied look of an owl that had just devoured its evening rodent.

"Bill Harris, director of the Central Intelligence Agency," he said in a tone that told Ben there would be no further introductions.

Ben's former boss paused to glower at him, his disapproval at Ben's presence as clear as if he'd flipped him the bird.

"You're all here to help us with a very unique problem," Harris continued. "Because there are a lot of rumors flying around, and everyone's department is working with different information, the president has asked me to bring everyone up to speed and get us all on the same page. So let's get right to it."

Harris nodded to Torozian, who used a remote to turn on a digital projector. A huge screen hanging on the northern wall blinked to life.

"Last night at 2100 hours," Harris said, "the video you're about to see was uploaded to a dark web forum called Baphomet. The video, please, Mr. Torozian."

The video began to play.

It opened with a black woman in her late twenties on the stoop of a building, sitting slightly apart from a group of female friends.

"Come on, Mack," one of the friends encouraged her. "Do the thing you told me about, the thing you found on Torsquare."

The woman, Mack, waved them off.

"Shit," one of the others said, "she probably can't even do it again."

The others reacted in a chorus, prodding Mack. She took the bait, standing up and tugging her sweatshirt's hood over her loose braids. She pulled a scrap of paper from the pocket of her jeans and began to read from it.

In the grainy video, her eyes appeared to cloud over as she pronounced a series of strange, guttural sounds. The other women stood up, shouting excitedly, clutching one another's arms, jumping in place. The camera changed position, and it became clear what they were reacting to: ten feet from Mack, a small sedan had left the pavement and was slowly rising into the air. The shot zoomed out wide and pointed up and down the street. There were no cables, cranes, or tow trucks in sight. The car rose to a height of about seven or eight feet, and in the wide shot other people on the sidewalks began to stop and point, their faces pasted with expressions of stark disbelief.

Then there came the loud blast of a truck horn, and Mack's head snapped up, distracted. The car dropped, crashing to the asphalt in a cacophony of exploding glass and bursting tires. Mack and the others began to scatter.

The video ended.

The recessed lights of the Situation Room pinged on. The faces around the table were grim. Whatever the hell Ben was supposed to have seen of importance in that video, he'd definitely missed it.

"Who is she?" a man at the far end of the table asked.

"We don't know yet, but the person who uploaded the video goes by the handle FarGone," Harris said, slowly circling the long table. "Low-level DoS attacks of inconsequential corporate targets. Kid's stuff—for now. We're watching them."

"Do we know how widely the video has been shared?" asked Lieutenant General Moore, the woman who had shaken Ben's hand on the lawn.

"That is difficult to determine," answered NSA Director Byrne. "Thus far we've had success keeping it off YouTube and the larger file-sharing sites. There are other videos like this, though. We're scrubbing everything we can find, but we can't be everywhere at once. They'll get out. The only question is when. After that . . ." She shrugged.

"What language is she speaking?" Moore asked.

"Our linguists believe the words may be ancient Sumerian," Torozian said. "We're still trying to find an expert."

"Where are we on countermeasures?" asked Walsh.

Countermeasures?

"I'm sorry," Ben interjected as Harris was about to respond, "but what was that supposed to be?"

"I think you just saw what it was," Torozian croaked.

"I don't have any idea what I saw," Ben said. "Countermeasures against what, exactly?"

"The girl's ability, Mr. Zolstra," Torozian said. "What she did."

"I still don't understand. What are you telling me? That a hacker and her friends pretended to levitate a car, and that's the reason the most powerful people in the country are gathered here today?"

"No, Mr. Zolstra," Walsh said, glaring at him. "We're here because this video is not a fake."

"Do I have to be the one to say the word?" Moore cut in. "Fine. It's *magic*."

Ben snorted, incredulous. "Really? *That's* the conclusion that the best intelligence services in the world have drawn here? Not that it's a green screen and some halfway decent CGI, but magic?"

"We've subjected the video to thorough analysis," Torozian said, "and, yes, that is our conclusion."

Ben sat back in his chair, gripping the armrests in frustration. All this pseudoscientific horseshit—telekinesis, future visions, mind reading—had been studied again and again, sometimes even by the Agency. It always added up to nothing. And the simple reason for that was what every rational person already knew: magic didn't exist.

"We located the original Torsquare post that one of the women referred to," Harris went on. "It went up yesterday at 1600 hours. It was a word puzzle, an easy substitution cypher. When solved, it read 'Merlin says.' Typing that back into the text field activated a function that opened a new window and generated the words that the woman in the video was speaking. We deleted the post, but it's already reappearing on various sites on the dark web. There's something else, too. Just before the puzzle appeared, someone calling himself Merlin posted this on the same forum."

Torozian leaned over and tapped a key on a laptop. Identical screens on opposite sides of the room sprang to luminous life, showing bright green text on a deep blue background.

" 'Your world is about to change,' " Harris said, reading the text aloud. " 'Your certainties will be undone. Your corrupt hierarchies will die. You may destroy yourselves, but you may ultimately liberate yourselves. The choice is yours. Can you handle freedom?' "

Torozian spoke to the group. "As you can see, it goes on like this for a while. It's a manifesto of sorts."

A manifesto. About the existence of magic. The national security brass had really outdone themselves this time. Ben felt the urge to get up and walk out of the meeting.

But then something floated up from the recesses of his mind, an old Arthur C. Clarke quote. *Any sufficiently advanced technology,* it went, *is indistinguishable from magic.* It was true. Brandishing a smartphone in the Middle Ages would have probably gotten you burned at the stake.

Is that what they were dealing with here? Some kind of superadvanced *tech*? Ben decided to hear them out.

Harris continued. "When Merlin finally gets to the point, he mentions a series of what he calls 'protocols' that are going to be released in the coming days, to random sites on the dark web. He says each one will be different, and each will, and I quote, 'challenge everything you think you know about the world.' "

Moore chimed in with a question. "So we're thinking this . . . levitation spell, or whatever it is, is the first of these 'protocols'?"

Harris nodded. "That is our current thinking. And as to your question about countermeasures, General Walsh, we already have agents working on it."

He walked to a door at the far end of the room and rapped on it twice. It opened, and a young man entered the room, looking nervous. He stood rigid at one end of the table as Harris presented him to the group.

"This is Agent Thompson. He's been working with the protocol since we discovered it. He isn't the only one we've got on it, but he's the best so far." Harris sat down at the table and removed a pen from a pocket inside his coat. He set the heavy Montblanc in the center of the table, then turned to the young agent. "Go ahead, Thompson."

Thompson's hands, hanging at his sides, were shaking. Ben couldn't blame him for his nerves—a guy just starting out, in a room with so many people who would happily make or break his career.

Thompson opened his mouth. Out of it came the same incantation in the same alien tongue that they'd heard in the video. Novak's pen began to tremble on the dark wood table.

"*Jesus Christ*," the woman sitting beside Torozian whispered.

Thompson said the words again. This time, the pen rose about two feet off the table. It began to traverse the table's length like a slow, miniature missile. Ben watched as the pen passed in front of one wide-eyed senior advisor, director, or Joint Chief after another. Then the pen wobbled and took a nosedive back to the table.

Ben looked over at Thompson. The young agent's forehead was beaded in sweat, and the underarms of his baby-blue Oxford were dark with moisture. It was clear the demonstration had cost him a tremendous amount of concentrated effort.

For a long moment, no one spoke. Ben was as speechless as any of them. Whatever it was that had just happened, no one here could explain it. That didn't make it *magic*—but it did make it uncanny.

Harris dismissed Thompson, then eyed Ben. "I assume you finally understand now, Zolstra, why we are all gathered here this morning."

"I'm beginning to." Ben ran a hand across his stubbled chin. "You're considering this . . . ability . . . as a new kind of weapon, is that right?" Harris raised his eyebrows, signaling him to continue. "If we follow that logic, it's fair to conclude that this may pose any number of security risks, depending on how powerful the telekinetic ability is and how far it extends."

Harris stood again and resumed his pacing around the table. "We believe the ability to perform these, ah, maneuvers"—he couldn't seem to bring himself to say "magic spells"; Ben didn't blame him—"is not equally present in all people. In fact, many of our agents have not been able to utilize the protocol at all."

"What determines their level of ability?" Walsh countered. "And how much power can one person yield?"

"Quite frankly, we don't know the answer to either question. That's part of what makes the threat so troubling."

Certain scenarios were easy enough for Ben to envision. Telekinesis would be an assassin's dream, for one: every hit made to look like a freak accident—no weapons, no fingerprints. Planes might be yanked out of the sky by terrorists hiding safely on the ground. World leaders snatched in the middle of speeches and sent flying through the air into waiting getaway vehicles.

"So do we have any idea what the next protocol will be," asked Byrne, "or when it will be released?"

"All we can confirm is that we do not believe it has been released *yet*. If it has, we haven't located it. As to what it could be . . . it's impossible to say. If telekinesis is real, the next protocol could be anything."

A laugh burst from a rotund man in a navy blue pinstripe suit. "This is absolutely preposterous."

"I don't find anything amusing about this threat, Secretary Meyer," Walsh said icily, "and it troubles me that you do."

"I agree with the general," said Harris. "This may seem harmless now, but imagine the damage that could be done if terrorists get their hands on this."

"Or North Korea," a woman in a naval uniform added.

"Precisely," Harris agreed. "That cannot be allowed to happen." He stopped directly across the table from Ben, training his hard gaze on him. He appraised Ben through his wire frame glasses. "So tell me, Zolstra, what would you do if you discovered a dangerous new technology that could easily be weaponized, and you still had no sense of its scale or scope?"

"I would learn as much as I could about it, while trying like hell to contain its spread," Ben answered immediately. "Then I'd find its creator and make sure from now on he works for us, and only us." Almost as an afterthought, Ben added, "And if he has a problem with that, I'd take him out."

Novak, turning in his seat to face Ben, unrolled a wolfish grin. "You just described your own mission to a T. You're tasked with putting together a team—of your own choosing—to do just that. Find out what we need to know. Who is Merlin? One person or many? What do they want? How can they be stopped? And what exactly is the extent of these protocols?"

Ben had to laugh at the man's presumption. "I'm *tasked*? I don't know if you got the memo, but I don't work for you people anymore, remember?"

"How could we forget, after the way you left?" Harris growled.

"But," Novak added, eyeing Harris sharply, "some individuals who have the ear of the president remember you differently. They remember how you were first in your cohort at the Farm. They remember a decade of intelligence gathering throughout Asia and the Middle East, running your assets like no one they'd ever seen, squeezing intel where no one else could. You knew the whole underworld of international terror, and its financiers and tacit supporters, as well as anyone."

"Better than most, from what I heard," Byrne chimed in.

"You kept your country safe," Novak continued. "You worked fast, you were adaptive."

"Thanks," Ben said, "but I don't need to hear my own résumé. What's your point?"

"The point is, you're what we need. Someone smart and experienced enough to command a field team with minimal oversight. Someone quick on the ground who can think like the enemy and anticipate their moves. You'd have access to everything, the full support and resources of the United States government. So what do you say? You in?"

Ben drummed his fingers on the arm of his chair. It was a tempting offer. Command of a handpicked team. The chance to be the first to hunt down a new kind of enemy. Unlimited funds for any supplies or operations he deemed necessary. But Ben didn't play nice with others in the best of times; after the circumstances surrounding his departure from the CIA, how could he ever trust these people again?

"If I were to do it, I'd need someone who can really work this . . . new physics." Ben couldn't call it magic. That was nuts. "I'm not talking about the pen trick Thompson did, either. I need someone with real strength."

Novak and Harris shared a look.

"You may meet that person soon," Novak said. "We've got a team chasing down a solid lead as we speak."

3

After the meeting adjourned, Ben and Novak followed their Secret Service escort back out of the maze of the West Wing. Harris's voice came booming from down the hallway behind them.

"*Zolstra!* "

Ben stopped. Out of the corner of his eye, he saw Novak wince.

"You said you'd keep him off my ass," Ben said, glancing at him.

"And I will," Novak said in a half-whisper. "Just don't say anything stupid."

"I'll say whatever the hell I feel like."

"So will I," Harris called, approaching fast. He was roughly Ben's height, but his gaunt, pale face, long arms, and dark suit gave him the look of an undertaker. "I don't trust you." He jabbed a finger toward Ben. "I don't like you. And frankly I don't want you here. You're here because my deputy insists, despite plenty of evidence to the contrary, that you're the man to be put in charge of this operation."

"Director—" Novak began.

"You don't trust *me?*" Ben said. "That's fucking rich. You fed Congress a steady diet of bullshit about our black sites in Eastern Europe for years. You said anything as long as they'd keep cutting the checks to fund your own personal Spanish Inquisition."

"It's called the *war* on terror, Zolstra," Harris said. His voice was calm, but a vein in his neck pulsed visibly. "If you can tell me how to wage war without hurting the bad guys, I'm all ears."

"That's pretty easy to say when you weren't the one in charge of the torture," Ben retorted. "I don't remember seeing you there in a freezing interrogation room, trying to avoid the puddles of watery shit and puke on the concrete floor from an all-night run on a hapless Afghani village idiot who just happened to be a driver for some Taliban warlord—"

Harris held up a hand. "Spare me the sob story. You knew what the job was, who these people were. If someone drives for a terrorist, guess what? They're a fucking terrorist."

"So screw Geneva, throw out the rule book, and just make 'em talk."

"You're goddamn right." Harris nodded emphatically. "If you're going to play against us, you'd better be ready to take your fucking medicine."

"There's that good ol' American moral clarity," Ben said, his voice heavy with sarcasm.

Harris got in his face. "If you didn't like it, you could have walked away."

"I did."

The Secret Service agents watched Ben and Harris square off, looking uncertain if they should intervene.

"Oh, yes," Harris acknowledged, "you sure did. But not before raising hell. I almost lost my job because of your little crusade against me, asshole. Jerking yourself off in Vermont, writing your letters to senators on the Committee on Foreign Relations, the Select Committee on Intelligence. I had to testify before Congress."

Ben had wanted Americans to know what was being done in their name. But all of Harris's testimony took place in closed session. Ben had heard about it through some contacts in the room. Nobody had cared what Harris was up to. After the terrible things he'd ordered done, and the agents he'd left traumatized for doing them, the master himself never had to answer for a damn thing.

Novak tried again to intervene. Although he was the shortest of the trio, he had the thick, wide-shouldered build of a college wrestler. He inserted himself between Ben and Harris, who were still staring at each other.

"We agreed to leave the past in the past," Novak said to Harris. "I've chosen Agent Zolstra because he has the contacts and the skills to lead this team. And"—Novak turned to Ben with raised eyebrows—"I'm sure Zolstra recognizes that whether he likes it or not, if he wants to be a part of this operation, then Director Harris is in charge."

Novak's eyes pleaded with Ben to grant Harris at least that much deference. Ben couldn't make himself agree even to that. The director and his methods were an indelible stain on both the intelligence community and on Ben's own history. Still, the mission was intriguing, and Ben had to admit he already wanted back in on the action. It was all Ben could manage just to keep his mouth shut.

That seemed enough to satisfy Harris, who straightened somewhat and nodded.

"If I catch even a whiff of insubordination, you're gone. Is that clear?"

The director didn't wait for a response. He turned and stalked back toward the Situation Room.

"Jesus," Novak said under his breath to Ben, shaking his head as they resumed their walk toward the waiting Secret Service agents, "you never make things easy on yourself, do you? I can already tell that before this is over, I'm going to regret going to bat for you."

"No one asked you to."

Novak let out a dry laugh. "Is that how they say 'thanks' where you come from?"

Ben ignored him, his mind already back on the mission. "How long before we know if the team was successful in capturing this secret weapon of yours?"

Novak glanced at his TAG Heuer. "I expect to hear that they've got her in custody any minute now."

4

Eila Mack clicked the play button on the video for what had to be the twentieth time. She'd been up since well before dawn, too excited to sleep. She dragged the timeline marker to exactly forty-eight seconds. That's when the video version of herself said the words that started levitating the car. She watched herself pull the hood up over her braids, her typical reaction to being photographed.

On the video, Mack spoke.

Esh-ka-lam, shu-rin-mah-ka-la, nish-tah-pah-kah.

With the prodding encouragement of her friends, she had gotten lucky; it was only her second time trying to use the magic words. The first time, just about an hour before the video was shot, she'd barely managed to slide her couch forward a few feet.

Mack looked at where she'd scrawled the words onto the inside cover of one of Ray's matchbooks from the off-track betting place. She caressed the edge of the matchbook lovingly. The rush she felt from the power of those words . . .

It was her friend Lasha who had come across the "Merlin protocol" somewhere in whatever dark corner of the internet she did her shady business in, and passed it along to Mack. Lasha was definitely involved in some secret hacker shit. Mack didn't ask questions.

"It's probably nothing," Lasha had said in her email. "But I know how you like this weird stuff."

Lasha always teased Mack about her interest in astrology, in Tarot, crystals. Mack could never quite explain that it wasn't like she *believed* in all of it, it was just that she didn't totally *dis*believe. It helped sometimes to make sense of things. To understand how she'd gotten to where she was.

Or how she might get out.

Now Mack was lying on the bed with Ray's laptop opened next to her, reading the words out loud again, in parallel with yesterday's video of herself. She still couldn't believe what she'd done. She'd lifted a *car*.

She pulled the timeline marker back to forty-eight seconds and let it play again. She turned the volume up as high as it would go and concentrated on practicing the odd, guttural sounds. She wanted to learn them by heart, to get them just right.

Esh-ka-lam, shu-rin-mah-ka-la, nish-tah-pah-kah.

And then it happened. The empty bottle of rye—the *last* bottle, the one she'd kept around instead of tossing it when it was finished fifty-six-days-and-counting ago, as a reminder that she was Done with That Trash—rose from the floor of the open closet. It was now floating in the air in the middle of the room.

She felt an exhilarating surge of blood through her body, and her mouth pulled back in an involuntary smile. *Magic!* Actual real *magic.* She was doing it again—and it was even easier this time.

She looked from one side of the room to the other. As she somehow sensed would happen, the bottle followed her eyes, winging effortlessly from side to side. She rolled her eyes, and the bottle made a little loop-de-loop.

Mack laughed like she hadn't done in God knew how long. She felt warm, like she was swaddled in a two-drink buzz. She looked up, and the bottle flew toward the stained ceiling tiles. She looked down, but before she could stop it, the bottle crashed hard onto the wooden floor and shattered into pieces.

The front door opened, then banged shut. "*What the fuck was that?!*" Ray. Shit. *Shit.*

She wasn't even off the bed before he stormed into the room, all two hundred muscled pounds of him. Fresh off the graveyard shift he hated, Ray's bad night was written all over his face. They were all bad nights lately. He flung his keys onto the dresser and stared down at the remnants of the bottle on the floor.

"What the fuck, Eila? I gotta come home to this?"

"I'm sorry." She scrambled to her feet. "It was an accident. I'll clean it up."

She tiptoed around the glass, careful of her bare feet. She was headed to the linen closet to grab the broom, but Ray planted himself in the doorway and refused to move. She stopped a few feet from him. Out of arm's reach.

"Is that my computer?" Ray's question was soft, but his nostrils were flared in anger. "The computer you know is private?"

Mack didn't speak. Sometimes it was better not to.

"I can't even believe you. You're lying on the bed, watching videos, drinking down your fucking bottle, while I'm working my ass off to provide for us. *And* you're using my computer. Without permission. Is that what's happening here?"

"Baby." Mack tried to smile. A taut face helped keep the tears in place. Ray hated tears. "I only needed to—"

The blow was sudden and harsh, Ray stepping closer to jab his fist into her gut. Never in the face—he was too smart to leave marks.

She doubled over, stumbling forward. Her left foot came down on something cold and hard. She gasped as the sliver of glass opened the flesh of her heel. Her left leg buckled and she sat down hard on the floor, narrowly avoiding more glass shards.

At once, Ray was towering over her, his hand raised to strike again.

Mack squeezed her eyes shut, raised her arm in a feeble defense, and waited. Somewhere she heard the strange words of the spell, repeating on a loop, and for some reason that was deeply comforting.

The next blow never came.

"What the fuck are you doing?! *How are you doing this?!*"

Ray's voice. He was scared. *Ray* was *scared.*

She opened her eyes. There was Ray, floating in the middle of the room just like the bottle had been. He was waving his arms and kicking his legs, frantic, but he was just . . . hovering there. He couldn't move an inch.

"Put me down, bitch!"

Her mind spun. *She* was doing this. She was levitating a two-hundred-pound man, and it had come so naturally.

Ray starting cursing her out again.

"Just be quiet!" she shouted, needing a moment to get her bearings. She waved her arms at him, like she was pushing an invisible box forward with both hands. Ray careened backward into the wall, the air rushing out of his lungs on impact. His elbows left gaping holes in the plaster.

God, that felt good. Mack's blood sang in her veins. She motioned Ray off the wall, and with little effort or conscious thought returned him to the center of the room, still suspended off the ground.

"What are you doing?" Ray was still catching his breath. "What the hell is this?" *This* was magic. This was *power*. She felt electric.

She leaned over and inched the glass out of her heel, inhaling sharply as she did so. She stood up. She stepped toward Ray, careful to keep the weight off her left leg. Ray flailed his arms to try to back away. *He* was trying to back away from *her.*

Mack smiled. She tasted iron in her mouth from where she'd bitten the inside of her cheek when she'd fallen. She spat a gob of blood on the floor at Ray's feet. Ray stared warily at her like he was seeing her for the first time. Like she was a different person. Maybe she was. She sure didn't feel like the same person she'd been before the words had come into her life.

"Baby," Ray said. He'd stopped flailing and now just hung awkwardly in the air. He was using his nice voice. How had she ever fallen for it? "I'm sorry I did that. You know how I get about my things. Come on, now. I forgive you, you forgive me. Put me down."

The man in front of Mack had never looked helpless before. Mean, sure. Plenty of times. Especially in the last two months since he'd gotten fired from the plant and had to start working security at the ministorage place. His temper had always been nasty, but lately it was quick, too. Helpless, though? This was something new.

She bent down and picked a large, sharp piece of glass from the floor. Holding the shard loosely, she stepped closer to Ray, who stiffened.

"Look at me, Eila." Ray cooed the name—*eye-luh*—that he'd earlier barked out like a curse. Mack did look at him. She wasn't afraid to. "Who was there for you when nobody else was? Who took care of you, baby?"

Mack hesitated. It wasn't total bullshit. Ray had helped her. When her little brother, Nathaniel, died, she was already living in Cincinnati, far from the support of her family in Pittsburgh. She was so devastated she could hardly feed herself. Lost her job at the hospital, was about to lose her apartment. Then Ray showed up—tall, broad, and so tender—and took her in. By the time she saw what kind of man he really was, she'd burned so many bridges she had nowhere left to go. She'd been living with Ray for three years. Three foggy years spent mostly drunk and under his thumb.

It was time to get her life back.

She held up the glass shard and pointed it at Ray's face with shaking hands. He winced.

"I'm leaving, Ray."

"No, you ain't." He spoke calmly, but he couldn't hide the fear in his eyes.

"I'm leaving," Mack repeated, more to herself than to him.

"Where you gonna go?"

"I don't know," she said. She reached over and grabbed the keys to Ray's truck from the dresser. "But I know how I'm gonna get there." Let Ray drive around in her purple Hyundai for a while.

Ray, still suspended in the air, now lunged forward suddenly, and was just able to snare Mack's wrist in his strong grip. She dropped the glass shard, screaming in pain as Ray twisted her arm behind her back.

"You ain't going no place."

Yes, Mack thought, *I am.*

She extended her free hand toward the lamp on her nightstand, the magic words already on her lips again. At once, the lamp was hovering above the table. Her fingers tingled. She could almost feel the lamp's contours in her hand as though she were actually touching it.

Ray wrenched her arm again and she cried out, but at the same time she willed the lamp to fly. And it flew—fast and straight—catching Ray square in the forehead. He howled and brought his hands to his face, reeling backward in the air and releasing Mack.

She pressed herself against the wall and out of his reach. Her body pulsed with pain. There was something else, too. A deeper ache that felt somehow connected to the energy it was taking her to keep using magic.

"You fucking bitch!" He kicked and batted furiously, futilely, at the empty air. "You dumb, freak-of-nature bitch!"

Blood was dripping into Ray's eyes from the gash in his head. The sight of it was indescribably satisfying.

She straightened herself off the wall. "I could kill you, Ray." There was no anger in her voice. "I could kill you, and I should."

"Fuck you."

Mack ignored him. "But I'm not gonna do that." She shook her head. "Because I'm better than you. Nathaniel's looking down on me right now—" She choked back a sob. "And he's not gonna see me become a murderer. So you can thank him for your life."

She turned away from Ray and moved toward the door. A glimpse of herself in the mirror over the dresser stopped her cold. She looked almost . . . luminous. Her mother's constant refrain from childhood came to her from across the years—*carry yourself right, and people will treat you right*. Well, she was going to be treated right from now on. She pulled her shoulders back and stood up taller. She took a halting step toward the door, clutching Ray's keys in her hand.

"I bet your brother was one punk-ass bitch," Ray spat. "I'm glad he's dead. One less punk-ass bitch in the world."

Mack didn't think. The rage was too blinding for thought. She just waved her hands and threw Ray through the glass of their bedroom window. There was a loud crash as his body slammed into the corrugated metal tool shed in the backyard. His low moan told Mack that he'd survived, but he wouldn't be getting up anytime soon. Good.

Her suitcase was buried under a mountain of clutter in the basement, so Mack just grabbed a couple of brown paper grocery bags from under the sink and shoved her clothes into them. Some toiletries. Her few items of jewelry worth keeping. She left anything Ray'd bought her. It wasn't much to show for her twenty-nine years of life. Then again, it hadn't been much of a life recently.

Ray's truck, the one he so clearly loved more than her, started up easily. Mack revved it in the driveway a few times. Let the bastard hear it as he lay there hurting. She pulled away from the house, watching Ray's little bungalow in the rearview mirror until it disappeared. It was so easy. In her daydreams, it had always seemed impossible. Of course, even in her wildest dreams she hadn't imagined being able to throw Ray through a window just by thinking it.

Without really planning it, she found herself on Highway 71 headed east toward Pittsburgh. Toward her family.

After about two hours, her stomach was growling and the gas gauge was nearly on empty. She eased the big truck into a gas station outside of Columbus and cut the engine. This was where things were going to get tricky. She'd been out of work and dependent on Ray for too long. She'd managed to sneak a little cash from Ray's wallet over the last year, and she had two credit cards that she had painstakingly avoided maxing out. She was going to need to be very careful about rationing her money until she got back on her feet. She opened her purse.

Her wallet wasn't there. She'd left it back on the dresser.

A sour dread pooled in her stomach. She forced herself to think.

The gas, at least, was an easy enough problem to fix. Many stations in this part of the country still let you gas up first before you went in to pay, and this looked like one of them. Mack jumped out of the truck. She cried out in pain as her injured heel, protected only by a thin sneaker sole, hit the asphalt. She half-limped to the pump and filled the tank.

Then she went inside and cleaned her bloodied heel in the bathroom sink. But as she emerged from the toilet into the station's minimart, she saw that food was going to be a little more work. Mack was the only shopper in the store—and the clerk was already scowling at his lone, dark-skinned customer.

The idea came to her, simple, perfect: *use the words.*

Outside, the only other vehicle besides Ray's big red truck was a banged-up beige sedan that had to belong to the clerk. Mack willed the words to cycle through her head again, then mouthed them as silently as she could while focusing on the sedan. She held her hands up—just slightly, as she pretended to browse the magazine rack—and soon she felt the car's plastic bumper press against her palms. She gave it a shove. Through the window, the car began to roll away, toward the frontage road leading back to the highway.

"Hey, mister!" Mack called.

The man stared at her. "What?"

"Is that your car?" She pointed at the vehicle. It had reached the frontage road and was picking up speed as it rolled down the road's gentle slope.

"Mother*fucker!*"

The man tore out from behind the counter, threw a warning look at Mack, then hauled his bulk through the door after his vehicle.

Mack didn't waste time. She helped herself to potato chips, honey-roasted cashews, two premade deli sandwiches, a bottle of iced tea, and a bottle of water, tossing one after the other into her purse. She doubled back for some beef jerky and peanut M&M's, then hustled out to the truck.

A hundred yards off, the attendant was still chasing his shitmobile. Mack flung her haul into the front seat of the truck, climbed in, roared down the frontage road in the opposite direction, and merged back onto the highway.

It was another hour before she heard the siren and saw the flashing lights.

Shit shit shit. She hadn't thought about cameras. Of course the owner would have checked his footage and given the cops her license plate. *Oh God, the truck.* Ray had probably reported it stolen by now. Mack had been free for all of three hours in the last three years, and she'd already fucked it up.

She checked the rearview. It wasn't the police cruiser she'd expected. It was a dark van. For a crazy moment, Mack thought about jamming the accelerator down and making a run for it. For an even crazier moment, she considered using the words to send the van off the road, or flip it over, anything. But this wasn't just her abusive boyfriend she was dealing with anymore. This was the *police*. Mack wasn't trying to get herself killed.

She pulled the truck over. The van stopped behind her. Two men got out and stepped toward the truck. It wasn't until they were at both side windows that she realized the men weren't wearing uniforms. Something wasn't right.

One of them knocked on the driver's-side window. He didn't show a badge.

"Roll it down, ma'am," the voice commanded.

"Okay, okay," she said, pretending to fumble with the controls. "Sorry. Just a sec."

"Right now."

A jolt of fear ran down her spine. These guys weren't cops. Out of the corner of her eye, she saw that the man at the passenger-side window had pulled a gun and pointed it at her. *Oh, Jesus. Oh, God.* If she floored the engine, right now, she might have a tiny chance—but more than likely they'd shoot her.

What about the words?

But there was no time. There was just the muted spit of two silenced shots, the crash of breaking glass, and darkness.

5

Novak's driver maneuvered the town car expertly through D.C.'s midday streets, heading northeast from the White House. Out of habit, Ben mentally catalogued the route to the undisclosed location where they were bound.

What was really on Ben's mind was the mission. The more he worked it over, the more the mystery of the Merlin protocols intrigued him. Who was "Merlin" and how dangerous was he? What was he after? What the hell was this new kind of physics that no one had any word for but "magic"? And how could they keep it out of the hands of the kinds of people Ben had spent too many good years of his life tirelessly hunting down?

"I got the call just before the briefing began," Novak was saying, seated next to Ben in the car's wide backseat. "A couple of unusual reports had come in a few hours apart. We'd already instructed the directors of our field offices to keep an ear open for anything . . ." Novak paused. "Well, we couldn't very well say *magic,* for fuck's sake. But we implied that it was possible they might see something strange, and that if they did, they needed to send it our way immediately."

"What reports?" Ben asked as the car went right, turning off the broad avenue and onto a street with warehouses lining one side and tumbledown homes along the other.

"First, Cincinnati PD. A man was taken to the hospital with serious injuries. He was ranting the whole time that his girlfriend had done it. Said she was some kind of witch who threw him all around the room with her mind."

"Sounds like he was on drugs."

"That was the obvious conclusion," Novak acknowledged. "The victim's got a few substance offenses on his rap sheet. It almost certainly wouldn't have been passed along to us if his story hadn't been confirmed, more or less, by a neighbor. She heard the couple fighting, then saw the man come flying out the window. 'Like he'd been catapulted,' she said. Big guy, too, apparently."

"You said a couple of reports. What else did you hear?"

"The other report," Novak continued, "was from the Ohio State Patrol. There was an incident at a gas station. Stolen gas and shoplifting. The owner caught the woman who did it on camera. She sent his car rolling down the street as a diversion."

"Nice trick."

"Yes. Especially because she did it from inside the store. Telekinetically."

The town car slowed as it approached a two-story house.

"You think it was the same woman?"

"It is. I authorized her capture just prior to entering the Situation Room. We're both about to meet her for the first time."

Novak nodded toward the house. In many ways, it fit in perfectly with the rest of the dilapidated block. The siding had so completely mildewed to a greenish brown that it was impossible to determine what color the place had once been. The windowsills were crumbling, and there were support posts broken or missing from the wooden porch railing.

But closer inspection revealed some significant differences. Unlike its neighbors', none of this house's windows were cracked or smashed. Not only that, but they were visibly thick, reinforced windows. Ben would've bet anything they were bulletproof. The front door, too, was painted brown and had the superficial appearance of wood, but Ben could see it was metal. Likely steel.

Novak noticed Ben's appraisal. "It doesn't look like much, but if anything goes south, this place can lock down tight."

It was a needless thing to say. Ben remembered the ins and outs of dozens of safe houses on multiple continents. Some he wished he could forget, places that had morphed into Harris-mandated torture chambers in the dark years after 9/11. Ben's stomach churned in disgust as images of the "enhanced interrogations" he'd conducted flashed through his mind.

The car shifted into park, jolting Ben back to the present. Novak instructed the driver to move the car around to another block, then stay put and return for them when he called.

Ben exited the vehicle and shouldered his duffel bag. He and Novak walked up the concrete path that cut through the front yard. The lawn was overgrown, scorched brown and dead in the summer heat.

"What else do we know about her?" Ben asked.

"For starters, we think she's the woman from the video."

Ben felt a rush of anticipation. *There's someone inside this house who can lift a car with her mind.* The thought was ridiculous, but if it was true he could learn a lot from her about what they were up against.

"Her name is Eila Mack," Novak went on. "Twenty-nine years old. Originally from Pittsburgh. Put herself through community college, then worked as a medical tech in a hospital until a few years ago, right around the time her brother was killed."

"Killed?"

"Hit by a drunk driver. He was about to start on a full ride at the University of Chicago. By all accounts a real bright kid. Mack started showing up for work drunk, got fired, dropped off the map."

Novak delivered the unfortunate woman's life story in a flat mono-
tone. Too much time in a business built on lies and emotional manip-
ulation had blunted his capacity for empathy. It was an occupational
hazard that Ben himself was only beginning to recover from.

Novak pressed a button at the door, then turned to face the camera
installed in a corner above it. There was a buzz, and the sound of a
metal latch releasing. Novak pushed the door open, and he and Ben
stepped inside.

The place didn't immediately look any better inside than out.
The floral wallpaper was cracked and peeling. The floorboards were
warped. There was some furniture that would have been old during
the Carter administration. A damp, musty smell prevailed.

"Everything's downstairs," Novak said, leading Ben through the
front hallway to a door near the decrepit kitchen.

They stopped at the door, and Novak once again knocked and
waited for a camera to confirm his identity. The door opened.

Ben followed Novak down a set of stairs into a small basement
room. It was a significant improvement over the condition of the rest
of the house. It was clean, for one, with freshly painted white walls
and modern track lighting. The window had been bricked up, and the
bricks, too, were painted white. There was a sofa that reminded Ben
of something from a dentist's office: clean and uncomfortable. Ben set
his bag onto the floor next to it.

Sitting at a simple, uncluttered desk was a young agent. She was
dressed casually in jeans, a T-shirt, a baseball cap. Her sidearm sat in
its holster on the desk in front of her. Multiple computer monitors
showed the outside and inside of the safe house from every conceiv-
able angle. But there was one display that Ben was drawn to immediately.

An entire large monitor was devoted to a single feed. It showed a
room that Ben figured had to be just on the other side of the closed
door next to the desk. On the screen, a young woman sat in a chair

in the center of the empty room. She wore a pair of stretchy leggings and a baggy olive-green tank top. Her hands and feet were bound to the chair with leather restraints, and she was gagged. One foot was wrapped in a thick bandage. She wasn't conscious.

Novak nodded to the agent at the desk. "Good afternoon, Agent Stevens. How's our subject?"

"Good, sir. They brought her in a half hour ago." The blonde agent's accent was pure Chicago, full of big midwestern vowels. "The tranq should be wearing off any minute now. She's been shifting a bit."

"Let's raise the light level in there," Novak said. "Bring her around."

"Yes, sir."

The agent tapped on the keyboard, and Ben watched on the monitor as the room brightened considerably. Mack's head lolled from one side to the other. Her eyelids began to flutter.

Novak motioned for Ben to sit on one side of the sofa then sat himself on the other. He crossed his legs at the knee. His buffed shoes shined in the light.

"What do you plan on doing with her?" Ben asked.

"Just what you said at the briefing. Find out everything we can about what she knows and what she can do. Her power is obviously substantial. We need to know its limits."

"So she's your science experiment from now until you're through with her," Ben said, unable to hide his contempt.

"Playing the fool doesn't suit you, Zolstra," Novak said bluntly. "This woman is a threat. She will be released when she is determined no longer to be so, and when she has exhausted her usefulness to the United States government. Remember, we're here because you wanted to meet someone who could work the protocol. Well, here she is."

He motioned to the screen, where Mack was slowly stirring.

"Have you thought about who you'll put on your team?" Novak asked.

"When did I say I was agreeing to the mission?"

"Don't tell me you're still playing hard to get after everything you've learned and seen."

Novak had known exactly what he was doing when he brought Ben to that briefing. Now that Ben had a sense of the magnitude of the potential threat if this "magic" really got out into the world, he couldn't turn his back on it all and hide in Vermont. Novak knew Ben well enough to know that he'd be duty bound, honor bound, to do everything he could to counter the danger. His country needed him—the *world* needed him. It was that simple.

"You're right," Ben said finally. "I'm in." Novak's smile of triumph was cut short when Ben added, "But I've decided I don't want a field team."

"What do you mean?"

"The more people who get involved in this thing, the slower I'll be able to move. Teams mean bureaucracy."

Novak stood and ran a hand through his salt-and-pepper crew cut. He started pacing the length of the small room. "So . . . what then? You're saying you want to do this *alone*?"

"Not alone." Ben pointed to the monitor. "All I need is a plane, and that girl."

Novak scoffed. "That's out of the question. And you're out of your mind if you think Harris would ever go for it."

Agent Stevens cleared her throat and called out from the desk, "Sir, the subject is awake."

Ben stood. He and Novak approached the monitor. Mack's face was wide-eyed with terror under the harsh lights, and she was struggling forcefully against her restraints.

Novak turned to Stevens. "Open the channel so she can hear me."

The woman did so, then signaled Novak with a curt nod.

"Hello, Eila Mack," Novak said. His voice must have been booming in the other room, because Mack immediately froze and stared straight ahead. "I've got your attention. Good."

Mack tried to speak, but the gag rendered the attempt meaningless. Even so, Ben could hear the panic in her muffled words, the edgy break in her scream.

"I'm going to ask you some questions. You can nod your head for 'yes,' or shake it for 'no.' Do you understand? Nod if you understand."

Mack looked paralyzed.

Novak repeated, slowly, harshly. "Nod your head if you understand."

Ben looked at Stevens and ran a hand across his neck, *cut the mic.* "Look, I get that this is your interrogation," he said to Novak, "but if you're already determined to be bad cop, let me be good cop. Ten minutes to see what she can do and if I can get anything out of her."

Before Novak could answer Ben, his phone rang. The deputy director eyed the screen, hesitating a second before swiping to pick up. "Director?"

Novak looked at Ben, concerned. There was a long pause. Ben could hear the drone of Harris's buzzing voice but couldn't make out the words. "I understand your feelings, sir, but—" Novak's face went red, and his lips—squeezed tightly together—went white. "I must strongly object to this course of—"

Novak lowered the phone from his ear. It was clear he'd been hung up on.

"Director Harris has . . . changed his mind," Novak said in a low voice, pulling Ben away from Agent Stevens. "You're not to be allowed to see or speak with the subject. You're off the mission."

Ben laughed incredulously. "Bullshit. Because I didn't bow and kiss his ring? Come on, Novak, give me ten minutes with her." When the deputy director seemed to waver, Ben added, "You know this is what I do."

Novak shook his head slowly. "Was there ever a time when you weren't a pain in everyone's ass?"

"Probably not."

Novak checked his watch. "Five minutes," he said, "and that's it. The director's on his way, and if you're not out of there by the time he arrives, he'll have my balls for breakfast."

Ben had no intention of being taken off the mission now—the challenge and thrill of it had its hooks in him—and this new threat was too important to leave things to the CIA to screw up without him.

Ben reached into his duffel and grabbed his pistol. He stuck it into his waistband along the small of his back as he moved toward the door, a plan unfurling in his mind. A bundle of zip-tied power cables ran along the wall from the desk, crossing the floor in front of the doorway. Ben turned back to Novak as though he'd forgotten to say something, and pretended to trip over the cables, unplugging them. The monitors on the desk went dark, along with the power lights on the desktop computers.

"Shit," Ben said. "Sorry."

Agent Stevens was already moving to plug the electronics back in.

"Just get in there," Novak grumbled.

Ben entered the interrogation room. The door closed and locked behind him. Mack was staring at him, her rounded jaw clenched tight, her expression a mixture of fear and defiance. *So you're a fighter,* Ben thought. *Good. You're going to need to be.*

Ben stepped toward her, speaking softly, looking straight into her copper eyes. "Listen to me very carefully. I don't have much time, because in less than forty seconds the computers will be back online and they'll be able to hear us again. I can get you out of here, if you do exactly as I say. But let me be crystal clear: if you try to fuck me over, I will not hesitate to take you out. Am I understood?"

This time, Mack nodded.

"Okay. Here's what's going to happen . . ."

6

Ben kept the gag on her, as Novak would have done, while he staged some preliminaries for the deputy director's benefit.

"Is your name Eila Mack?" Ben asked.

When she nodded, Ben took a step closer. "Do you have any . . . unusual abilities?" A slight hesitation, then another nod. "Will you show them to me, with the understanding that if you attempt to use them against me or escape, you will leave me no choice but to use this?" Ben showed her his gun before tucking it back away.

Mack's eyes widened in apparent fear, and she nodded again. She was playing along perfectly.

Ben unfastened the restraints that bound Mack's wrists and ankles, then removed her gag. "Do not speak unless you are answering a question or demonstrating your abilities." He took out his wallet and tossed it onto the concrete floor between them. "Pick it up."

Mack leaned forward and reached her hand down.

"Not like that," Ben said.

Mack closed her eyes for a moment, then started to say the words that Ben had heard her use in the video. His wallet leaped from the floor to hover at his eye level.

Even though he'd known what to expect this time—his plan hinged on Mack's ability to do what he'd seen in that clip—Ben was still awed. Not to mention impressed by how effortlessly Mack seemed to wield her power. Agent Thompson had looked about ready to pass out after floating a pen for a few seconds. Mack seemed like she could do this for hours with one eye closed.

Ben plucked his wallet out of the air and returned it to his pocket. "Good."

Crackling from the speaker in the ceiling preceded an announcement from Novak's rough voice. "The director is two minutes out," he said. "Wrap it up and get out of there."

"We're going to try something bigger," Ben said to Mack. "Go ahead and stand up."

Mack did so.

"Pick up your chair," Ben said.

She had hardly spoken more than a few syllables this time before the wooden chair was floating in the air between them. It rotated slightly like a shiny new car on display at an auto show.

"It gets easier every time I do it," Mack said with a hint of pride, lowering the chair to the floor.

Let's hope so, Ben thought.

Novak's voice echoed into the room again. "Time's up," Novak said. "That's enough fun for now. Sit the subject back down and restrain her. I'll take over from here."

This was the moment.

Ben turned toward the camera on the ceiling and shook his head. "I need more time," he said. "You can see we're making progress here. I'm not coming out yet."

Ben knew exactly what would happen next.

The door to the room buzzed and then opened. Novak stormed in. He didn't close the door behind him.

"Zolstra, I don't know what the hell you think you're—"

"*Now!*" Ben shouted.

Novak left the ground, confusion etched on his face as he hurtled through the air and struck the back wall of the room.

"*Gently,*" Ben reminded Mack, running for the door.

Ben entered the small room at the bottom of the stairs. Agent Stevens, caught completely by surprise, had only just scrambled to her feet. No sooner had she managed to free her sidearm from its holster than Ben wrested it from her hands. He leveled the gun at her, then used it to motion toward the interrogation room.

"Inside," Ben said. "Now, please."

She glared at Ben and walked into the room. Ben followed. Mack still had Novak pinned to the wall. The deputy director looked shaken, but his eyes narrowed at Ben.

"You shit," Novak said.

Ben motioned to Mack. "Let's go."

Mack dropped Novak to the ground, and she and Ben left the room, closing and locking the door behind them.

Ben went to the desk and spoke into the mic. "You can tell Harris the mission's still on, and I just chose the first member of my team. I need someone with her power. Whoever Merlin is will have plenty of his own."

Ben watched on the monitor as Novak stepped as close to the ceiling camera as he could, and stared up into it. "You don't fucking get it," Novak said. "If you do this, the mission is *you*. The director is going to come down on you with everything he's got."

"Then that's how it is," Ben said.

Ben clicked off the mic. He left Agent Stevens's gun on the desk, then grabbed his duffel bag, pulling its strap securely across his chest. He and Mack ran up the stairs, Mack clutching the railing to take the weight off her injured foot.

They were back on the ground floor of the house now. Golden shafts of afternoon sunlight shone through the grimy windows, illuminating a cloud of dust motes in the air.

Ben threw open the front door, and he and Mack bounded down the sagging wooden stairs and onto the brown lawn.

They needed a ride. Ben scanned the street. The few cars parked on the largely abandoned block were caked in dust and looked like they hadn't moved in weeks or longer. A few had flat tires, others had broken windows. Even in the unlikely event that any of them still ran, they wouldn't be fast.

Then he spotted something up against the side of the warehouse across the street, half hidden behind a bush: a motorcycle. It was old, but clean. It had been driven recently.

"Come on," Ben said.

They ran to the bike—Mack limping a bit, Ben pulling her arm over his shoulder for support. No one was around. There was a camera on the wall that could probably spot them, but they didn't have the luxury of worrying about that right now. Priority number one was to put as much distance as they could between themselves and the safe house, before the director showed up, appraised the situation, and called in an intercept team.

Ben was hoping the motorcycle was too old for the owner to have bothered with much in the way of security, and when they reached it he saw he was right. The Yamaha XS Eleven, which was a few years older than Ben was, had no lock on the fork or the ignition.

He grabbed the ignition wiring and followed the wires down with his hand until he felt the place where they connected to the starter solenoid. He snapped open the plastic connector.

"You're stealing this thing?" Mack said.

Ben flicked open his folding knife and cut out a small section of wire, stripping the ends. "Don't have much choice."

He crouched down. He bent the piece of wire he held into a U, then slid both ends into the wire cap running to the starter solenoid. "What we just did in there could get us both locked up for life." He tested the headlight switch, smiling when it came on. "We're going to play our cards right, so it won't come to that. But we won't have any cards to play if we don't get moving right now."

Ben wiggled the handlebars. When they didn't turn the front wheel, he stood up and took a step back. He lifted his leg and brought his boot down on them with as much force as he could—once, twice—until a snapping sound told him he'd busted the steering lock. He grimaced as he set his smarting foot back on the ground.

He straddled the bike and started the engine, then slid his cell phone out of his pocket. He held it in both hands, snapped it in two, and tossed the pieces into the grass. Ben wasn't about to carry what amounted to a tracking device with the CIA on his trail. Besides, he had his burners in the duffel.

"Do you have a phone?" Ben asked Mack.

"I—I don't have anything. They took it all." Her voice was edged with panic. She shook her head as if to clear it, and a lock of wavy hair fell out of its loose braid and partially covered the smooth brown skin of her face. "I don't even know who 'they' were. I don't know who *you* are. I don't know what the fuck is going on!"

There was a screech of tires from down the block. Ben turned and saw a black town car racing toward the safe house. Harris.

"Look, I'll explain everything, but right now we have to go." He tapped the seat behind him.

Mack climbed on. She put her arms around Ben's stomach and linked them.

Ben fired up the bike and gunned it. The old machine still had kick, and Mack clutched him tight as they roared away from the warehouse and into the street.

Ben watched the town car in the side mirror. The driver slowed, then stopped in front of the safe house.

Ben turned right onto a busy street and began weaving through cars.

"Why do we still need to go so fast?" Mack shouted.

The shriek of a police siren sounded from somewhere behind them. Novak or Stevens must have called them.

"That's why," Ben said.

He steered the bike around a delivery truck that had stopped with its hazard lights flashing.

"Turn around," Ben said, "and tell me who's after us." The tiny side mirrors were all but useless, giving him little sense of depth or perspective.

He revved the engine faster, watching the speedometer climb as the tachometer tilted into the red. His eyes were watering from the wind. He leaned down lower and blinked back tears.

"I see two cop cars and a motorcycle," Mack shouted over the engine's roar. "They're coming fast."

Ben shot through a red light, then veered left, jumping the bike over the grassy median into oncoming traffic. He clenched his jaw to keep from biting his tongue as the bike swerved onto the road again.

"*Holy shit!*" Mack screamed.

Horns blared on both sides of them as Ben powered the bike up the dotted white line between the lanes.

"How about now?" he called back.

"The cruisers got stuck back at the intersection," Mack shouted. "But the motorcycle is getting closer."

Ben checked his mirror. The police bike was heavy, muscular. Lots of power. It was gaining on them, and the cop hadn't even opened his chopper up yet. Ben had to think fast. If they didn't lose the pursuer soon, he would continue to radio their exact position to air support. Ben was sure that area helicopters were already being retasked to track them. Once they were spotted from the air, they would really be up shit creek.

"Are you holding on tight?" Ben asked.

"*Now* you ask me that?!"

Ben opened the throttle even more and took the bike up onto the

sidewalk. Shocked pedestrians leaped into the street or pressed themselves against buildings or chain-link fences as the bike blew by. The
whine of the wind and the engine at this speed made their curses and
Mack's screams of protest nearly inaudible. They zoomed past a bak-
ery and a greasy spoon diner.

The cop hadn't followed them onto the sidewalk, but he was still
edging closer along the road. Ben leaned the bike low and curved into
a corporate office park. It was a complex of at least ten concrete and
glass buildings, with smooth black tarmac curling around them, con-
necting the various parking lots, entrances, and exits. This was going
to be make-or-break. Ben's ride wasn't exactly agile, but he was counting on it to outmaneuver that beast the cop was riding.

Ben leaned to follow a broad curve, using the opportunity to look
back and gauge the distance from their pursuer. The cop was still closing in, even on the curve, leaning hard, his knee inches from the black
top. The guy knew how to ride.

As they straightened out, Ben pushed the bike the hardest he had
yet. There was a long circular drive that led in a wide arc uphill to the
entrance of one of the buildings, and Ben raced up it. He was going
so fast now that the trees lining the approach blurred into a wall of
green. From his vantage at the top of the driveway's rise, Ben quickly
surveyed his exit options below.

The helicopters would arrive soon. It didn't matter if they could
lose one motorcycle cop if there were eyes on them from above. But
leaving the complex wouldn't help if they couldn't ditch the cop,
either.

"How close is he?" Ben shouted.

"I don't know." He could barely hear Mack. "Forty feet? Thirty?"

Christ. Ben rocketed down the opposite side of the ramp, then
darted around a long, low building. In his side mirror, it looked like
the cop was right on top of them. Ben could even make out the man's
face now—youngish, teeth grit in determination, wisps of blond hair

poking out from his helmet and lacerating his cheeks. This guy wasn't going anywhere. Ben was out of ideas.

He felt more than heard the whisper in his ear. Something strange and incantatory. He watched in the mirror as the blond cop, motorcycle and all, began to rise into the air like a marionette on giant strings.

It was *her*. Ben slowed, mesmerized. That Mack could exert this much focused power, even in the midst of chaos, was beyond impressive.

Ben let off the gas completely now, looping back to come alongside the flabbergasted officer.

"Gently," Ben reminded Mack over his shoulder, bringing the motorcycle to a stop. He didn't want to hurt anyone. That wasn't what this was about.

The cop was maybe a dozen feet in the air. He starting fumbling the pistol out of his belt with shaking hands, when his bike suddenly dropped out from underneath him and crashed to the ground. He cried out in fear, still floating, and dropped the gun.

"Whoops!" Mack said. "It slipped."

In the side mirror, Ben saw the ghost of a smirk on Mack's face, and knew it had been no accident.

"It's all right, just set him down." The damage to the police motorcycle looked sufficient. The cop wouldn't be able to follow. "Someplace *soft*," he added.

Mack guided the officer over to some bushes at the edge of the parking lot, then unceremoniously let him fall—from a bit higher than necessary, Ben thought. But the man was already scrambling to his feet, shouting at them.

Ben revved the old Yamaha again. He looked back at Mack admiringly. "You're incredible," he said.

Mack smiled. The first one he'd seen from her. It was worth the wait.

7

Novak stood in the doorway, watching with a queasy feeling in his stomach as Director Harris turned the corner and advanced down the corridor toward the Project Merlin command center at Langley. Even from a distance, Novak could read Harris's scowling, livid face.

He was about to get the earful he'd been spared when Harris had raced from the safe house in pursuit of Zolstra. Novak had been the one pushing to bring Zolstra in on this, after all. He'd forced the issue with Harris, who despised the troublesome ex-agent. He'd cajoled Harris, appealing to the director to set his personal acrimony aside, convincing him that the needs of the mission took precedence over the grudges of the past. He'd believed in Zolstra.

Then the bastard outsmarted him and disappeared with an asset of incalculable value. Now here Novak stood, holding the fucking bag, waiting to be whipped like a disobedient pup. He could only hope some good would come of Zolstra's gambit, and that he managed to come through with something, anything, that could help the Agency get out in front of the Merlin protocols.

Director Harris stormed down the hallway, his wingtips stomping against the floor as though the tiles had personally offended him.

"Sir," a young aide, leaning out of a doorway, called after him, "the committee chair is asking again about the—"

"Not now," Harris said without looking back. "Tell the congressman if he can't be patient he can go fuck his mother."

Harris blew right past Novak into the large suite of three rooms that had been set up only the day before. Novak cringed, recognizing that his dressing down was going to be public.

Two dozen handpicked agents—some glued to computer monitors, others huddled in pairs over maps or documents, a handful standing up and talking animatedly in front of a huge whiteboard—all hushed and straightened a little when Harris entered the room.

"Where the fuck is Zolstra?" Harris barked.

A trim black man, his blue Oxford shirt wrinkled and damp under the arms after a sleepless night spent in this very room, swiveled around in his chair and looked up at Harris. Smart and driven, Walters had been Novak's right-hand for years.

"As of now, we can put him on the outskirts of Annapolis approximately three hours after leaving the safe house," Walters said. With a click of his mouse, an image appeared on one of the large screens mounted on the wall at the front of the room.

It had been taken by a gas station security camera that mainly captured the two cars at the pumps below it but also grabbed a section of the road in the background. Despite being badly pixelated, the image showed Zolstra clear enough. He was astride a motorcycle, with Mack behind him, her arms around his waist.

"After that?" Harris asked. He still hadn't so much as looked at Novak.

Walters shook his head. "After that the bike disappears." He halted, correcting himself. "I mean, not *disappears*. It doesn't become invisible. We just lose it—"

"Christ, I understand what you mean, Agent Walters."

Novak wondered what other former figures of speech would soon take on an inconveniently literal meaning in this new world. *I see right through you? You read my mind?* How much more did Merlin have in store for them?

"We're confident the motorcycle hasn't left Annapolis," Walters continued.

"I want a list of everyone Zolstra's ever had contact with in the city," Harris said. "We'll take a look at all of 'em, but prioritize anyone with skills that might be useful to a fugitive."

Fugitive? Novak had thought he might be able to talk Harris down a little, to make the director see that it was possible that Ben was off doing exactly what they needed him to—but Novak didn't like the implication of Harris's word choice at all.

"Skills such as?" Walters asked.

"Special ops guys, forgers, infosec types. And watch anyone he was in the field with. While you're at it, I need pictures and full profiles of both Zolstra and Mack sent to the FBI, the NSA, our pals at Interpol . . ."

Novak cleared his throat. "Excuse me, Director," he began, "but do you think treating Ben Zolstra as a fugitive is the correct play here?"

Harris trained his gaze on Novak. His owl eyes burned through his wire frame glasses. Novak felt a cold twinge in his gut.

"Are we talking about the same Ben Zolstra?" Harris kept his voice unsettlingly low. "Are we talking about the man who turned a gun on one of my agents and my own deputy director? Who locked them in an interrogation room?" Now his volume began to rise. "The same man who ran off with the most important weapon we had in a new war that we're already losing?"

"What I mean is—"

"The Ben Zolstra that *you let fucking escape with Eila Mack?! Is that who we're talking about?* Because to me that sounds like the textbook definition of a fugitive. What do you think, Agent Walters?" Harris kept his eyes on Novak.

The other agents in the room pretended not to be glued to what was happening.

Walters gave Novak an apologetic look before answering. "Sounds like a fugitive, sir."

Harris nodded approvingly. "Somebody's thinking straight around here."

Novak swallowed hard. He had to defuse this. "I know it looks bad . . ."

Harris snorted.

" . . . But I think we need to consider the man we're dealing with. What's happening here is classic Zolstra. He's gone to ground before but always in service of the mission. Remember Bangkok? How long did he spend getting in with that arms dealer . . . Kovit? *Weeks* he didn't check in. He's always chafed at what he sees as intrusive oversight. It's a pattern with him."

"I agree, it is a pattern. One that we indulged for far too long." Harris's voice was acid-edged. "A pattern of deliberate disrespect, of undermining authority, and of putting our agents and our nation in unnecessary danger. And it's a pattern that will no longer be tolerated. Which is precisely why I took him off this operation!"

"Perhaps if we waited a day or two for him to check in—"

"Check in? Zolstra *isn't on a mission for us anymore,* do you understand? He may be off to rob a bank for all we know."

"I'd say that's very unlikely."

Harris ignored him, speaking to Walters instead. "You have your orders. Get started."

"Right away, sir."

Walters stood and walked over to a pair of young agents who sat with laptops open in front of them at a long table to the side of the room. Detailed maps of the entire Eastern Seaboard were spread out on the table. Walters leaned down to deliver the new orders to the agents.

"*You* wanted Zolstra on this mission." Harris stabbed a finger toward Novak. "He's your fucking responsibility. I want him, and Mack, back here. *Now*."

Harris turned to go. "If you'll excuse me, I have to go inform the president that we've lost our most powerful weapon."

8

The drive should have taken about an hour, but with Ben keeping off the main roads as much as possible it took them over three. By the time they hit the Eastport neighborhood of Annapolis, it was dusk.

Ben steered the Yamaha along the quiet, tree-lined streets. Mack's grip around his waist had slackened. After being abducted and imprisoned, and then spending three hours on the back of a motorcycle with the hot summer air whipping at her, she had to be exhausted.

Ben took the bike down a narrow lane and up into the short drive-way of a beige house, stopping next to an old Ford Explorer. The place was shaded—hidden, really—by a stand of robust fir trees.

He killed the motorcycle. The silence that ensued was immediate and total, though as the ringing in his ears stopped, Ben could make out the familiar evening chorus of crickets. He and Mack got off the bike.

"So the guy that lives here, he's your friend?" Mack asked.

"He's . . . the guy we need."

Ben and Gabriel Garcia went way back, but they weren't exactly friends. Gabe was an asset, ex-military, now an off-book contractor that Ben had cultivated and only later come to trust. Hopefully he could still be trusted.

"The important thing," Ben said, "is that he's my guy, and the CIA doesn't know about him."

Ben started toward the front door.

"I need to get some things straight before we go any further," Mack said.

Ben turned around. "I understand," he said. "But first we need to get inside and out of sight."

Mack ignored him. "Earlier, you told that other man that you needed somebody with my power. What did you mean by that? What do you need me for?"

On the street, a middle-aged couple walked by with a little puff ball of a dog on a leash. They were staring at Ben and Mack with frank suspicion. Ben gave them a wave and nod, but they gawked as they passed. *Fuck.* For all Ben knew, Harris had already managed to get their pictures on the news.

"Later. Inside. I promise."

Mack looked like she was deciding whether to dig in her heels, but she relented.

As they started up the front steps, the screen door creaked open. A shirtless Latino man in board shorts and flip-flops appeared in the doorway.

"I'd ask you what the hell you're doing coming here unannounced," the man said, "but you'd get all 'national security' and probably wouldn't tell me anyway."

"A pleasure as usual, Gabe," Ben said. He motioned to Mack. "This is Eila Mack."

Gabe hid his wary expression behind a disarming smile. "Gabriel Garcia. Pleasure to meet you. Any friend of Ben's . . . probably shouldn't be. He's a prick, you know that, right?"

Mack shook Gabe's offered hand. "Well, this prick just saved my ass," she said with a smile, "so watch your tongue."

Gabe burst out laughing. "I like your fire." He stepped aside. "Come in."

"Actually, could you open the garage?" Ben asked. "I need to stash the motorcycle."

"Sure thing, boss," Gabe said, retreating back into the house.

A moment later, the garage door rumbled open, and Ben wheeled the old Yamaha inside the large space, parking it next to a candy-apple-red Camaro of similar vintage.

"That is a beautiful car," Ben said as Gabe closed the garage door behind him.

"She will be, if I ever get her running."

Gabe walked to a refrigerator against the back wall of the garage. He opened it, crouched down, and reached inside. There was a clinking of glass, and he emerged holding three bottles of beer.

Ben held up his hand. "Thanks, but we're going to need to stay sharp."

Gabe shrugged, then slid two of the bottles back into the fridge. He banged the cap of the third off against the edge of a long wooden workbench.

"Well, it's my house and I'm toasting anyway," he said, hoisting his bottle aloft. "To old pains in the ass, and lovely new acquaintances." He winked at Mack, then took a big swig of beer. "So," he said, pulling the bottle away from his lips, "what do you need, Zolstra?"

Ben explained everything that had happened as quickly as he could, starting with the moment that morning when Novak and Wei had rolled up to his place in Vermont.

When Ben finished, Gabe let out a low whistle.

"That all sounds pretty fucking unbelievable, man."

"I know," Ben said. "But it's real. Someone, or some group, put this information out into the world and told us to have a blast destroying ourselves. The question is, why? What's Merlin's game? And how do we find whoever Merlin is and stop them? That's why I'm here."

"How can I help?"

"Wait a minute," Mack interrupted. "Your mission is tracking down Merlin in order to stop magic? Why do you automatically assume magic is such a bad, dangerous thing?"

Ben smirked. "Says the woman who a few hours ago threw a police officer across a parking lot with her mind."

"You did?" Gabe's eyebrows rose, impressed.

"No, seriously," Mack insisted. "You're talking about stopping magic, but I have it, and I like it. It feels *great*."

"It feels great until our enemies turn around and use it on us," Ben said. "With so many unknowns, it's safer to keep a lid on it."

"You're not talking about safety," Mack scoffed. "You're talking about control."

Ben bit his tongue and turned to Gabe. "Look, can we go inside? We need to get started."

They moved into the house. Gabe's place was a disaster. It was also a monument to his singularly brilliant, obsessive mind.

A torn leather sofa largely obstructed the main hallway. There were greased engine parts lying on top of newspaper spread over the kitchen floor. There was a full-size basketball hoop on the wall of what would have been, in any other house, the living room. And everywhere—in piles on the floor, on tables and counters, balancing on the carpeted stairs—there was electronic detritus. There were the dismembered corpses of computers: motherboards, fan blades, wires of all colors. There were coils of cables, modems, speakers, and keyboards. There were monitors large and small, flat and curved. Disk drives, cameras, batteries of every description. There were also larger, intact machines whose dubiously legal purpose Ben could only guess at.

"Sorry about the mess," Gabe said as he led them into a downstairs room that contained a number of mismatched chairs. "It's the maid's day off."

He invited them to sit in one of the battered chairs.

"All right," Gabe said when they'd settled, "what do you need?"

"Information, and lots of it," Ben said without hesitation. "I need you to find out where the protocol and manifesto were uploaded from, and anything you can about who did the uploading."

Gabe spoke with similar definitiveness. "User info will be tricky. But the IP address of the computer that was used for the upload, I can get you. Might take a while if your guy's a pro . . ."

"Do what you can," Ben said, "but get started right now. We don't want our leads to get any colder."

Gabe pulled his chair up to a half-built desktop computer that sat on a card table, and tapped on the keyboard to bring the screen to life.

Ben leaned down and picked up a laptop that balanced precariously on a pile of deconstructed computer parts. "Does this thing work?" Ben asked.

Gabe nodded without looking back over his shoulder. Ben opened the laptop so both he and Mack could see it.

"While Gabe starts on the trace," he said, "we need to find out everything we can about this . . . thing."

"*Magic,* you mean?" Mack said. "You might as well get used to calling it what it is."

"I don't *know* what it is. That's what we're trying to find out."

Mack rolled her eyes. "Where do we even begin?"

It was a good question. What did they know so far about how this all worked? Ben closed his eyes. He pictured Agent Thompson, saying the strange words, levitating the pen. He heard Mack whispering into his ear as she yanked the officer from his motorcycle . . .

"Words," Ben said, eyes snapping open. "You need words to do it, right? You have to say something?"

"Yeah, except that when I really focus, I can almost just *think* them and that's good enough."

"But it's fair to say that the ability hinges on language?"

Mack pursed her lips and nodded. "Sure, I suppose."

"In our meeting at the White House, Torozian said they thought the language might be ancient Sumerian. That can't be a very common field of study. So let's start by looking for a scholar, a professor somewhere, who can confirm that and translate. If words can be used to do this, maybe we can find the words to stop it."

Ben and Mack huddled over the laptop, cross-referencing scholars of ancient languages and magic. It turned out to be an unmitigated waste of time. Instead of esteemed professors at accredited universities, the search results were one New Age crank after another, with each supposed "expert" claiming the ability to tap into the earth's mystical energy to solve Ben's problems with love, or career unhappiness, or male pattern baldness. One even referred to himself, in his glowing About Me section, as a "Solution Astrologer."

"This is such horseshit," Ben said, exasperated, leaning back into his chair. He set the laptop on the floor. "We shouldn't be surprised we can't find anyone. No serious person would ever admit to believing in magic."

Mack stared at him, her face reddening. "Excuse me?"

Ben looked at her. "You know what I mean. Nobody with a reputation to protect could afford—" He broke off.

"What? What is it?"

"It's just . . ." Ben sat up straighter. "A lot of the academic game at a university is about a person's reputation. How much they've published, how seriously they're taken in their fields."

"So what are you saying?"

"I'm saying nobody's credibility would survive in academia if they said they believed in magic. Someone admitting to something like that would be laughed out of any legitimate institution." Ben ran a hand through his hair. "So maybe . . . maybe that's who we need to be looking for."

Mack frowned. "People with bad reputations?"

"Sort of," Ben agreed. "Disgraced academics. Ex-professors. People who held high positions and got fired. Maybe we can start to filter our search that way?"

It didn't help. The web search continued to be fruitless. Time was ticking away. Right now, Novak's men would be poring over CCTV footage from every gas station, bank, toll booth, and whatever else they could find with a camera within a hundred miles of D.C., hunting for them. The longer Ben and Mack stayed put, the harder it would be to move.

More importantly, every second that went by with these protocols out in the world, and without Merlin in custody, meant the risk of more dangerous terrorists and criminals, and a higher potential for devastating attacks.

It was another half hour before Ben finally found what he was looking for.

There was a handful of small news items, mostly from the UK press. Each contained no more than a paragraph or two about Dr. Desdemona Heaton, a disgraced former Oxford scholar. Most featured the same photo of the pale-skinned, white-haired Heaton, dressed in academic regalia at some formal function. The tone of the puff pieces was also invariably mocking. The woman was a laughingstock.

She'd been a scholar of mystical religion. Two years before, during a speech at an academic conference, she'd made her career-ending claim. She told the crowd that, based on a lifetime of research, she'd concluded that not only was magic real but that for centuries it also had been kept under wraps by a collection of ancient families known as the Possessors.

Ben read on, navigating to some of Heaton's published works. Her careful arguments connected the dots between disparate phenomena, drawing lines between the rise in the economic and social status of certain families and the accounts of unexplainable events that frequently accompanied them. Some of the names were expected. Heaton cited members of the House of Medici as prominent Possessors. But most were unknown to Ben. Something about the relative anonymity of the names—the fact that she didn't traffic in the usual conspiratorial litany of supposed secret society members like Da Vinci, Dante, Napoleon, Paine, and the rest—lent a certain credence to her claims.

Then there was the fact that Heaton was also one of the world's foremost scholars of ancient Sumerian.

The day before, Ben would have dismissed it all as superstition, baseless conjecture, wishful thinking. But it had been a hell of a strange day, and he felt differently: this Heaton woman might be the real deal.

Reading about these so-called Possessors, and how in Heaton's estimation they had abused a formerly sacred trust to their own advantage, Ben was reminded of Merlin's manifesto. *Your world is about to change. Your certainties will be undone. Your corrupt hierarchies will die.* What was the connection between Merlin and these Possessors?

"We need to talk to Heaton," Ben said, as much to himself as to Mack.

Another search turned up her current whereabouts. She'd been hired as an adjunct professor at a tiny, undistinguished college outside Edinburgh, Scotland. Academic exile. But she had no listed contact information of any kind.

"Gabe, let me use your phone."

Gabe had moved to the floor, where he was sitting, cross-legged and still shirtless, typing rapidly back and forth on the two laptops open before him. He reached into the pocket of his board shorts and tossed Ben his phone without looking up.

Ben caught it, and dialed the main number of the Scottish college. He hung up on the first ring, remembering that it was the middle of the night there.

Mack yawned and stood up. "Bathroom?" she said.

"Down the hall." Gabe pointed. "Across from the vacuum tubes."

When she'd gone, Ben addressed Gabe, "What have you got so far?"

"Tracing the upload back to the source is harder than I antici-pated," Gabe admitted, scratching at the stubble under his chin. "The protocol was released using a worm, and there are so many replicated copies around it's a goddamn chicken and egg situation: Which came first? For every ten dead ends, I take one step in the right direction." He shook his head. "I'll get there, but it won't be fast."

"All right, well keep at it," Ben said. Something else nagged at him. "Gabe," he began, thinking out loud, "everyone keeps calling this thing magic. But all I see is a way of manipulating objects in space and determining their motion. Where I come from we call that phys-ics, you follow me?"

"Maybe. Keep going."

"I'm just thinking about Newton: for every action there's an equal and opposite reaction, right? So what's the opposite of this protocol?"

"You mean like a . . . counterspell?"

"Something like that. Do you think you can play around with the wording of this thing? Chop it up, run it backward, I don't know. See if you can alter it in any way. The more we know the better."

"Sure, but let me ask you something." Gabe looked thoughtful. "Have you tried using the words yourself yet?"

Ben shook his head. It hadn't even occurred to him.

"Well, aren't you curious?" Gabe goaded. "What if you're, like, a wizard or whatever?"

Ben grinned. "You have the thing open on your computer? Let me see it."

Gabe turned one of the laptops in Ben's direction. Ben started to read Merlin's words aloud, the foreign syllables thick and clumsy in his mouth. When nothing happened, he repeated them with all the concentration he could muster. This time, the object of Ben's focus,

Gabe's cell phone, shifted about a quarter of an inch on the seat next to him. Even that much labor had winded him.

"Dude," Gabe cackled, "you totally suck at magic, bro."

"Let's see *you* try, jackass."

Gabe's shot was better, but only marginally. After repeating the words a few times, and squinting and squeezing up his face so hard that Ben half-worried he might burst a blood vessel, Gabe managed to tip over a lawn chair that had been propped against the wall. He, too, looked exhausted by the effort.

Ben's appreciation for Mack's abilities had grown exponentially in only a few minutes.

"All right, we both suck," Gabe said breathlessly. "Look, as far as trying to reconfigure the spell, I'll do what I can. But listen, Ben, I like you. We're tight and all, but this ain't charity." He gave Ben a pointed look.

"I know." Ben nodded. "And while you're at it, I'm going to need you to put something else on my tab."

Gabe's eyes narrowed. "What?"

"Passports. I got mine from an out-of-Agency contractor, so my aliases shouldn't be compromised, but Mack's going to need a few. Let's make it three."

"Three what?" It was Mack's voice, closing in from down the hall. She reentered the room.

"Passports," Ben repeated.

"Just what the hell do I need three passports for?"

"Two for backup," Ben said, looking from Mack to Gabe, then back to Mack. "And one because we're going to Scotland."

9

Ben leaped up from his chair, his mind and senses sharp with the anticipation of action, as Mack stared, openmouthed.

"Dulles and Reagan are out," Ben said, "obviously."

"There's a small airfield about twenty miles northwest of here, on the way to Baltimore. I know the guy who owns it."

"Can he be trusted?"

Gabe nodded. "I've used him before. He'll come through."

Professional courtesy meant Ben didn't ask what exactly Gabe had needed to transport through a remote airfield.

"The bike's been compromised by now," Ben said. "We'll need a car."

"I can take you."

"How fast can you be ready with the passports?"

"Hour and a half. Two at the outside."

"Stop it!" Mack shouted. "Both of you just . . . *stop*!"

Ben and Gabe turned to her. Mack's hands were clenched into fists at her sides. Her chest rose and fell rapidly.

"What makes you think I'm going with you?" Mack said to Ben. "Your mission, or whatever it is, has nothing to do with me. I'm in deep enough shit as it is. I mean, the CIA is after me, and you want me to leave the *country*?" She laughed. "I don't even care who Merlin is, or what he wants, okay? I just want to go back to . . . to . . ."

She seemed to lose her steam all at once as the reality of the situation hit her full force. Her eyes fell.

"Back to the guy you threw through a window?" Ben asked. It came out harsher than he'd intended.

Ben crossed to Mack and put a firm hand on her shoulder. "Look, if we don't keep moving, Harris *will* catch up with us. And it'll be even worse for you than it would have been before, because now they know the threat you pose them. I wish we could afford to wait until morning to call and see if this Heaton woman is around in the summer, but we need to go now to have a fighting chance."

Mack threw up her arms, brushing Ben's hand away. "A chance to do what?"

"To find this professor who can help us, to learn what we need to know about the Possessors, to get to Merlin." The operation had already coalesced in Ben's mind. "You said you don't care about the mission, but stopping the spread of these protocols means we can keep people safe. We can save lives. You worked in a hospital, right? Don't you want to save people?"

"Why are you even doing this?" Mack persisted. "Why do you even care? You might as well turn me in to them and disappear."

"I can't do that."

This wasn't about protecting Mack; it was clear this woman could take care of herself. This was about not sitting idly by while a destabilizing force potentially greater than the world had ever known was unleashed piece by devastating piece. He may not understand this "magic," but it was real and it was more terrifying than any threat he'd seen.

"I need you," Ben finally said. "I meant what I told Novak. Whoever Merlin is, he's obviously powerful. I'm going to need someone who can match him if he's going to be stopped. But it's your choice:

you could help save the world, or you could sit here and watch it all go to hell on TV."

Mack looked down at her feet. She snorted and shook her head in evident disbelief. Then she leveled her gaze on Ben.

"All right," she said. "Let's go to Scotland."

Gabe's beat-up Ford Explorer—more rust than metal at this point in its long service—rolled through the open barbed wire gate of the rural Maryland airfield just before one in the morning. Gabe angled the SUV toward a hangar to the left of the gate, which had also been left open in anticipation of their arrival. The huge door slowly slid shut behind them as Gabe brought the vehicle to a stop in the center of the lit end of the cavernous space. Parked at the other end of the hangar, in shadow, Ben counted four planes: two small prop planes, and two private business jets. Ben, Gabe, and Mack opened their doors and stepped out.

The man who had closed the hangar door stomped toward them with a grim look on his face.

"You know I don't like new people around here, Garcia," the man said gruffly, his voice echoing in the vast space.

"Couldn't be helped, Klipp," Gabe responded. "This is important."

The man harrumphed. He was short, broad shouldered, and looked as solid as a boulder.

Gabe made the introductions. "These are the people I was telling you about. This is Ben Zolstra"—the hand that shook Ben's was stubby and calloused, with spots of engine grease under the fingernails—"and this is Eila Mack."

Gabe turned to Ben and Mack. "This is Sergeant Klippman. A good man and a mean son of a bitch."

"Sergeant?" Ben said.

"Marine Corps."

"My brother was a Marine." Ben pressed his thumb against John's ring as he spoke.

"We don't say 'was,'" Klippman chided. "Once a Marine, always a Marine."

"Yeah, well, he's dead," Ben said, "so I say *was*."

"Shit." Klippman rubbed at the back of his neck. "I'm sorry to hear that. Did he die in combat?"

Ben nodded. "Afghanistan."

Gabe cleared his throat to break the silence that followed. "I told Ben you might be able to help him."

"I didn't get many details on the phone," Klippman said, turning back to Ben. "So what is it you need? You looking for a place to lie low for a bit?"

"We need a plane," Ben said matter-of-factly, "with enough fuel to get to Scotland. I imagine that G5 back there would do it." He pointed at one of the jets in the rear of the hangar. "You'll also have to not file a flight plan or passenger manifest."

Klippman let out a single, booming laugh. He looked to Gabe, jabbing a thumb in Ben's direction. "This guy kidding me?"

"No," Gabe said, "I'm afraid he's not."

"Well, I'm afraid you're out of fucking luck, my man," Klippman said to Ben. "This isn't some kind of rental service. Now, if you want to hide out for a few nights, that'd be all right. Got a cot or two in the back, and I think there's a cookstove around here someplace."

"What we need is the plane," Ben repeated.

Klippman slowly shook his head. "You're not hearing me," he said. "What you're asking me to do is ten different kinds of illegal. I'm trying to help you out, but I'm not trying to see the inside of a cell."

Ben gritted his teeth, his blood starting to rise. This was their only shot to get out of the States. They'd never make it through any commercial airport, Harris would see to that. And they'd be stopped at any land border crossing. But they could slip out on a tiny jet before Harris's net closed any tighter around them.

"What if I could show you something that you'd never seen before?" Ben asked. "Something dangerous. Something that you could help us stop before it gets out of control."

Klippman folded his arms across his barrel chest, and raised his eyebrows. *Well?*

Ben put an arm around Mack and led her a few paces away from the others.

"You ready to show off?" he asked her.

"Yeah." Mack nodded, a smile turning up the corners of her lips. "I think so."

A moment of hushed chatter later, they rejoined Gabe and Klippman. The Marine looked restless.

"If you've got something to show me, let's see it. Otherwise, I think we're done here."

Ben nodded toward the G5 again. "How much would you say that jet weighs?"

"I don't want to play games."

"Me neither," Ben said. "How much?"

Klippman pursed his lips. "Fully fueled? About ninety thousand pounds."

"Pretty heavy." Ben turned to Mack. "Think you can lift it?"

"No problem," Mack said, rubbing her hands together.

"What the hell is this?" Klippman asked.

But Mack was already whispering the words of the protocol, the foreign syllables flowing ever more effortlessly across her lips. She stared at the jet, her gaze hardening in intensity. Her hands reached out toward the plane.

Klippman snickered but abruptly stopped when the business jet began to wobble. Ben looked back at Mack, who was now reciting the words through gritted teeth, her face reddening.

Slowly, the front wheel of the jet left the concrete floor of the hangar.

"*Madre de diós*," Gabe said under his breath.

The plane shuddered, then parted with the ground completely. Mack grunted with evident strain. Her hands shook violently, and her breath was ragged and shallow. The jet floated uncertainly a few feet in the air.

"That's good," Ben said in her ear. "Now don't drop it. Set it down nice and easy."

As soon as the wheels were back in contact with the earth, Mack fell to her knees, sucking down air in great gulps. Ben helped her to her feet, though she continued to look unsteady.

"A little harder than a fucking Ford Focus," she gasped.

Klippman stared at Mack. His lips moved, but he seemed unable to find the words he wanted to say. Ben walked over and clapped him on the shoulder.

"Wha—what . . . was that?" Klippman finally said.

"*That* is why we're here. If we don't move fast, there are going to be more who can do what she does. Maybe lots more. Maybe thousands. Millions. And they won't all be so friendly."

Klippman nodded dully, his face still a stupefied mask.

"We're working with the government to stop this," Ben said. "And I have an idea of how to do it. But we have to get to Scotland. There's someone else we need."

"I can't . . . the plane's not mine to give."

"Sergeant, I know I'm asking a lot of you. I understand the position I'm putting you in. But you swore an oath to defend the Constitution against all enemies, foreign and domestic, didn't you? You help us stop this power from falling into the hands of our enemies, and you'll be a hero twice over."

"Okay, enough," Klippman growled, "you've made your point."

"You'll help us?"

"If you're really with the government, why do you need me?"

"This is a need-to-know black op. The more people in on it, the harder it is to keep something this sensitive under wraps." Ben felt a twinge of guilt lying to the Marine, but he was their only ticket out. He fixed Klippman with a penetrating stare. "Can we count on you, Sergeant?"

Klippman frowned, then gave him a curt nod. "I'll give you a plane," he said. "But stop calling me Sergeant, will you? Call me Klipp."

"Thank you for helping us, Klipp," Mack said.

"The G5 you just . . . lifted . . . is owned by a rich asshole from Bethesda. It's a trophy for him more than anything. He comes around once a year. He'll never know it's been used." Klippman started walking toward the jet. "I'll get it prepped."

The more Ben thought about it, the worse an idea it seemed heading out without logging a flight plan. There were too many ways for that to go south, and Ben didn't want to make it across the Atlantic only to be shot down by British air defenses.

"Forget what I said earlier," he said to Klippman, "go ahead and log the flight under the owner's name, and put us down as passengers on the manifest." They could use the fake names from one set of passports.

Klippman nodded without stopping. "Can do."

"Oh, and one last thing, Klipp," Ben called out.

This time Klippman stopped and turned. "What's that?"

"You're not gonna like it," Gabe warned, a smile playing on his lips.

"None of us knows how to fly a plane," Ben said. "Except you." He grinned. "You were a Corps aviator, and a damn good one, if Gabe is to be believed—which he sometimes is. So what do you say: Will you be our pilot? Ready for the mother of all black ops?"

Klippman snorted incredulously and looked at Gabe, though by this point he knew better than to ask if Ben was kidding.

"What the hell," Klippman said. "Let's ride."

10

It started with a loud crash that woke everybody up. Workie sat upright on his bed and strained his eyes, looking into the dim hallway. It was after lights out, so he couldn't see much past the bars of his cell. But across from him, he caught the outline of Chicago, also sitting up and squinting. Workie figured they were both thinking the same thing: *a crash* that *loud, with tearing metal and shit? What the hell did* that *mean?* The Broad River Correctional Institution wasn't near major roads, or any other damn thing for that matter. That was kinda the whole point.

Giggles, whose little slit of window looked out over the front of the facility, shouted a report from two cells over.

"It's a truck," Giggles said. "An armored truck. Busted right the hell through the front gates."

"Beautiful," Chicago said with a groan. "Guess we'll be spending all week fixing that shit."

Chicago thought the crash was an accident. Workie supposed he did, too.

Then the gunshots started. *Ratta-tat-tat-tat.* Fast and loud.

"They're shooting the guards," Giggles announced.

Workie's cellmate, Roach, rolled over in his bed and asked who was doing the shooting.

Giggles giggled. "Whoever the fuck just got out of that truck."

There were more shots. Roach sucked his teeth and said it sounded like firecrackers.

Bullshit, Workie thought, *it sounds like fucking gunshots.*

That was when Giggles really started losing his shit. They could hear the straining springs as he jumped up and down on his bed, laughing like he'd just inhaled two whippets.

"There's four of 'em," Giggles yelled. "They're throwing the guards around."

"What do you mean?" Chicago asked.

"Like with their hands and stuff," Giggles said. "Throwing 'em into the buildings. Breaking them. Breaking them in half." Giggles was hysterical. "Like magic," he kept saying, "like fucking magic."

Minutes later all the cell doors opened at once. Workie and Roach looked at each other. *Is this for real?* They got up and stepped into the hall.

A spray of rifle shots made Workie hit the deck, but Roach was too slow. He got blasted. Blood spurted from his neck as he fell. Workie knew right away he was dead.

A guard at the end of the hall was shouting at them to get the fuck back in their cells or he'd kill every last one of them. Workie knew he wasn't playing. He started to crawl backward into his still-open cell.

Then the guard flew up into the air and some force started shaking him back and forth until he dropped his gun. Chicago darted out from his cell and pounced on the rifle like an alley cat, then turned it toward the guard and let it rip. The bullets tore a dozen holes in the CO and the bastard still hovered in the air.

"Well well well," said the voice of someone having a good time.

At the opposite end of the hallway, Workie saw a tall guy in a Gamecocks sweatshirt looking at them all and grinning like a politician. When the guy put his hand down, the side-of-beef of dead guard finally hit the floor with a wet thump.

"If y'all don't want to stay in here," the guy said, "now's a pretty good time to move y'all's asses."

So Workie moved his ass.

11

In the back of the White House press briefing room, Novak thumbed through a mountain of texts and emails as he waited for the fireworks to start. Linda McAllister, the president's press secretary with perpetual fresh-from-the-tanning-salon bronzed skin, was about to take questions. After what had happened a few hours before, Novak knew the reporters weren't going to be asking about the jobs report, the infrastructure bill that was stalled in Congress, or any of the other nonissues McAllister had been speaking about for the last ten minutes. The questions would be about the South Carolina prison break that freed three dozen inmates in a way that nobody could quite explain. As if by magic.

The protocol was getting out through the dark web, and despite the best efforts of the intelligence agencies to plug the leaks, they simply didn't have the manpower to keep the dam from bursting for much longer.

Novak opened a text from Walters, back at Langley.

Seoh says they're getting closer on upload.

That was a sliver of good news mixed into all the shit. Agent Seoh, the head of the Merlin tech team, was a baby-faced ex-hacker who'd wisely decided that working for the government was a more attractive option than spending twenty years to life in prison. She was smart, fast, and she worked around-the-clock as long as she was kept well supplied with energy drinks. If Seoh said they were close, it wouldn't be long before they found the terminal from which Merlin had done his dirty work.

At the front of the room, McAllister signaled that she would now take questions. Hands shot up from every seat.

"Go ahead, Mark," the press secretary said, her voice already wary.

"What can you tell us about what happened in the South Carolina prison break? The reports coming in are very unusual, not to say troubling. Is this—?"

"I don't have all the information at this time. What I *can* talk about is the record job growth we've seen in the—"

"Sorry, you have no comment on the prison break?"

"As I've said, information is continuing to come in." McAllister pointed into the crowd. "Jane."

"Thank you," a blonde woman said. "Witnesses at the correctional facility have said that people were being thrown through the air . . . uh . . . that guards were being . . . crushed by some unseen force—"

"The president does not wish to comment on—"

"Just to follow up," Jane continued, "some people are suggesting that there might be some sort of chemical leak in the area, and that some of these stories might be the result of induced mass hallucination. Residents in the area are reportedly panicking, fleeing their homes. They're getting mixed messages from the police. What can you tell them—?"

McAllister's face hardened. "I'll say again, the White House will address the situation in South Carolina at the appropriate time and in the appropriate manner."

"What does that mean?" shouted a man near the front. "This happened over four hours ago. Why has there been no response? Why has local law enforcement been told not to speak about this?"

Another reporter jumped in. "Why has there been no video of the incident released, even though there were cameras throughout the prison? Is there something being covered up here?"

"One at a time," McAllister snapped, "and wait until you're called on. I'll take one more question . . . *not* about the prison break." She pointed at a gray-bearded man near the rear of the auditorium. "Sam, go ahead."

"Was what happened in South Carolina *magic?*" The man's voice put quotes around the word. "Some witnesses are saying that—"

"This isn't Harry Potter, people," McAllister said, with an unconvincing laugh. "Lots of worked-up imaginations out there, I can tell. But I can assure you that the explanation for the prison break will prove to be not nearly as exciting as you all seem to think. That's all, thank you."

McAllister, chased by a babel of shouted questions, stepped down from the podium and through the door that led back to her office. Novak followed after her.

"They smell blood," McAllister said as Novak closed the heavy wooden door behind him. "There's only so much longer we can contain this." She sat heavily into her desk chair. "That's the second question about magic in the last two days. I have to give them something."

McAllister had been broadly briefed about the developing Merlin situation.

"No, you don't," Novak said. "You can't."

"How come you intelligence people have never understood rule one of public relations? Stonewalling doesn't make a story go away, it makes it bigger. People speculate and freak out like you saw in there."

"Until we can reassure the country that we have the situation under control, we cannot acknowledge the reality of what is going on."

What he didn't say was that he was afraid that soon the evidence of magic would be irrefutable—and so would the fact that the government had been caught totally unprepared to deal with it.

Novak's phone rang and he swiped to answer.

"We think we've got something on Zolstra," Walters said. "A plane."

Novak cupped the phone closer and turned away from McAllister. "Go on."

"It's a Gulfstream registered to a pharma lobbyist named Savas Demir. He keeps the jet stored at an airfield outside Baltimore. He logged a flight plan to take it to Edinburgh in the middle of the night. The unusual timing automatically triggered a system alert we'd set up. The thing is, one of our guys just spoke with Demir. Says he had no idea it was taken."

"What are they saying at the airfield?"

"No one's picking up. The guy who runs it is a former Marine, Sergeant Maxwell Klippman. So far we haven't found any direct connection between him and Zolstra."

"Well, keep looking for indirect ones. This is Zolstra, I can smell it."

Even as he said the words, Novak hoped he was wrong. Despite everything, he found himself rooting for the aggravating ex-agent. Harris couldn't see that what was at stake now was bigger than any personality conflict. Whatever problems Novak had with Zolstra's methods, he rarely had cause to argue with the results.

Zolstra wasn't just running from capture, Novak knew, he was running *toward* something. In his mind, he was still on the mission, just doing it his own way. But what the hell did he expect to find in Scotland?

Whatever it was, Zolstra wasn't going to get it. Novak's hands were tied. Harris wanted him and Mack brought in. Novak sighed, ready to give Walters the order to send the jet's call number and flight plan to their assets in the UK so they could intercept the plane at the airport.

He hesitated. He didn't have to give that order. Not right away at least. Of course, he needed to bring Zolstra in eventually—but maybe he could buy him a little time first.

"I'm going to take this to the director," Novak lied, "and see how he wants to proceed from here. Sit tight, Walters."

He disconnected the call.

"Anything I should know about?" McAllister asked coyly.

"Absolutely not." Novak turned to leave. "Remember, keep a lid on this story."

He put his hand on the doorknob.

The press secretary called after him, "For how much longer?"

"It won't be long now."

One way or another, the truth would soon come out.

12

Livingston College was not what Ben had expected. Instead of medieval turrets and towers of weathered stone, tall spires, and Gothic arches, the small school looked surprisingly modern, as though it had been assembled from flat-pack boxes like an IKEA couch. Its long, low main building was a love song to right angles, all thin wooden slats and huge panes of darkened glass.

Ben and Mack stepped out of the taxi that had brought them from the airport. A few wisps of Mack's loosely braided hair were immediately swept up on the breeze.

"I feel like I might be the only black person within fifty miles of here," Mack said with an easy laugh, looking around at a few white students walking across the campus. "Aren't we trying *not* to draw attention to ourselves?"

Ben smiled. "Just don't let the celebrity go to your head."

They'd traveled all night—and, with the time difference, well into the next day—watching from the plane as the peninsulas and islands of western Scotland appeared like mirages after the long hours of unbroken black sea and sky. Out of the mist, the craggy shores shimmered toward them, dotted here and there with clusters of stone houses. The moors followed, dressed for summer, rich and emerald green even in the gray of the overcast day. Then the plane left even those behind, and only the green and purple of grasses and heather blanketed the earth below, crisscrossed by narrow country lanes and spotted with lakes.

Now, at last arrived at Heaton's college, Ben and Mack passed through the glass doors labeled ADMINISTRATION BUILDING. The student worker at the front desk frowned when they told him they were looking for Heaton. Apparently she wasn't any more popular here than she'd been at Oxford. The kid directed them down a corridor toward the back of the building.

They moved down the hall, a sense of unease gnawing at Ben. They'd come so far and risked so much to meet one woman, to chase down one lead.

Mack expressed her own doubts. "What if this professor can't help us? Do you really think Gabe will be able to trace Merlin's upload?"

"Absolutely."

There'd been no reason for Gabe to join them in Scotland. He was most useful to them back home in his digital lair. Klippman was waiting for them at the airport in Edinburgh. The Marine had agreed to pilot them, transitioning quickly from grudging to enthusiastic in his support of the mission. Ben had even caught him whistling as he readied the jet and planned their route. It was just what Ben had suspected when they'd been introduced: despite his early protestations, Klippman proved eager to get back in the action. Ben had felt the same tug when Novak visited his farm in Vermont. Civilian life for men like them lacked urgency and clarity of purpose. It was like living with no heartbeat. Walking death.

Next to a closed door was the placard they'd been looking for:

DR. DESDEMONA HEATON, PROFESSOR OF MYSTICAL RELIGION AND OCCULT STUDIES.

Ben and Mack shared an anxious look. He knocked at the door.

"Enter."

It was not the voice of an aging female professor. It was a young voice, male, with a minor trace of Scottish brogue.

Ben opened the door into an office in such a state of evident disarray that it could've given Gabe's place a run for its money. All four walls were lined with leaning, sagging bookcases stuffed to the gills with thick tomes, two or three volumes deep. Tall stacks of yellowing papers took up most of the floor, each weighted down with whatever object had been at hand. On top of one stack sat a cobblestone; on another, a tiny, leathery skull. The room smelled of mildewing books and sweet tobacco smoke.

A giant wooden desk stood in the center of the office, wide and two-sided, like a partner desk from an old accounting firm. Two people sat at it. On the left side, in front of the door, sat a young white man with a dark, trim beard. He was typing at blazing speed on a desktop computer. On the right side, near the window, sat a white-haired older woman who Ben recognized as Heaton from the news articles he'd read back at Gabe's. As they entered the room Ben and Mack stood awkwardly in front of the desk: there was no other place to sit.

"Good afternoon," Heaton said. Her voice was gravelly, but her accent clipped, upper-crust English. "How may I be of service?"

"Dr. Heaton, my name is Ben Zolstra, and this is Eila Mack. We have some questions for you about the . . . phenomena of your expertise."

"You want to know about magic," she said simply.

"Yes. But what we need to discuss is sensitive." Ben glanced at the young man.

Heaton pursed her lips. "Lucas Adin is my research assistant, and the most capable student I've ever worked with. He has my complete confidence." Lucas tugged at the bottom of his tweed vest and sat up straighter.

Ben glanced at Mack, who shrugged. What choice did they have?

"This is the situation," Ben said. "Someone has leaked the knowledge of how to manipulate objects using telekinesis onto the internet.

The same person has promised more revelations to come. We're working on behalf of our government, trying to track that person down and stop them. We're hoping you can tell us what you know about the people you call the Possessors, and anything you've learned about how we might counter these protocols."

Heaton picked up a delicate wooden pipe from its holder on the desk in front of her. "Protocols?" She shook loose a match from a small box.

"Spells," Mack clarified. Ben winced at the word.

Heaton struck the match against the box, then brought the pipe to her mouth and puffed it to life. The woodsy, almond-vanilla aroma of pipe tobacco filled the small room. Heaton stared at Ben. The pictures he had seen failed to capture the way it felt to stand before her and be appraised by those pale blue eyes.

"Very well," Heaton said through a mouthful of smoke. "I'll answer your questions. In fact, in some strange way I believe I've been expecting you. But we can't talk here. Will you join me at my home for dinner? Please give me a few moments to sort out my things."

"We'll wait for you in the hall."

Once out of the room, Ben dialed Gabe back in the States.

"Zolstra!" Gabe answered on the second ring, cheerful as always. Ben could almost see his flip-flops and smell his Pacífico with lime. "You make it to Scotland? You wearing one of those plaid skirts yet, man?"

"We're on the ground. How about you? What kind of progress have you made on tracking the uploads?"

"Closing in. I should have the terminal pegged soon. Looks like it's gonna be in Asia."

Asia, not exactly a small target. "Okay, call me when you've got it. What about finding a way to counter the protocol. Any luck there?"

"Working on it."

"How's it looking for me and Mack? Are we public enemies number one and two yet?"

"Got five different TV stations on. No coverage about you so far."

That should have been good news, except it could just as easily have meant that Harris knew they were out of the country. Had he already located the missing plane?

Ben thanked Gabe and disconnected the call.

Moments later, Ben and Mack were in a large sedan, being driven by Heaton away from Livingston and out through gently rolling fields. Here and there, fragments of weather-beaten stone walls appeared in the gray haze. After cresting a gentle hill, they steered off the lane and onto an even narrower stretch of road, lined with oaks on one side.

Finally, a two-story house appeared a hundred yards in the distance. It looked venerably old but also modest—a compact place made of stone, with three small rectangular windows cut into both stories, and a chimney sticking up from the slate roof. Heaton stopped the car in front of the house.

"My humble abode," she said with a warm laugh.

Once inside, the professor popped into a back room, and could be heard informing her cook to prepare for extra dinner guests. Then she reentered and poured herself a single malt scotch on the rocks, unconcerned when Ben turned down a glass. Mack also declined, though Ben couldn't help noticing that she eyed the amber liquid with longing. He recalled that Novak had mentioned Mack's drinking getting her into trouble.

They all sat in the comfortably appointed front room, Mack at one end of a long sofa, Ben and Heaton across from her in two high-backed armchairs.

"Nice place," Mack said.

"You're kind, but I know it isn't much. I lived in my previous home for nearly twenty-five years." A wistful look came over Heaton. "A lovely place. Huge windows. I could bathe in sunlight. Within walking distance from the university, too." She cleared her throat, returning to the present. "But I'm afraid I find myself in rather reduced circumstances lately."

Heaton took a sip of her drink. Mack was looking around the room skeptically, as if the circumstances didn't seem too reduced to her.

Heaton gave her scotch another taste, then waved a hand in front of her, as though clearing the air. "It's all in the past now," she said. "No sense in combing over it again and again, I suppose. Especially at my age. One must look to the future."

"The future is exactly what we're here to talk about, Dr. Heaton," Ben said. "How can we stop all this? There must be some way, something you've come across in your years of research that could point us in the right direction."

Heaton looked at Ben like he was an unruly student. "Americans always want to jump right to the solution without taking the time to understand the problem. If we're going to talk about the future, we have to talk about the past. We'll need to start at the beginning."

"The beginning of magic?" Mack said eagerly. "You mean you know where it came from? Why some people can do it, and"—she threw Ben a smug look—"others can't?"

Back on the plane, once they'd gotten well into international waters, Mack had helped Ben try to use the words of the protocols again. She explained how to hone his focus, how to connect the words with an intention, but it was no use. Although his attempts to master this new—weapon? technology? science?—were wholehearted, all he'd managed to do this time was make a cocktail napkin flutter. Yet Mack herself seemed to be such a natural. Why?

Heaton threw the rest of her drink down the hatch. "I believe I do know the answers to your questions, my dear."

"So how far back does . . . all this go?" Ben asked.

"Is it so hard for you to say *magic*, Mr. Zolstra?"

"Yes," he said, "it is."

"Ah, I see. You're a man who values the life of the mind. A man of reason and logic. A tactician, perhaps. You consider belief in magic to be a ridiculous superstition."

Ben nodded. "I do."

"Then how do you explain the phenomena you're here to ask me about?"

"I don't *need* to explain it. I'm only saying that when you jump to the conclusion of calling something 'magic' just because you can't understand it, you cross the line that separates science from myth."

The tinkle of a bell sounded from somewhere deeper in the house.

"We'll have to continue this in the next room," Heaton said pleasantly. "Dinner is served."

The dining room, like the rest of the house, was small but elegant. Ben, Mack, and Heaton sat at an oval table of stout, burnished wood, in upholstered chairs whose high backs ended well over their heads. Portraits of distinguished Heatons from distant eras adorned the walls. Spread before Ben and Mack on the oval table were sets of bone china plates, weighty silverware, and heavy crystal goblets. The candles in the brass candelabra cast a dim, flickering light onto the walls, leaving the room's corners smudged in shadow. Heaton motioned toward the tender slabs of meat on the bone and the large bowl of indeterminate mush that accompanied them.

"Mutton curry is one of my favorites," Heaton said. "And no one but my grandmother ever made a better rumbledethumps than my cook, Mrs. McQuarrie."

"A better what now?" Mack said.

Heaton jabbed a spoon in the direction of the mush. "It's potato, cabbage, onion, and cheese. Quite delicious even to an American palate, I should think."

When the sound of metal scraping on plates had subsided a little, Heaton picked up the conversation where they'd left off.

"What I have spent my life researching is something I'm afraid I can only call magic. So for the duration of what I am about to explain, when I say 'magic,' Mr. Zolstra, perhaps you'd be comfortable thinking of the word as a shorthand for 'science we don't understand yet.'"

Ben swallowed another bite of the tender mutton. "You call it anything you want, Professor," he said. "As long as you can help me stop it."

"I suppose I should begin," Heaton said, sipping red wine from her goblet, "by admitting to you that I don't have all the answers. I don't have the whole story, for the simple reason that generations of people have gone to great lengths to keep that story from being told."

"These are the Possessors you've written about," Ben said.

"Are they like the Illuminati?" Mack asked.

"Not exactly. The conspiracy fanatics who say the world is controlled by some secret cabal that pulls all the strings behind the scenes are right in some ways and wrong in others. Most of what I've been able to uncover suggests these families are generally inclined to use their power to secure a somewhat more personal gain. I don't know that they've played much of a role in picking kings and popes and presidents and such."

"But why do they have the power to begin with?" Mack asked. "What makes them so special?"

"Thereupon hangs a tale," Heaton said, the twinkle in her eye exaggerated by the glinting candlelight. "As near as I can tell, there was a time when magic was available to everyone. In the Western imagination, this has been conceptualized as Eden: the world before the Fall."

"Adam and Eve's Eden?" Mack asked.

Heaton smiled, clearly thrilled to explain her life's work to a captive, willing audience. She leaned forward conspiratorially. "Think about what their lives were said to have been like. According to Scripture, before the poor couple was cursed for disobedience, they were immortal. They could talk to animals. They frolicked around in the woods, naked as jaybirds, and weren't stung, bitten, or clawed by any living creature. It was paradise. It was *magical.*"

Ben frowned. "You're not telling us that Adam and Eve were real."

"Oh, heavens no," Heaton said, "only your fundamentalists say that. No, what I'm suggesting is that there was a time when what we call magic was simply a natural part of life. Something that humans could control as effortlessly as we now move our own limbs—and probably just as thoughtlessly. And that time has been collectively remembered as myth."

"Okay, so what happened?" Ben said. "What was the Fall that kicked us out of Eden, so to speak?"

"Language," Heaton responded. "Specifically, writing. More specifically still, ancient Sumerian cuneiform writing."

Heaton set down her heavy wine goblet with an authoritative *plunk.* The motion caused the flames of the candles to sputter. The room seemed to darken and close in around her. The portraits appeared to glower at them from above.

"In the earliest days, magic was everywhere"—she spread her arms out wide—"and it was very weak. But with the advent of sophisticated and abstract language, humans suddenly had the ability to specify, to describe, to command the world around them, magic included. As a consequence"—she began to bring her hands closer together— "two things happened: magic was able to be commanded in a more focused way, and so it also became more concentrated and powerful. This is when the first, simple spells would have been created, maybe nothing more than little nursery rhymes that were passed down from mother to child. However, as time passed and written language was devised"—Heaton brought her hands together in front of her until they were only inches apart—"magic became *much* more narrowly focused, and many times more powerful."

"But how could that happen?" Mack asked.

Heaton thought for a moment. "Consider sunlight," she said. "You step outside and it's everywhere. You expose your skin to it, and it warms you. This was the case with magic for most of human history: it was merely a form of diffuse energy that was shared more or less equally."

Ben tried to picture what a younger, more innocent humanity might have looked like, prancing and happy, but it all seemed as phony as a Hallmark card.

"However," Heaton continued, "if you take a few well-placed mirrors, or a magnifying glass, you can focus that same energy and use it to burn something, or start a small fire. This was what language allowed. But if you *really* want to harness the sun's energy, you build a giant solar farm with thousands of huge photovoltaic panels, and then you can use that energy to power a whole city. That's what writing did with magic. And just the same way only titans of industry can own a solar farm, so it is with magic today."

Ben swallowed another spoonful of casserole. "Your image of the solar farm doesn't totally make sense to me," he said. "If I want to feel the sun on my skin, I can still step outside. It doesn't matter if someone else has a bunch of solar panels or not."

"Yes, that is where the analogy breaks down," Heaton agreed. "What happened with magic was something different in kind. It was more akin to someone inventing a device to block out the sun entirely, preventing it from reaching anyone but those whom they specifically allowed."

"But who would do that?" Ben asked. "Who even could?"

Heaton raised her eyebrows. "That," she breathed, "is where the Possessors come in."

As blue moonlight crept through the arched window of leaded glass and crawled across the floor, Heaton held court. Information rushed out of her in a torrent—decades of research from a life spent poring over tablets of ancient Sumerian records, the complex genealogies of prominent world families, the densely layered symbology of mystical texts from across the globe.

Heaton's brilliant mind touched on a kaleidoscopic array of topics and historical events, making connections between seemingly disparate phenomena, and knitting it all together into a comprehensive web. Although it was all fascinating, Ben's attention homed in on what she had to say about the Possessors.

According to Heaton, there was a group of powerful families in ancient Mesopotamia—no more than fifteen clans, as far as Heaton could identify—that formed an alliance to strengthen and consolidate their regional dominance. Writing was a recent invention, still the exclusive province of elites like themselves, but its capacity to direct and intensify magical energy had become clear. These ancient families feared the threat to their power that the widespread dissemination of this knowledge might mean. So they made an accord: from then on, only they and their descendants would be allowed to use magic; they would destroy any others who attempted to do so. These families must already have included the most naturally powerful magicians then known to the world, and with the combined force of their focus and will, they tethered the use of all magic to a series of complex incantations in their language, ancient Sumerian. This meant that anyone who didn't have knowledge of the specific spells that these first Possessors wrote would be entirely unable to perform magic.

All at once, in order to do magic, you had to know the right words—and those words had been the Possessors' most closely guarded secret for more than five thousand years. Until an unknown agitator who called himself Merlin started releasing them to the whole world two days ago.

After dessert, Heaton invited them into her book-lined study. The layout was essentially the same as the front room, two armchairs facing a sofa, though in here there was also a massive rolltop desk at one end of the room, and a long, high table at the other. Both surfaces were piled with antiquated, leather-bound volumes, their covers and spines cracked and peeling.

"You know, Professor," Ben said, taking a seat in one of the armchairs, "two days ago I would have thought that everything you've said tonight was complete nonsense."

Heaton looked amused. "And now?"

"After what I've seen her do"—Ben cocked his head toward Mack— "it makes about as much sense as anything else."

Heaton's eyes lit up. "*You* can do magic? What does it feel like?"

"You know how when you're drunk you feel kind of invincible?" Mack said. She immediately looked ashamed. "I mean," she faltered, "it feels, you know . . . nice."

"You *must* show me something."

Mack turned toward the fireplace, her lips moving soundlessly. A moment later, a flaming log floated a few inches up into the air, then dropped back onto the grate in a shower of sparks. Heaton clapped her hands like a delighted child.

"How strong are you?" she asked.

"I'm . . . not sure," Mack said. "I can lift a plane. Is that strong?"

"Dear me, yes! Like any natural ability, there are variations in people's capacity to use it. But your natural talent is like . . . like . . . oh, who's a good sportsman?"

"LeBron James?" Ben offered.

"I don't know who that is"—Heaton frowned—"but I'll take your word for it."

Mack beamed at being called the LeBron James of magic, but Ben felt only a cold hardness inside. He stood and began to pace the room. While they were dining in luxury, some pathetic loner with delusions of grandeur might be planning to use "magic" to kill the president; some other sick fuck could be figuring out how to use the protocol to immobilize and rape his victim; even infrastructure that had once

seemed secure—dams, bridges, tunnels—might prove highly vulner-
able to telekinetic attack. This esoteric, ancient knowledge could leap
from the dark web to the World Wide Web at any time, spreading like
an angry cancer. Meanwhile, they sat here talking and spinning logs in
the fireplace. Ben had heard so much tonight, but he'd learned nothing that might help him solve the problem.

Or had he?

Ben stopped pacing and turned to Heaton. "It's all about language,
you said, right? The first Possessors wrote the spells, and those spells
controlled the magic that was already out in the world by limiting
who could perform it."

"That's correct . . ."

"So if they could put *some* limitations on how magic is used,
wouldn't it be possible to limit it further? What if there's a . . . *binding*
protocol of some kind out there—some words that could limit the use
of magic even more, or get rid of it entirely?"

Heaton looked thoughtful. She reached into one of the deep pockets of her cashmere sweater and produced the wooden pipe she'd had
earlier in her office, and a round, flat tin of tobacco.

"I have encountered some perplexing tablet fragments in my research," she continued, gently packing her pipe. "No more than a
handful, I hasten to add. But I have seen a few intriguing suggestions
of something along those lines, Mr. Zolstra. Phrases like 'the finishing
words' and 'the words-never-to-be-said' could very well refer to a kind
of binding spell. I admit they've always baffled me."

Heaton struck a match and puffed her pipe to life. "Even if such
a thing exists, you had better believe only the highest-level Possessors
would know about it, and it would certainly take someone of truly
phenomenal magical ability to utilize it."

"What do you mean, 'highest-level'?" Mack asked. "Are there different types of Possessors?"

Heaton let out a billow of smoke. "Now we're entering into serious speculation on my part," she admitted. "But after they spread out from Mesopotamia, there seems historically to have been very little interaction among Possessors from different regions. I suspect the families may be organized into regional . . . sects, I suppose you could call them. And I would further surmise that, given their historical obsession with hierarchy, each sect must have some kind of leader."

Ben leaned against the high table and looked at Mack. From what he'd seen, magic came as naturally to her as breathing. If they could get their hands on this binding protocol, she might be powerful enough to use it. Ben's gamble to make a run for it with Mack was starting to look like the good bet he'd hoped it would be. Now he just needed to find someone who knew the spell.

"Professor," Ben said, "you've spent your whole life researching and trying to track the Possessors through the centuries, but do you know where any of their descendants are *now*? Have you ever actually met any of them?"

"I'm afraid the trail grows quite cold around the time of the Black Death in the fourteenth century. It could be that many of the Possessors perished. Perhaps whole family lines were extinguished—though it's equally possible they just became better at hiding themselves."

Heaton took a ruminative pull on her pipe. It seemed like she was trying to decide whether to continue. "I always suspected a colleague of mine at Oxford was a Possessor. Dr. Carlton Braithwaite was an anthropologist who had absolutely no reason to be as interested in my arcane research as he was." Heaton smiled. "He was eccentric and unfailingly charming, and we became friends. I honestly think his pull with the administration was the only thing that kept me and my 'embarrassing' research off the chopping block. He hadn't been retired three months when they sacked me."

Ben leaned toward Heaton. "What made you think he was a Possessor?"

"The way he would tease and prod me about my research. There always seemed to be a kind of logic to it. He would give me these subtle jabs here and there, nudging me toward some alleys I hadn't ventured down, or away from dead ends. When I followed his lead, I invariably discovered something interesting."

"I'd like to see him. Where is he?"

"Far, far away, I'm afraid," Heaton said with a rueful smile. "After he retired, he left the United Kingdom for a little island off the coast of Thailand. The only time I've heard from him since was last Christmas, when he sent me an invitation to pay him a visit. At least I assume it was an invitation, albeit a cryptic one. He sent me a postcard with nothing on it but a pleasant greeting and some latitude and longitude coordinates. Imagine that."

"I'll do better than imagine it," Ben said. "Do you still have the postcard?"

"Yes, I believe so."

Ben nodded. "Good. Let's go to Thailand and pay Braithwaite a visit, then."

"Are you serious?" Mack said.

"If there's a real chance that he's a Possessor, then it just became our best option."

Heaton shook her head. "He'll never talk to someone he doesn't know—*certainly* not about any association he has with the Possessors."

"I'll take my chances."

Heaton pursed her lips thoughtfully. "No," she finally said, "you'll take me with you."

Ben wasn't sure he'd heard correctly. "I appreciate your enthusiasm, but you should stay here, Professor."

"Oh, to hell with your 'appreciation,'" Heaton barked. She took a step toward Ben, who tried not to smile as the diminutive septuagenarian stabbed a crooked finger up toward his face. "First of all, Carlton is *my* friend," she said. "Second, the two of you are at the center of the most important events to happen in my particular field in centuries. Third, and most pertinent, you don't know where Carlton lives. *I* do."

Heaton held Ben's gaze for a moment, then nodded triumphantly and dropped her accusatory stance. "I'll go pack my bag. In the meantime," she added brightly, "who wants more coffee?"

13

It was nearing four o'clock in the morning when Ben looked out the window and spotted the approaching headlights of Heaton's assistant's car coming up the long driveway.

"He's here."

Ben's voice rang loudly in the muted stillness of the old house. Mack and Heaton, who'd been half-dozing on the sofa, shook themselves awake.

"I still don't know why we had to involve Lucas in all this," Heaton said.

"A taxi driver could remember us," Ben said, "and if we take your car and leave it there, that makes it much easier for them to place you with us."

Headlights swept the sitting room in a bright flare as Lucas's vehicle curved to a stop outside the house. Ben opened the door and walked out to meet the young assistant as he stepped from a small black sedan.

He wasn't prepared for Lucas to shove past him without so much as a look in his direction, and go storming into the house.

"Desdemona," Lucas half-shouted as Ben entered behind him, "tell me you're not really considering going off on this insane . . . adventure." His brogue was more pronounced now that he was upset. "It would be dangerous for someone half your age. This is foolhardy . . . and I don't want you to go!"

"Lucas, really," Heaton said, amused. "I don't exactly need your permission."

"If Carlton Braithwaite is a Possessor," Lucas went on, still fuming, "there's no telling what he might do to protect himself. These people have no trouble killing to hide their secrets. You taught me that."

They went back and forth in hissed whispers. Ben almost wanted Lucas to change Heaton's mind. He wasn't looking forward to babysitting a senior citizen while tracking down Merlin. But Heaton was intractable: she wouldn't give up Braithwaite's location unless she could come along, and Ben had no time to hunt for the postcard among all the books, research papers, and ephemera in her house on his own. Heaton was a tough old bird—and Ben had to admit that she was probably right that Braithwaite would be more inclined to talk to her than to an American former agent. Bringing her with them, though a pain, was the right play.

Heaton finally took Lucas's hand. "I'm very touched by your concern for me, truly. But I get along just fine when you're not around. Besides, Carlton was well aware of my work for years. If he'd wanted to dispatch me, Lord knows he'd had ample opportunities."

Lucas pulled absently at the chin of his neat beard. "I don't like it," he muttered. "Let the Americans go and get themselves killed. You should stay here."

Enough of this. "Hey," Ben said, putting a hand on Lucas's shoulder, "the professor's coming with us, and you're taking us to the airport. Clear?"

Lucas whipped around and stared at Ben, his hands twitching themselves into loose fists.

Really? Ben thought, staring down at the grad student that he both towered over and outweighed. *You want to do this?*

Lucas took a deep breath and smoothed back his hair with both hands. "I'll be in the car," he said quietly to Heaton, before leaving without another word.

Ben, Mack, and Heaton followed him outside. Ben tossed Heaton's bag into the trunk but kept his own duffel with him. Just as he was hopping into the backseat next to Mack, his phone buzzed in his pocket with two new texts from Gabe. Ben swiped to open them as Lucas started the car.

Tracked the protocol and manifesto to the same computer terminal. They were uploaded from an internet café in bangkok. Will send coordinates.

The follow up, predictably, read,

Hey, don't you like to bangkok?

Ben smiled and shook his head. He sent a response:

Good work. Also that joke is so old it hasn't been funny since the last time you got laid.

What did it mean that the initial uploads were done from Thailand—the very place they were now headed to see a suspected Possessor? It had to be more than a coincidence. Was *Braithwaite* Merlin? Had they found their man already?

No streetlights shone as Lucas piloted them cautiously through the countryside, and their headlights illuminated little more than the ghostly predawn fog. At this rate, it would take them closer to forty minutes to reach the airport. Which wasn't a concern. They had their own plane and pilot.

Ben called Klippman to make the arrangements.

"Agent Zolstra," the gruff Marine said, "I await your instructions about the plane."

"We're coming your way now," Ben said. "I hope you gassed her all the way up, because we're heading—"

"You're coming right now?" Klippman interrupted.

"Like I said, we're on our way, and we should be there—"

"Sorry." Klippman cut him off again. "You're kind of breaking up."

Ben glanced at his screen. The connection was fine, full signal strength. Then, before Ben opened his mouth again, it hit him: Klippman was trying to shut Ben up, to keep him from revealing his position or his destination. Klippman was telling him someone was listening in.

"Roger that, Klipp," Ben said. "I'll give you the full rundown when I get there. In the meantime, be ready for our arrival in about three hours."

"Got it," Klippman said. Ben heard the relief in his voice. "See you then."

They disconnected.

"Three hours?" Heaton said. "We're much closer than that."

"You know that, and *I* know that, Professor," Ben said. "But whoever was listening in on the call doesn't know that. And by the time they figure it out, we'll be long gone."

"What?" Mack said, worried. "Who was listening?"

"It's gotta be Harris. *Shit.* They must have an intercept team waiting for us at Edinburgh."

"Well that settles things," Lucas said with satisfaction. "I'll bring us back to your home, Desdemona."

Heaton looked to Ben.

"No, you won't," Ben said. "We're not sunk yet. Take us to Glasgow. We'll get on the next commercial jet headed for Thailand."

Ben took out his phone. A quick search turned up a KLM flight leaving for Bangkok in less than four hours.

"Won't they stop us?" Mack asked. "How do you know they haven't stationed people at every airport?"

Ben turned to look at her. Mack's eyes were pink and puffy from lack of sleep, but her umber skin was smooth and lustrous in the moonlight. Her loose braids had separated even more throughout the night, and strands of hair fell around and into her face. Ben fought an urge to brush them behind her ears. Looking at her, barely over five feet, you'd never know the power she had inside her.

"It's a risk, but a calculated one. Harris's guys think we're headed for Edinburgh to meet up with Klippman. And we've all got working passports. If we can be wheels-up in the next few hours, we may be able to beat them out of here."

Lucas reluctantly altered their route toward the Glasgow Airport.

"Who is this tosser with his brights on?"

Ben turned in his seat, squinting into the high beams, and spotted the vehicle Heaton was referring to. A sports car had just turned onto the road a quarter mile behind them, and was now racing toward their sedan.

"Whoever he is, he's coming fast."

Lucas's eyes shot to the rearview mirror and went wide with fear. "And he's not alone."

A second and third car had joined the first, forming a tight pattern: one in the lead, the others side by side immediately behind, taking up both lanes.

Lucas's grip on the steering wheel tightened anxiously.

"It's okay, Lucas dear. It's probably kids out for a joyride," Heaton said unconvincingly. "Just let them go by."

The country road allowed only one lane of traffic in each direction, but there were no other cars around at this hour. Nothing prevented the vehicles from blowing past them.

The cars got closer and closer until Ben saw that all three were customized BMWs, their drivers hidden behind darkly tinted windows.

"Floor it," Ben said, alarm bells going off.

Lucas hit the clutch and downshifted the manual transmission, causing the car's engine to rev hotly in response. Then he stomped on the accelerator and sent the vehicle galloping forward, hurtling away from the approaching cars.

"Is it them?" Mack asked. "The CIA?"

Ben craned his neck to look behind him again. It was too dark to see anything through the lead pursuer's windshield except for a pair of leather-gloved hands on the wheel. "Unclear."

Lucas turned sharply to the left, taking them onto a smaller side road. The first car easily made up the distance they'd opened and was practically on their bumper. The others were right behind. Their engines growled—a trio of hungry wolves nipping at the heels of their prey.

Suddenly, the first car leaped forward, colliding hard with the rear of their sedan. Heaton cried out as they began to lose traction on the dew-slick road.

Ben watched Lucas wrestle with the steering wheel. He seemed to be losing the battle for control as their vehicle's tail end slid out wider and wider.

The pursuing cars backed off slightly, and then the lead car zoomed up and bashed into them again, buckling their trunk and spidering the glass of the rear window, before easing off once more.

Lucas's car was wrenched completely sideways, perpendicular to the roadway. They came to a fast, hard stop. The engine roared as Lucas mashed the accelerator down—but they didn't move.

"Get us going!" Ben shouted.

"I can't! We're stuck!"

The BMWs had stopped in the middle of the road about sixty feet behind them. They idled ominously, bright halogen headlights illuminating curls of fog.

"My door!" Heaton yelled. "It won't open!"

None of them would; something was holding them shut.

"I think . . ." Lucas turned to Ben, his face white with terror. "I think . . . maybe they're using magic."

"Oh, God," Heaton said. "It's them. It's finally them."

The Possessors.

They must have been watching Heaton. They probably had for years. Were they trying to stop them from reaching Braithwaite?

"They'll kill us," Lucas shrieked. "Can't you do something?"

Ben was already reaching into the duffel bag at his feet. He pulled out his SIG Sauer pistol and racked the slide.

"We won't need that," Mack said, unbuckling her seat belt.

Ben stared at her.

"I'm not dying tonight," she said.

Ben rubbed at John's Annapolis ring. "Me, neither," he said. "Let's try to keep at least one of them alive."

"*Alive?*" Lucas echoed.

"For a little chat. If they really are Possessors, we may not need to go all the way to Thailand to get the answers we need."

"That's lunacy," Lucas protested. "How do you expect to contain their magic?" He reached back and gripped Mack's arm, hard. "You can't really think you're strong enough!"

Mack shook him off but didn't answer.

Heaton eyed the idling sports cars. "What are they waiting for?"

As if in response, the first car's engine revved loudly. Then it peeled out and sprang forward, a missile headed right for them. Ben and his team were pinned down, unable to move their vehicle or abandon it. The collision would be side on, easily crumpling Lucas's small sedan like an aluminum can.

Ben leaned across Mack, raised his gun, and unloaded a full clip at the car. The fusillade shattered their own window, but barely marred the other car's windshield. It was bulletproof, by magic or design. Ben thought quickly of blowing out another window for them to escape but knew they'd never get out and away in time—the crushing impact was mere seconds away.

Then Ben heard Mack's whispered incantation. He saw her raise her hands in front of her, palms out toward the oncoming car.

She didn't stop the BMW. Instead, with a groan of effort that seemed torn from her deepest core, Mack lifted the oncoming car from the road. Her hands flew up and she wrenched herself backward onto the seat, sending the sports car flying over their own, spiraling like a thrown football, missing them by inches.

There was an ear-splitting crunch as the car slammed back onto the road roof-first and was dragged along by its momentum for at least twenty feet before it came to a stop. The wreck was quickly consumed by fire.

The remaining cars stayed put. A door opened. The silhouette of a driver stepped out and stood in place, one hand on the door and the other on the roof, assessing the situation. The other driver emerged and did the same. It was too dark and distant to make out any features, but they appeared to be talking, deciding their next move.

Ben knew his. He slammed a fresh magazine into his pistol, then lined up his shots. He would take one out, and only wing the other—

Just then, Lucas's car jerked forward. They could drive again. Ben cursed and lowered the gun as Lucas smashed through a wooden fence and into a field in order to get around the destroyed BMW that was blocking the road.

"Stop," Ben ordered.

Lucas was incredulous. "Are you mad?"

"Stop the fucking car!"

Lucas hit the brakes and they lurched to a stop past the wreck. Ben raised his gun again, but the other drivers were already back in their cars. "Shit."

The souped-up sports cars turned around and tore back up the road in the direction they'd come from, their taillights quickly receding to red pinpricks in the dim predawn.

"Why aren't they coming after us?" Heaton said.

It was a good question. Were they intimidated by Mack's ability, or just regrouping and getting more backup?

Ben pushed his door open. "Stay put," he called over his shoulder.

He approached the destroyed vehicle, using his arm to shield himself against the heat of the engine fire. He squinted through the flames and saw that the head and face of the lead car's driver—a middle-aged man, suspended upside down by his seat belt—were awash in blood. A shard of glass protruded from a burbling wound in his neck.

When the blaze became too intense, Ben dropped to the ground and crawled the remaining few feet with his head down. He reached through the busted side window to check the driver's pulse. Nothing. No ID in the pockets of his pants or his windbreaker, either.

The BMW creaked, groaned. Began to shift. Ben propelled himself away from the vehicle just as the roof supports buckled, crushing the inside of the car along with any further answers it might have provided.

Ben got back into Lucas's sedan and shut the door behind him. He shook his head at three sets of questioning eyes.

"He's . . . dead?" Lucas whispered.

"Yes."

Mack looked half-dead herself. Pale and sweating, still breathing hard. Lucas stared straight ahead, frozen.

"Hey," Ben snapped, "we don't know if those other cars are coming back. We need to get to the airport. Let's hit it."

Still looking shaken, Lucas shifted the car into drive.

14

Mack's strength still hadn't returned by the time they pulled up to the departures area at the Glasgow Airport. The magic had really taken it out of her. Her heart alternately fluttered and pounded—a strange sensation that made her feel like she kept switching quickly back and forth between a hard sprint and a deep middle-of-the-night drunk. She'd seen people come into the hospital in that state before. Usually it was some kind of panic attack; that diagnosis didn't quite fit in this case.

I guess these magic hangovers are their own brand of bitch, Mack thought.

As they got out of the car, Heaton's assistant tried again to convince the professor not to go along with Ben's plan, insisting she'd be safer staying in Scotland.

"After what just happened, Lucas," Heaton replied in a shaky voice, "I find myself quite unable to agree."

Mack watched Ben rest a hand on the car's roof and lean down to the driver's-side window. "Thanks for the ride."

Lucas nodded once but said nothing.

"Listen," Ben continued, "the professor says you're a great researcher.

If you want to keep her safe and bring all this to an end sooner, do something to help us."

"What's that?"

"See what you can find out about who might have been driving those cars. Find the police report from the crash and let us know the identity of the dead Possessor. Any lead helps."

"Fine," Lucas said without looking up at Ben.

The grad student sped away in his newly beat-up sedan, leaving the rest of them standing at the curbside in the cold light of dawn.

Ben steadied Mack with an arm around her shoulders, as she put one leaden foot in front of the other, and they moved through the sliding glass doors toward the ticket counters.

Heaton, who hadn't stopped looking behind them the whole rest of their drive to the airport, anticipating a second assault, was obviously upset by what had happened. But she hid her fear behind what Mack imagined was British stoicism.

The international terminal was already bustling. Ben stopped them as soon as they stepped inside the doors.

"There's one thing I need to do before we get on a plane for the next twelve hours," he said.

Whatever secret spy thing Mack thought he was about to do, it certainly wasn't what happened next.

Ben pulled out his phone and dialed. "Mom, it's me," he said.

Mack and Heaton shared a surprised look. Mack wondered if "Mom" was an agent's code name.

"I'm okay," Ben continued, "but I'm going to be gone for a while. I don't know how long." There was a pause. "I'm sorry, you know I can't say more." Another pause. "I *am* coming back, I promise. Listen, I need to go. I just wanted to let you know that things are about to get pretty hairy. Everywhere. You'll know what I'm talking about when you see it. Just . . . keep the guns loaded and don't trust anybody, all right?" Ben glanced at the floor. "You too. Good-bye."

As soon as he disconnected, Ben looked at Mack and Heaton, registering the amusement in their faces. "What?" he demanded.

"Nothing, dear," Heaton said with a slight smile.

"With my dad and brother gone, I'm all she's got left."

That was apparently all the explanation they were going to get, because the next thing Ben did was gesture toward the KLM ticket counter.

"That's us," he said, snapping back into his usual mode of casual command. "Remember, everything just like we talked about in the car. Harris is after me and Mack, so if there's an alert out, they'll be trying to spot the two of us together." He turned to Heaton. "They probably don't know about you yet, Professor. You and Mack go up together and put two tickets on your card, then I'll go get my own with cash. We'll pass through security apart, and wait at the gate separately."

Ben reached into his duffel bag and pulled out a plain gray baseball cap that he pressed low onto his head. He nodded at Mack and Heaton. It was time.

Mack and the professor stepped into line together, Mack leaning slightly on Heaton as strength gradually returned to her body.

"I hope your friend knows what he's doing," Heaton whispered.

Mack looked back at Ben. He was pretending to read a newspaper that someone had left on one of the plastic chairs near the door. He was waiting to join the line until there were enough other passengers between them.

"We don't have a lot of choice," Mack hissed back. "If we stay here, the Possessors either kill us like they just tried to, or the CIA eventually finds us. Getting out of this country is the only chance we've got."

"But what if we're walking right into a trap?"

One of the passengers in front of them, a balding man carrying a suitcase held together mostly by duct tape, cocked his head in their direction. Mack elbowed Heaton and glared at her. *Enough talking.*

When they reached the counter, they were both sweating in spite of the terminal's unnecessarily aggressive air-conditioning.

Heaton was a tongue-tied mess as she bought the tickets. She twice asked for tickets to Taiwan instead of Thailand, and then fumbled the answer they'd agreed upon when asked what their relationship to one another was. She was supposed to tell the ticket agent that Mack was her research assistant and leave it at that.

But when the pasty-faced agent with the permed hair asked what kind of research Heaton did, she responded unthinkingly, "Oh, I research magic."

Heaton, knowing what she'd done, immediately eyed Mack in horror.

"Magic?" The agent looked up from her screen, her face wary. "What do you mean, magic?"

Mack jumped in. She slapped at Heaton's arm. "You're cruel," she said, forcing a laugh. She turned to the agent. "The professor's just teasing me. She doesn't appreciate my interest in astrology. Classic passive-aggressive Libra behavior, if you ask me."

The agent smiled grimly. "I hear you. My husband's a bloody Libra," she said—or at least Mack thought that's what she said, her Scottish accent was so thick she couldn't be sure.

Somehow they managed to purchase their tickets for Bangkok and move into the security line without saying or doing anything else too red-flag raising. Ben joined the line about ten minutes later, far behind them and not making eye contact. He was empty-handed. Unlike Mack and the professor, he'd had to check his bag because of the handgun that was locked in a small case inside it. Mack breathed a sigh of relief. They'd all cleared the first hurdle.

As they neared the conveyor belts and scanners of the security checkpoint, Mack couldn't help noticing all the ceiling cameras pointing their way. That was normal, she reminded herself.

Also normal was that group of uniformed security agents huddled behind their bank of monitors, supervising everything. Mack was only imagining that they were scrutinizing Heaton and herself more closely than the other passengers. Obviously they were just doing their jobs as they whispered to one another, their eyes flicking from the screens in front of them to Mack and Heaton before them. When one of them turned away and started speaking urgently into her walkie-talkie, that was completely normal, too. All of this was normal.

Wasn't it?

Mack and Heaton neared the scanners. Mack wondered if they had secret technology to detect her elevated heart rate or her dry mouth. They must not have, because both Mack and Heaton passed through without any problem.

"Let's wait at that bookstore over there," Mack said, "and make sure Ben gets through okay."

"The plan was to go to the gate, Eila," Heaton reminded her. "I think we ought to—"

"I've got a bad feeling. Please."

Heaton relented. From their vantage point in the small bookstore, Ben was obscured behind the security equipment, personnel, and the other waiting passengers, but after a few anxious minutes spent thumbing through magazines and reading the back covers of the latest paperbacks, Mack saw Ben come into view again.

He also got through the scanner—but then something went wrong. One of the supervisors from behind the monitors approached Ben and waved him over to the side, toward a door with a security keypad on it. Ben protested, trying his best to look like an annoyed passenger who didn't want to miss his flight, but that only attracted the attention of a second agent, who approached Ben from behind and laid a hand on his shoulder.

Oh God.

Ben held up his hands, indicating that he wouldn't put up a fight, and started walking in the direction security was pointing him.

"What do we do?" Mack asked Heaton.

"I think we have no choice but to follow the original plan," Heaton said apologetically. "If one of us is stopped, the others go to the gate and get on the plane. It's better than us all getting caught."

"Screw that," Mack said. "We can't just abandon him."

Ben hadn't left her back in Harris's little basement torture chamber, and Mack wasn't about to leave him here.

Ben, still keeping his head down to avoid the cameras, was nearing the locked door now. The security guard in the lead leaned down to punch in the code on the keypad. Mack had to do something. Create some kind of distraction . . .

She conjured up the words of the protocol, waking them from where they lay dormant in a corner of her mind. She began to speak them in the faintest whisper, keeping herself half-hidden behind a rack of Scottish-flag key chains and decals. Then she lined up her targets, envisioning what she was about to do. Finally, when she felt primed and ready, when her intention was firm and directed, she released her magic.

The security agent had gotten the door open, and Ben was stepping through the doorway, when the alarms on the metal detectors started to sound. First one, then a second, then a third, as Mack magically nudged each detector with sufficient force to set it off.

Soon the alarms on all five detectors were screaming and flashing red. At the same time, she stopped the conveyor belts for x-raying baggage and held them in place. It was a complete jam-up at the checkpoint as agents scrambled to figure out what the hell was happening.

No passengers could be allowed through without proper screening, of course, and soon grumbles and even shouts began to erupt from the irate crowd. All the while, the grating sound of alarms continued to add to the chaos.

The agents who were about to interrogate Ben were suddenly getting called for help from all their subordinates. They looked at each other, momentarily at a loss, until the lead supervisor shook his head and waved Ben away before plunging into the disorder and confusion of the unfolding mess. Ben didn't need to be told twice. He speed-walked away from the checkpoint and toward the gate.

As he passed the bookstore, he shot Mack a half-smile from under his baseball cap without breaking stride.

They sat on opposite ends of the crowded gate's waiting area. The minutes ticked by so slowly Mack would have preferred to spend them beneath a dentist's drill. Every time an announcement broke in over the loudspeaker, each time a new uniformed attendant or employee walked by, Mack felt a jolt of agitation. Heaton did, too. They squeezed each other's hands on the armrest between them.

Even when they were finally walking down the Jetway, being greeted by the flight attendants, settling into their seats, Mack remained certain that at any second, one of Harris's men would shove his way onto the plane and push himself up the aisle toward them, his gun drawn and pointed straight at Mack's face. They were never getting out of this country, never getting off the ground.

It wasn't until they'd passed through the layer of ground fog and burst through the clouds into the bright morning above that Mack realized they'd actually done it. The plan had worked. The plane had taken off with all three of them aboard.

They were going to Thailand.

15

The mood in the Project Merlin command center at Langley was grim. Zolstra had slipped the net. Harris was fuming. The junior agents were hunched over their workstations as though trying to will themselves out of sight of any hostile superiors.

"How did Zolstra know we had Klippman?" Harris demanded incredulously of no one in particular. "How did he fucking *know* not to go back to the plane?"

"He reads people," Novak said. "Or maybe he and Klippman had a signal word arranged in advance."

"Is that what the pilot said?"

"He's not talking."

"Well, *get* him talking," Harris said. "Get him on a plane back to the States and put the screws to him for God's sake. He's got to know something about where they're headed. *Jesus Christ!*" Harris kicked out at a wheeled office chair, sending it crashing into a vacant workstation. "Is there any chance Zolstra is still in the UK?"

"Doubtful," Novak answered. "Before he hung up he asked Klippman to make sure the tank was topped off. They're going far."

"*You.*" Harris wheeled around on a young agent who was huddled over a computer screen showing satellite footage of the Edinburgh area. "What's the outside range of a G5?"

The wide-eyed agent keyed in the query. "Seven thousand, seven hundred miles, sir."

Harris groaned. "Our search area is half of the goddamn world." He ran a hand through his slicked-back hair. "Okay, I need video of everyone leaving the UK in the last four hours. I'm talking planes, trains, coach buses, cars. Names alone aren't going to work, since they'll be traveling under false passports. And let's alert MI5."

"Maybe we should . . ." Novak began, then changed course. "I'll put agents on it immediately."

Harris turned to Novak, his eyes narrowed. "Will you?"

"What do you mean?" Novak asked. "Of course."

"I mean"—Harris leaned in close enough that Novak smelled his aftershave—"how come I had to find out about this stolen jet from Agent Walters and not from you?"

Novak's mind raced, playing back the circumstances that had led him here. After Novak had made the decision to sit on Walters's information about the plane—just for a little while, he reminded himself, to give Zolstra a shot at gathering useful intel—Harris had paid a visit to the command center when Novak was out. Walters had passed the news about the discovery of the jet to Harris, who'd initiated the UK operation that had just failed.

"I was at the White House, leaning on McAllister to keep a lid on the prison break," Novak said, hushed. He hated the nervous edge he heard in his voice. "It was an oversight. The reporters were getting aggressive—"

Harris was having none of it. "Tell me right now—are you on Zolstra's side?" he asked. "Or on the side of this agency?"

Novak swallowed. "The Agency is my life, sir."

Harris's eyes hardened behind his glasses. "Deputy Novak, are you working with Zolstra?"

"Absolutely not."

Harris kept Novak pinned in place with his stare for a long moment, then finally nodded. "Good. Now what do you want to say to me? Something's on your mind."

Novak tried not to let his relief show. "It's nothing."

Harris's face made it clear that Novak had no choice but to continue.

"I was going to say . . ." Novak began, trying and failing to think of a convincing cover and plunging headlong into the truth, "that once we locate Zolstra and Mack, maybe we shouldn't bring them in right away."

Harris raised an eyebrow but said nothing.

"Zolstra clearly has a lead. If we let him pursue it—while keeping an eye on him—he can lead us to exactly what we want."

Harris shook his head. "The idea's not terrible, but it's too dangerous to keep them out there. Zolstra clearly can't be trusted, and Mack is still the most powerful weapon we know of on this new battlefield. Bringing them in, as soon as possible, is priority one."

Just then Walters emerged from the room where the tech team was still working around the clock trying to track down the location of Merlin's initial upload. He strode briskly toward Novak and Harris, and nodded in greeting. He looked eager to share something.

"What have you got, Walters?" Novak asked.

"We've almost tracked the upload, sir. Right now, based on the pattern of server jumps Merlin's worm made early on, the team is saying there's a pretty good chance that the initial upload was onto a terminal based in Asia."

"How good a chance?" Harris asked.

"At this point they said they'd place the likelihood of an Asian upload at about eighty-five percent, maybe higher. Bangkok is looking like a good candidate."

"Novak," Harris said, "before you and Walters do anything else, take a close look at recent Asian-bound flights out of all Scottish airports."

"Do you think Zolstra had some way of knowing about the upload?" Walters asked.

"We still don't know who he met up with in Annapolis," Harris said. "Someone might be passing him intel."

Novak suspected that he might have learned the identity of Zolstra's Annapolis contact, but he kept quiet. He wasn't totally certain of the connection yet. And in any case he never knew if it might prove helpful to be able to secretly back-channel with the rogue agent, outside of the glare of Harris and the rest of the Project Merlin team.

A sudden burst of commotion drew their attention. An exclamation of excited voices came from the smallest of the three rooms of the command center, which was connected to the main space via a doorway near the conference room. Novak, Harris, and Walters rushed across the larger room and squeezed through the door.

Seven agents in various stages of dishevelment looked up at them from their computers as the senior agents entered the room. The place was dimly lit, the air stale with the odor of unwashed bodies. Luminous screens filled with multiple active windows, all dense with code, were reflected in the agents' glasses and their reddened eyes. The tech team had been working harder than any of them, and for longer.

A round-faced young woman leaned back in her chair and smacked her gum in Novak's direction. Agent Seoh was the youngest in a room already full of peach-fuzzed hacker-babies. Novak, at fifty-six, felt like Methuselah around them.

"The next protocol is out," Seoh said, scowling. "It appeared on about a dozen sites all at once and is spreading like a motherfucker."

The next protocol. As though telekinesis weren't enough, some *other* type of magical ability was making the leap from fantasy into reality.

"Well," Novak said warily, "what is it?"

Seoh shook her head. "It's just the code and a little message: *now you see me, now you don't.*"

Novak felt the blood drain from his face. It couldn't be . . .

Invisibility.

16

Avigdor Dolgin blinked his eyes in the watery dawn light that crept in under the curtains of the estate on Smolenskin Street. It was too early. What had awakened him? The familiar, cold fingers of fear clenched around his stomach. Anxiety—about what, exactly? about nothing, everything—had been his companion since his earliest days on his mother's kibbutz.

But here, Dolgin reminded himself, there was nothing to fear. He was no longer a little boy, and he'd never been so well protected in his life as he was now.

Dolgin had been prime minister for four months—sixteen weeks of sleeping and waking in Beit Aghion, a Jerusalem compound as well fortified as a military garrison.

Then why this feeling now? Why this clammy skin, this palpitating pulse?

His wife, lying next to him in bed, sighed contentedly in her sleep and pulled the covers up to her chin. Had Dolgin ever slept with such ease? Would he ever?

He groaned and sat up, putting his bare feet on the cool tiles. He rolled his shoulders, wriggled his toes. At his age, the body woke up piece by piece instead of all at once.

Coffee. The image of a steaming cup popped into Dolgin's head with almost surreal clarity. He felt his anxiety subside. Remembering anew every morning that coffee existed was one of life's only unfailing joys.

He stood, his knees grumbling with the effort, and ambled toward the kitchen.

Something caught his eye as he passed through the wood-paneled dining room. A trick of the light, a shimmering in the air. Dolgin blinked it away. He rubbed the sleep from his eyes and shuffled into the kitchen.

He filled the electric kettle from the faucet, then flicked it on. Reaching into the cupboard for a cup and saucer, he felt it again. That jolt. A sour jet of acid in the stomach. The stupid, ancient flutter of primeval panic, as though he were dodging cheetahs on the savannah instead of standing safely in his own kitchen.

It was the stress of the job, of course. Enemies within and without. An unruly Knesset. He would soon, as his wife never tired of suggesting, speak with his doctor about taking medication.

There was that haze again, in the corner of his eye. This time it wouldn't blink away. Dolgin turned toward the odd vision, watching in disbelief as a shimmering form appeared in the air near the kitchen doorway. It grew more solid, and took the shape of a person.

A man he'd never seen stood before him. A scowl on his face. An Uzi in his hands.

The cup and saucer fell from Dolgin's trembling grip and shattered on the kitchen tiles just as the first shots blasted from the gun.

17

The Bangkok sun was a hammer. Ben's shirt stuck to his back, and he squinted through the cheap sunglasses he'd picked up from a street vendor. The asphalt of the narrow, stall-lined lane was hot under his feet.

The tourists were likely waiting out the heat in air-conditioned comfort, since things were pretty quiet in this part of the Banglamphu district. It was the workaday locals who were out and about: a shriveled old man using a wooden broom to sweep the area around his rice porridge cart; two bald monks, swaddled in saffron robes, holding out their alms bowls toward a greengrocer; a teen buzzing by on a motorbike, trailing a cloud of exhaust mingled with cigarette smoke.

Mack and Heaton shined with perspiration and took in the scene with obvious excitement.

The shock of the deadly pursuit back in Scotland was finally receding, but Ben remained on high alert. Now they had two groups tracking them—the Possessors and the U.S. government. All he could do was hope they had the head start they needed.

"Almost there," he said. "Gabe's directions say the internet café is on this block."

Ben's phone buzzed in the pocket of his shorts. He slid it out and glanced at the screen. Gabe was calling.

Ben answered. "Speak of the devil."

"Where you guys at?"

"Almost to the café. I've got a lead on something bigger, too. A binding protocol that might stop all magic."

"That's great. And the sooner the better, man," Gabe said. "Shit's getting real. Someone assassinated the Israeli prime minister this morning. Somebody *invisible*."

Ben stopped in his tracks, his mind struggling to get a hold of what Gabe was telling him. Heaton and Mack looked at him quizzically.

"You're sure this is really the next protocol," Ben asked, "and not just an unverified story?"

"They're being vague on the news and in public statements, but the chatter I'm hearing through Mossad sources makes it pretty fucking clear. The guy walked into the compound unseen, blew away Dolgin, his wife, and half the guards, then walked right back out again."

Ben led Mack and Heaton to the side of the street, into the shade. He leaned his back against the cool brick of a building. This was exactly the scenario they'd been afraid of. "Is the existence of the protocols themselves widely known yet?"

"No. The feds are still doing a decent job of scrubbing magic-related posts and videos as they appear—but it's Whac-A-Mole, man. Things are getting through. Things are starting to happen. People know something's up."

"How bad?"

Gabe sighed heavily. "Not end-of-civilization bad—yet. But there's a lot of shit going down. Assaults and robberies, mostly. People know the cops can't stop them, so . . ."

They needed to get that binding spell fast.

"But hey," Gabe continued, his tone brightening, "it's not all doom and gloom. I've been tinkering with the protocols, like you said. I think I may have figured something out."

"Hold on," Ben said. He toggled the call to speakerphone and motioned the others closer. "Okay, I've got Heaton and Mack on. Go ahead, Gabe."

"Why, hey ladies, everybody enjoying the tropical—?"

"The *point*, Garcia."

Gabe laughed. "All right, these protocols are just English transliterations of what are basically lines of command code," he said. "As Ben suggested, they might be able to be rearranged or altered to code for different things. I've been trying to figure out if they're reversible."

Mack chimed in, "Reversible how?"

"I wanted to know if I could recode the invisibility protocol to do the opposite thing—to reveal instead of hide, you know?"

"Merlin's next protocol is invisibility," Ben informed the women.

"Dear me," Heaton whispered.

"What'd you find out, Gabe?" Ben asked. "Did you manage to do it?"

In this dangerous new world, what was essentially an antistealth technology would be an incredibly valuable tool for authorities trying to keep the public safe. Even for Ben's own mission, the ability to reveal what was magically hidden could mean the difference between success and failure.

Gabe cackled again. "I don't know, man! You forget that I'm magically useless! But I've written a few variations for Mack to try out."

"Well, send them over."

"And the original invisibility protocol, too!" Mack added.

"Will do."

Ben thanked him, and they disconnected.

"I can't wait to practice the new protocols," Mack said, her eyes lit with excitement.

"Soon," Ben said. "But first let's get to this café and find out who Merlin really is."

Two minutes later, Ben spotted their destination beneath a bright purple awning. They squeezed between two stalls—a woman frying noodles with shrimp, and a man grilling hunks of chicken on long skewers over a charcoal grill—and came to the door of the internet café they'd crossed the world to find.

Ben pushed through the glass door into the shop. A row of identical black PCs lined each side wall, while a ceiling fan lazily circulated the hot air. There was a counter at the back. A chubby young man leaned on top of it, his thumbs tapping quickly on his phone's screen. A handful of teenagers sat at the terminals, silently engrossed in computer games. One of them had brought his mud-caked dirt bike inside and parked it in the middle of the concrete floor.

This was ground zero for the upload that had changed the world? Ben tried to picture Braithwaite, the elderly, ivory tower Brit, setting foot inside this dingy place. He couldn't make the image fit.

"Help you?" the worker asked, seeming bored and tired with the effort.

"We're looking for someone who came in here a few days ago," Ben said.

The kid looked back down at his phone. "Lotta people come here. You wanna use a computer?"

"No. I wonder if you remember somebody who came in on Wednesday, and stayed for a few hours. Probably not Thai. Maybe an old man? Someone who acted strangely? Secretive?"

"Don't remember," the worker said without looking up.

Ben wanted to grab the kid's phone and chuck it across the room. Mack had a different idea. She whispered to Heaton, who removed her wallet and handed Mack a wad of bills, Thai baht they'd obtained at the airport. Mack walked to the counter and leaned across it so she was inches from the worker. The kid's eyes widened, traveling from the money in Mack's hand to the loose neckline of her tank top.

"Think harder," Mack cooed. "You don't remember anything?"

The worker reddened. "Sorry. Lotta tourists in here every day."

Ben spotted a small camera in the corner of the ceiling behind the counter. "What about that?" he said, pointing to it. "Does that thing work?"

The worker looked up at the camera, then back down at the bills Mack held. He nodded. Now they were getting somewhere.

After the financial negotiation had concluded, the kid sat them down at an empty computer terminal and pulled up the video files. Each day of the past week was stored as a folder that was filled with a series of files—one low-res video for each hour. Ben's pulse quickened in anticipation. They were going to see Merlin.

The kid clicked to open the video for the first hour the store had been open that day, 7:00 a.m.

"No," Ben said, "it would be earlier that that."

In the Situation Room briefing, they'd estimated the first upload had been around four in the afternoon, D.C. time. It was eleven hours later here, which would have put the time at roughly three o'clock on Wednesday morning. Ben told the worker to play that video.

The kid shook his head. "No one here then. Shop's closed."

"Well," Ben said, "I guess someone didn't care that it was closed."

At Ben's insistence, the worker opened the late-night file and began scrubbing through the poor-quality footage. There was nothing, just empty banks of computers, faintly illuminated by the light from the street. Then—

"Look!" Mack exclaimed.

On the video, one of the monitors sprang to life. It wasn't possible to make out what the display showed, but over the next fifteen minutes of video, the computer screen changed multiple times as various windows appeared to open and close. Yet there was no one in the store. Had the computer been hijacked somehow?

Then Ben saw that in all the darkness and graininess, he'd failed to notice something critical: the computer's mouse had moved. A number of times.

They scrolled back through the footage. The video hadn't been deliberately cut and pasted back together in order to hide someone. Instead, they could actually see the small movements of the mouse, with no one manipulating it.

"The bastard was invisible," Ben muttered. They weren't going to see their quarry after all, because he'd been smart enough to hide himself, even then.

"*What the fuck!*" the young worker exclaimed, leaping back from the monitor. The game players in the shop looked over, startled. "The fuck is this?"

The kid stared wide-eyed around him like he'd just discovered the place was haunted.

Ben stormed out of the store, followed closely by Mack and Heaton. *"Dammit!"*

They'd blown one of their two leads.

"Guess it's down to your pal Braithwaite," Ben said. "As of right now, we have to operate under the assumption that he is Merlin. We'll hire a car and leave for Pattaya City at dawn. The drive shouldn't take more than two hours."

"Then why don't we go right now?" Mack said.

"Too late for today," Ben said, with a nod toward the setting sun. "The professor's coordinates put Braithwaite's compound on a tiny island in the gulf. Navigating unfamiliar ocean in the dark? Bad idea."

"Then what do we do for now?"

"I don't know about you two," Heaton responded with a wink, "but I could use a drink with a little umbrella in it."

18

Not only had Mack never seen anything like Bangkok at night—she'd never *imagined* anything like it. It was a luminous dream world. She longed to stop and stare at all the people, the lights, the colors, the bustle of ten thousand things in motion at once. She breathed in the competing smells of tropical flowers, motorbike exhaust, grilling meat, cigarette smoke—even the warm, humid air itself smelled somehow foreign, heavy with all the life of this place. And the music! It was everywhere: bumping from the clubs, pouring from shopfronts, blasting out of tiny speakers from street stands and dirt bikes and the little three-wheeled *tuk-tuks* that buzzed around like flies at a barbecue.

"Better keep up so you don't get lost."

Ben took Mack gently by the arm, dragging her out of her reverie and down another long row of stalls at the night market they'd been exploring for the last half hour.

They needed clothes. According to Ben, what he'd packed wasn't entirely suitable for this heat, while the only things Mack possessed were the outfit she was wearing when the CIA picked her up and a sweater borrowed from Heaton. As long as they were stuck until the next morning, Ben said he wanted to do something useful. Heaton, meanwhile, was content to keep her eyes peeled for Thai jewelry.

As much as Mack was enjoying the city, she was eager to get back to the hotel and practice the new protocols Gabe had sent over. She could feel the power inside her calling for release, refusing to take no for an answer.

"It's crazy that it's business as usual here," she said, looking around at the swarms of tourists and haggling shop owners. "No one knows what's out there."

"If the protocols are getting out as fast as Gabe says they are, by tomorrow morning magic could be everywhere."

They were shuffling along an endless row of stalls displaying everything from colored-glass lamps and golden Buddhas to knockoff purses and crates of old Asian vinyl records. People swirled around them—Thais in skimpy club clothes mixing with tourists in Teva sandals.

"Oh, so you're calling it magic now?" Mack teased.

"Only because it's easier than saying 'science we don't understand yet,'" Ben said with a grin.

Mack wasted no time in procuring a pair of sundresses, a trio of breezy shirts, some undies and a bra, and a pair of loose-fitting pants. It wasn't high fashion, but it worked. For a moment, she could almost have convinced herself that she was just a normal tourist on some tropical shopping vacation, and not an international fugitive.

"You know," Heaton said thoughtfully, "all my life people have considered me a kook for believing in magic. I never thought I'd live to see it released into the world."

"It won't be out for long," Ben said. "Not if we do our job." He slowed to inspect a table of ornamental daggers. "If Braithwaite is Merlin, then we're closer than ever—which means things could get a lot more dangerous. We'll have to be ready tomorrow for any kind of reception he might throw at us."

Heaton sighed. "It will be sad, though, won't it?" she said. "If we eliminate magic and take it away from people again, what makes us any different from the Possessors?"

"What makes us different, Professor, is that we're trying to save the world, not just hoard our power," Ben said.

But what about my own *magic?* Mack thought. Even now her body thrummed with its sinuous energy. Was it wrong of her to hope that maybe she could find a way to keep some magic for herself?

They finally stumbled upon the jewelry section of the bazaar, with at least twenty stalls hawking a fantastic array of accessories—everything from necklaces, rings, bracelets, and earrings, to more exotic arm bangles and tiaras.

"*Now* we're talking," Heaton said.

The old woman was fearless, diving right into the fray. She tried things on and showed them off with a flourish. She shook her head and clucked her tongue dramatically when the quoted price was too high. The workers who were minding the stalls shouted back at her in Thai, then switched to trying to cajole her as Heaton threatened to walk away.

When the professor had finally found a necklace that pleased her, she made it her business to find one for Mack, too: a golden chain ending in a vertical bar pendant.

When they caught back up to Ben, he was clutching a few newly purchased shirts and a pair of cargo shorts. "I suppose we should eat," he said grudgingly, as though eating were some kind of human weakness. "Then get to bed. We're gonna be up nice and early."

Heaton asked, "So, which restaurant are we going to?"

"You don't go to a restaurant in Bangkok," Ben said. "They have some of the best street food in the world."

"How do you know so much about this place?" Mack asked.

Ben shrugged. "I spent a little time here. With the Agency."

He hailed a *tuk-tuk,* and the three of them crowded into the back-seat of the motorized tricycle. There were no doors or windows, just a canvas roof stretched over their heads, strung with colored light bulbs. It felt like they were getting on a ride at an amusement park. Ben told the driver where to take them, and the little vehicle tore off through the crowded streets, weaving around full-size cars, sometimes missing them by inches.

They were wedged in tight on the small bench seat, and each time the driver cut a sharp turn, they all fell against each other, Ben's muscular body pressing against Mack's own.

The *tuk-tuk* pulled to a stop near a huge, bustling crowd. Ben paid the driver and helped them out of the vehicle. The area was filled with the scent of food—charring meat, frying oils—and all around them on the pavement were thin, metal tables filled with people stuffing their delighted faces with noodles and grilled meats of every sort.

Ben was all business as he led them from one food stand to another, ordering a little bit of everything for everyone. "Trust me," he kept saying, "you should try this."

Mack rolled her eyes at him before realizing, with a twinge of surprise, that she actually did—trust Ben, that is.

They snatched a sidewalk table just as another group was getting up, and unloaded their bounty onto the center of it.

Everything smelled so good, but Mack hesitated before digging in.

"What's wrong?" Ben asked.

"Nothing," Mack answered truthfully. "I mean, nothing *yet*. It's just that all this . . ." She made a circle with her arm, encompassing the whole bustling night around her. "This may be the last normal night before everything changes."

"Maybe, dear," Heaton said, giving Mack a gentle smile. "Take a little advice from a woman of a certain age, and enjoy yourself tonight."

They ate. The cuisine was sweet and hot and sour and salty and rich all at once. Mack devoured the noodle dishes with lime and roasted peanuts, the stir-fried pork with basil, the sausage, the crispy little crepes.

When they'd cleared the table of all but scraps, Heaton puffed out her cheeks and said, "I think it's hotel time for me." She pushed her stool away from the table. "I'm going to get a cab, darlings."

"It's actually not that far," Ben said. "We can all walk back together."

"No, no." Heaton waved at him like he was a pesky housefly. "You two can walk. I'm an old woman, I need the cab."

"Well, if you're sure . . ."

"See you in the morning, kids," Heaton said with a wink. "Tomorrow we're going to give old Carlton the surprise of a lifetime. I do hope he doesn't have a weak heart."

"Or a private security force," Ben said.

After she'd gone, Ben and Mack started walking. The night was cooler than the day, but the air was still sticky. Ben had gone quiet.

"So is Thailand how you remember it?" Mack asked.

He nodded. "Pretty much."

They covered another half-block in silence, letting the sounds and colors of Bangkok at night whirl around them.

"What are you thinking about?" Mack asked.

"You go first."

They continued walking, their steps slower now, as though neither of them really wanted to get to the hotel too fast.

"I guess I was thinking about my brother," Mack said. "I was wondering—if Nathaniel were still alive, would he be able to do the things I can do? Could he do magic, too? He was smart. He could be here helping us."

A man stumbled out from between two cars on the street and pushed by them on the sidewalk. Mack's arm brushed Ben's as they moved aside, and they stayed close even after the man had passed.

"It's been three years since that drunk driver hit him, but I still think about him every day."

"I don't think you're supposed to get over it. My brother was killed two years ago, and I don't want to ever forget about him."

The path to their hotel took them alongside the riverfront. The breeze picked up as they approached the water. Goose bumps skittered along Mack's arms and legs. Across the wide river stood the sharply peaked roof and spires of an enormous Buddhist temple. The building, brightly spotlit, glowed golden in the night.

"Can I ask you something?" Mack said. She took Ben's silence as permission, and continued. "I get that you were a CIA agent, and then you left, and they brought you back for this mission. But the way you talk about them, there's bad blood there. What happened? Why'd you leave the CIA?"

A party boat cruised by in the water in front of them. The thump of house music competed with the shouts and laughter of the drunken revelers who swayed perilously close to the railings on the top deck.

Their hotel—a narrow, three-story building—was coming into view.

"It's a long story," Ben said.

Mack rested her hand on his arm, his skin warm beneath her touch. "I've got time."

Ben tilted his head, looking at the sky. Then he let out a loud breath. "After John was killed, things kinda . . . got foggy for me. We kept bringing in these suspected terrorists, and the Agency was encouraging us to do whatever we had to do to get information out of them. Ignore all the usual rules and just make 'em talk. I was fucked-up about John, and I . . . we had some rough interrogations. It wasn't right."

"I'm sorry," Mack said. "Is that why you wear your brother's ring? To remind you not to let things get foggy again?"

Ben spun the ring on his finger. "Yeah, I suppose that's as good a way to put it as any."

Mack closed her eyes and listened as the boisterous sounds of the party boat receded into the distance, replaced by the gentle lapping of the water against the wooden pilings beneath them. Somewhere far away in the vastness of the city, a motorbike's engine ripped through the night, echoing off the buildings. Closer, a man and a woman were laughing together.

Ben cleared his throat and continued. "This was Eastern Europe. The old Communist Bloc. We were operating out of a former detention center for the Soviet secret police. And one day it was like I woke up. I saw myself—where I was, what I was doing. I started realizing that so much about what we in the intelligence world were doing wasn't right. So I walked."

"But if you just left, then why does Director Harris hate you so much?"

Ben let out a single, bitter laugh. "Probably because I tried to get him fired. He was the one pushing us to go further, the architect of it all. When I left, I made sure that a lot of important people knew what he was up to." He shook his head. "But that was me being naive. As it turned out, nobody cared."

They reached the hotel. The elevator swept them up and deposited them onto their floor. Mack's and Heaton's rooms were side by side; Ben's was just across the hall. They stopped in the hallway and faced each other.

"We should get some sleep," Ben said.

But he made no motion to go. He looked down at her. He was so close she could see the gold flecks in his eyes, could smell the salt of the hot tropical day drying on his skin.

"Do you . . . ?" Mack began.

Do you want to come inside? That's what she nearly said. If this was the last night of normal life before the whole world went crazy, why not spend it in the arms of a good man?

But then she remembered what they were here for. What they might be walking into tomorrow. The new protocols she still had to practice. There was no time for messiness.

"Do you really think this Braithwaite guy is Merlin?" Mack asked instead.

"He's the best lead we have."

"What if he doesn't give us anything? What if he's already gone?"

"I don't know," Ben said. "I guess I'll have to think of something."

He took his key card from his pocket, turned around, and opened the door to his pitch-black room.

Then he, too, seemed to hesitate. "Well," Ben began, looking over his shoulder at Mack, "'night."

He went inside, and the door closed behind him, leaving Mack standing alone in the dim corridor.

Forget him, she told herself. *I have spells to practice.*

19

Novak yanked out a chair from underneath an unused computer console and sat down heavily. He rubbed at his eyes, at his face. Walters, with trademark good timing, approached with a steaming mug of coffee in each hand.

Novak reached for one. "Thanks."

"Oh no, these are both mine."

"Funny."

Walters passed Novak a mug, then lowered himself into a chair.

"No progress on magic?" Walters asked, jabbing a thumb in the direction of the conference room, where a handful of agents were practicing with the protocols.

Novak shook his head.

"Well, then you look like you could use some good news."

"Sure, you got some?"

"Could be." Walters bobbed his clean-shaven head noncommittally. "Zolstra's headed south in a rented car."

"Leaving Bangkok?"

"Looks that way. We're tailing them."

As soon as Agent Seoh's hackers had come through with the location of Merlin's upload, the CIA had obtained video footage of the

internet café from a bank's camera across the street. They'd spotted
Zolstra and the two women entering the place and leaving a short
time later. It had taken a bit longer to find the hotel where they'd registered, but Novak was able to retask three active field agents to make
the rounds. It was only a matter of time, and a fistful of baht, before
they found a front desk worker willing to talk.

Novak had finally convinced Harris to give Zolstra room to operate. Harris had, at least for now, seen the wisdom of letting one of the
government's best-trained hounds track his scent. Provided they could
keep tracking *him*.

The reprieve wouldn't last long, Novak knew. Given the horror of
the invisible assassin in Jerusalem, Harris would soon insist on bringing Mack in and finally cultivating her as a weapon.

But for now they still had one active lead. A bull-headed ex-agent
who remained on the hunt. If he was headed to the south of Thailand
it meant he had a reason to. Novak had to believe that.

So where the hell are you going now, Zolstra?

"One more thing," Walters said. There were dark bags beneath his
eyes. Jesus, did Novak look as tired as he did? "The tech team's saying
the dam's about to burst."

"How long?"

"A matter of hours, maybe less."

In a few hours, everyone in the world would learn that magic was
real, that there were talents available to them beyond their wildest
fantasies. And people—from government officials on down—would
make it their business to learn how to use them to rob, rape, and kill
with impunity.

"All right, thanks, Walters," Novak said. He stood, coffee in hand.
"If you'll excuse me, I think it's time to light a fire under some asses."

Behind a glass dividing wall that separated the conference room
from the rest of the command center, the three agents that Novak
had entrusted with figuring out how to use the protocols were

heatedly debating something. He could see them, pantomiming in broad gestures, as he approached. Agent Thompson, who had demonstrated his embarrassingly feeble telekinesis skills during the Situation Room briefing three days earlier, was tapping pointedly on a whiteboard with a marker. His shirtsleeves were rolled up, his tie loosened, his hair a greasy mess. Like everyone else, he hadn't slept in days.

The whiteboard behind Thompson took up the better part of the wall, and it was awash in disconnected groups of words, swooping arrows, and muddied erasures. What Thompson was pointing to was a gibberish phrase: the just-discovered invisibility protocol. Despite his sorry performance at the White House, Thompson was still the best they had at working with the damn things.

"It's not about the *words*," Thompson was saying to the others as Novak approached. "It's about the *focus*. Yes, the words need to be there, but . . . but you're missing the point."

"What point?" Agent O'Neill put her hands on her hips and shook her head. Her red ponytail swung back and forth behind her. "If it's not about the words, what good are they?"

Thompson sighed. "I don't know. There's something . . ." He stared up at the ceiling, blinked. "When you use them you can feel it. The power is *in them*, for sure. But at the same time, if you don't . . . harness and direct it correctly, nothing happens."

"But how are we supposed to increase our focus?"

"How indeed," Novak interrupted, moving into the room.

The agents turned, startled.

"So, Thompson," Novak continued, "can you use it yet? The new protocol?"

Thompson's head awkwardly split the difference between a nod and a shake. "It's harder than the last one. Instead of focusing on making something move you have to focus on making something . . . not exist. It's tough."

Novak just raised his eyebrows. He needed results, not excuses.

Thompson got the picture. "But I've got a start on it."

"Very good," Novak said. He lowered himself into a chair and stared at the young agent. "Let's have a demonstration."

Thompson paled. "Yes, sir." He set the whiteboard marker down on the table in front of him. "We've been practicing with this marker—"

Novak exploded. "*I'm not interested in another fucking pen, Thompson!*" He slammed his hand down on the table. "Eila Mack can throw a police officer and his motorcycle across a parking lot! Could you try to do something not pathetic, for Christ's sake?"

"What would you like me to use, sir?" Thompson's voice quavered.

"Yourself," Novak said. "Use yourself."

"Sir, I don't think—"

"Hamas can do it," Novak said. "As they showed the whole world in Jerusalem. ISIS can probably do it, and they don't have the luxury of the time you have, since they're quite busy cutting off heads and dodging fucking airstrikes in the middle of the *fucking desert!*" His voice, which had risen to a sharp intensity, went suddenly cold and calm. "Make yourself invisible and you might be half as good as a terrorist."

Thompson nodded, then closed his eyes. The agents he'd been talking with stepped behind Novak, giving Thompson the stage. The man's brow wrinkled and his eyes moved beneath their lids.

"He's focusing, sir," O'Neill explained unnecessarily.

Novak merely glared at her until she looked away.

Thompson's mouth began to move, and a small hissing escaped his lips. The sound was guttural, alien. Novak was the least superstitious person he knew, and even he felt the hairs on the back of his neck rise as Thompson recited the strange words.

Thompson continued to murmur, and as he did so Novak's

attention was drawn to the agent's abdomen. The left side of his stomach was beginning to blur, like the heated air above a boiling pot. The blurring spread across Thompson's body, and gradually the area became more and more transparent, until Novak could see, through Thompson's belly, a few smeary and unfocused words written on the whiteboard behind him.

By this time, Thompson's face was red and wet with perspiration. He'd evidently reached the limit of his ability, a fact confirmed seconds later when Thompson opened his eyes. He drew a deep breath, like a skin diver coming up for air, and held up his hands in front of his face. He appeared puzzled that he could still see them, then he looked down at where he'd produced nothing more than a wavy, semi-translucent band roughly six inches thick across his stomach.

Dismay creased his face. "Son of a *bitch*," he said. "I really felt like I was getting somewhere."

Even as he spoke, the area he'd obscured was becoming more opaque. In seconds, it had returned to normal. Thompson winced and faced Novak, dutifully awaiting judgment.

Novak slowly raised his coffee mug to his lips and took a long, loud slurp. "That was exceptionally disappointing, Thompson." He stood and began walking out of the glass-enclosed conference room. "Keep practicing," he called back over his shoulder.

What more could he say or do? This kid was the best they'd been able to find in the Agency. Was there somebody stronger in ability, in some other department or agency, or maybe some soldier someplace? Possibly. But even though it was apparently mere hours from being the biggest story in the world, magic was still officially unacknowledged; the government hadn't publicly confirmed its reality. They couldn't very well hold tryouts.

It was why Harris wanted Mack so badly. It was also why Zolstra had to come through and deliver something big that they could use to fight magic before Harris lost what little patience he had left and decided to spring his trap. Of course, Novak could try to guard against that eventuality—but it would mean doing something drastic. He would have to go behind his boss's back and make contact with an asset of Zolstra's he had tracked down: a man named Gabriel Garcia.

20

For Ben, Pattaya City had all the exotic charm of Miami Beach—which was to say, none at all. It looked like a classic product of heedless overdevelopment: a beautiful stretch of pristine coastline marred by high-rise hotels and garish condos, and a bay filled with pleasure yachts for the rich. But Ben wasn't too put out; unlike the rows of bikini-clad beachgoers, he wasn't here on vacation.

It was Heaton who spotted the newspaper in the gutter as they made their way toward the rental boats. "It's begun," she said.

"What?" Ben and Mack asked at once.

Heaton picked up the paper. The banner headline shouted about the continued escalation of the Israeli assassination affair. All signs pointed to Iran as the culprit behind the invisibility attack. The gears of war were turning again in the Middle East, and the United States looked like it was going to be dragged into a conflagration that experts warned would amount to World War III.

But what Heaton's thin finger was pointing to was a little article near the bottom of the page:

Recently Surfaced Videos May Suggest Reality of "Magic"

Harris's men hadn't been able to keep the videos and protocols consigned to the dark web. They'd gotten out, which meant that soon they'd go viral and be everywhere: everybody with internet access would want to try to test their magical ability. How many people would turn out to have real power, equal to Mack's or greater? One in a thousand? What would it be like to live in a world where even one out of every *hundred thousand* people had the abilities of a superhero?

"It'll be the headline tomorrow," Ben said.

"And probably every day after that," Heaton agreed grimly.

Then there was Harris, who would certainly not stop hunting them. It was an unfamiliar feeling; Ben was used to being the hunter. Had the CIA already tracked the upload to the internet café? If Gabe had managed to do it, they must have. How much else had they learned? They had to know about Heaton by now, but Ben's gut told him they didn't know about Braithwaite yet, though eventually Harris would decide to look at Heaton's former associates and colleagues, and they'd put together Braithwaite's current whereabouts. That's what the CIA did, better than almost anybody.

They stepped onto the plasticized dock of the marina. Fortunately, the booming commerciality of the place meant there were plenty of speedboats available for rent. Once Mack and Heaton climbed aboard the sleek, blue-and-yellow craft, Ben steered them out of the bay and toward the coordinates Braithwaite had sent Heaton. He flattened the throttle when they hit open water. The powerful engines drove the boat onward, bounding over the tops of the waves.

Heaton's voice came to Ben, thin and reedy on the wind. "Must we go quite so fast?"

Ben turned to where she and Mack were seated on the bench behind him. Mack looked okay, but Heaton's already pale skin had acquired a green tint, and she clutched her floppy sun hat in one hand, and her stomach in the other. Ben backed off the throttle a bit.

Soon the water was turning a lighter blue, the seafloor rising as it

approached the tiny island that poked above the surface right ahead
of them.

"How are we supposed to get anywhere near it?" Mack asked.

Ben had started to wonder the same thing. The island couldn't
have been much larger than the span of two football fields, and it was
composed mostly of a single, craggy rock formation. Stone pinnacles
jutted out of the water all around it, protecting the small strip of sandy
beach like the teeth of an angry sea monster. Ben slowed the boat to
a crawl.

If the island wasn't much, the lone building that stood on it was
something else entirely. The long, wooden structure was a marvel. It
was built into the island in such a way that it appeared to be a natural
outcropping. It undulated fluidly with the edges of the rock wall behind it and the sea in front. In a few places, it had been constructed
around spires of rock that poked up right through the solar-paneled
roof. The side of the house that faced the beach was made entirely of
sliding glass walls; it was like an extended covered porch, filled with
long rattan sofas and planters of tropical flowers.

"This doesn't look like a place you can build on a professor's pen-
sion," Mack said.

"No," Heaton agreed, "it doesn't."

The obvious expense of the endeavor was encouraging. Heaton's
conclusion that Braithwaite was a Possessor was already looking much
more plausible.

"I'm going to circle around the back and look for an easier approach," Ben said.

After a few passes, Ben found what he was searching for: a thin,
metal dock between two massive outcroppings of rock. Like the mi-
croisland itself, the dock was all but invisible unless you were actively
looking for it. The baby-blue speedboat that was already moored there
was covered in a matching blue tarp; from fifty yards out, it was expertly camouflaged with the surrounding water.

If they couldn't exactly anticipate *magical* defenses, Ben could at least scan the area for conventional ones: guards, cameras, mounted weapons, trip wires. Finding none, he slowly brought the craft alongside the dock, then jumped out and tied them off.

The dock ran straight for roughly forty feet before it disappeared into a narrow tunnel carved into the solid rock. Ben fished his pistol from his bag and tucked it into his waistband before leading Mack and Heaton into the unlit tunnel, which darkened with every step, abruptly ending at a heavy wooden door. In its center, barely visible in the murk, was an iron knocker. It was a strange geometric figure that looked like a thin triangle, pointing to the right, with four straight bars running vertically across it.

"Oh my God," Heaton whispered. "It's a Sumerian ideogram. This symbol dates from around the time of the Ur dynasty."

"That's fascinating and all," Mack said, "but what does it mean?"

"It means to fetter, or to shackle." Heaton stared at Ben through the gloom. Her demeanor had changed to one of sober reverence, like she was about to set foot on sacred ground. "It's the mark of the Possessors."

Ben felt a rush of vindication. He had been right to bring them halfway around the world. He only hoped Braithwaite would cooperate now that they'd found him.

"So what now?" Mack asked.

"Now I guess we . . . knock?" Heaton said hesitantly.

Ben turned to her.

"Go ahead and do the honors, Professor."

Heaton practically hummed with anticipation and purpose as she stepped forward, raised the iron knocker, and struck the door three times.

They waited. The seconds passed into a minute. Ben took the knocker in his hand and rapped harder at the wood.

Still no response. From the far end of the tunnel came the sound of the sea as it slapped at the dock pilings and splashed against the moored boats. It echoed, distant and distorted, in the narrow space.

Ben tried the doorknob. He gave it a turn, and the door clicked open, unlocked. He pushed it inward, revealing a rough-hewn stone hallway that ran for about two dozen feet, then appeared to open into a sunken, rock-walled living room. The sound of jazz twinkled softly in the air.

"Hello?" Ben called. "Carlton Braithwaite?"

There was no response. Ben made a hesitant step over the threshold, then stopped. Who knew what kind of magical traps this Possessor might have rigged up?

"Are you picking up anything about this place?" Ben asked Mack in a near-whisper. "Any weird . . . signals or anything?"

"I'm not a freaking radio," Mack said. "And everything about this place is weird."

Ben drew his gun and moved slowly, cautiously, down the cave-like hallway. Mack and Heaton trailed him.

The pentagonal living room looked like a 1970s pleasure palace. Piles of soft pillows were scattered around on the red leather couches built deep into the sunken floor. A bearskin rug—unmistakably real and complete with glass-eyed head—lay in the center of the room. A Miles Davis tune played on a staticky radio, the muted trumpet floating out from a pair of speakers hung in the corners of the ceiling.

"Carlton," Heaton called as she moved into the next room. "Where—?"

Her question contorted itself into a piercing shriek.

Ben rushed after her, his finger on the SIG Sauer's trigger.

Heaton was standing in the middle of a large kitchen, both hands pressed to her face, and breathing so hard that Ben worried she would lose consciousness. She was staring at the body of a man lying facedown on the floor. His back was a gruesome mess of slashes and stab wounds, and a syrupy puddle of slick, dark blood spread out around him. A blood-covered paring knife lay close by.

Something twitched beneath the man's torn T-shirt. As Ben leaned closer, a small crab scampered out through a hole in the man's shirt, its pincers stained red. Heaton screamed again.

Ben tucked the gun back into his waistband. Whoever had done this was long gone. The smell of the body's decay was Ben's first clue, but so was the congealed look of the blood and its dried, flaking edges. He had been dead for at least three days—as long as the first protocol had been out.

Ben motioned for Mack to take Heaton out of the room, which she did, trying to avoid looking directly at the body in front of her.

As Ben examined the area, one detail in particular stood out to him as significant. On the kitchen table there was a sterling silver teapot and a small ceramic pitcher for milk. Two half-filled teacups sat next to them.

Ben returned to the living room with a glass of water for the professor, who accepted it with a nodded thanks.

"What . . ." Heaton struggled to speak. "What *happened* here?"

"Was it—oh, Jesus—was it them? Harris's guys?" Mack looked like she was going to be sick.

Ben shook his head. Aside from the fact that it would have made no sense, government assassins were professionals: two bullets to the head. And they cleaned up after themselves. They didn't stab someone in the back in a chaotic pattern and flee the scene, leaving this kind of mess—not to mention DNA evidence in a half-drunk teacup— behind them. This was strictly amateur hour.

"I'm sorry about your friend, Professor," Ben said. His words of condolence were rote, but well intentioned; not everyone was as familiar with death as he was. The bright tones of Davis's trumpet contrasted jarringly with the somber atmosphere.

Heaton turned to him. "What if it was the Possessors?"

Mack, who still held a comforting hand on Heaton's back, asked, "But why would they kill one of their own? Braithwaite was a Possessor himself."

"Maybe for the same reason they tried to stop us back in Scotland," Heaton said bitterly. "To protect their secrets."

Ben considered the idea. It was possible. According to Heaton, the Possessors were well connected enough to have eyes everywhere. They could have found out Braithwaite and Merlin were the same person, and come here to shut him up for good.

"It fits, in a way, Carlton being Merlin," Heaton added. "All the little nudges he gave me on my research, like he wanted me to know the truth. Perhaps he simply tired of the secrecy and wanted to come out with the whole thing."

Except it didn't fit at all. Yes, it was a reasonable assumption that Merlin was a Possessor; who else would know their most guarded secrets? Yet the wording of the Merlin manifesto crackled with righteousness and rage at an unjust order. *Your world is about to change. Your certainties will be undone. Your corrupt hierarchies will die. You may destroy yourselves . . .* They were hardly the words of a Thailand-bound retiree who had benefitted from those same hierarchies his whole life. And whoever Merlin really was would have to have known that the Possessors would come for him with a fury—he wouldn't have been caught off guard and literally stabbed in the back by someone he'd invited in for *tea*.

"Professor," Ben asked, "was Braithwaite technology savvy?"

Heaton shook her head. "Dear me, no. In fact, he was the last person I knew to buy a mobile phone." She smiled sadly. "Old-fashioned to the core, that one."

"Does that strike you as a person capable of designing a sophisticated computer program to disseminate secret information on the dark web?"

"Not in the slightest. Carlton would have thought 'dark web' was something that collected in a disused attic." She stared at Ben, putting it together. "He wasn't Merlin."

"No," Ben agreed. "But maybe it was Merlin who killed him. The fact that they were both in Thailand must be more than coincidence."

"But why?" Heaton's voice cracked.

"Maybe Braithwaite was on to him, trying to stop him from releasing the protocols to the world, from betraying their ancient secret."

Ben started thinking out loud. "Let's assume they're part of the same secret order, and they know each other. Or at least know *of* each other. So Braithwaite invites Merlin over. They sit down to tea. Braithwaite tries to talk him out of what he's about to do—maybe even threatens him with what'll happen if he goes through with it. Merlin gets upset, grabs a knife . . ."

Ben trailed off and began examining the room's shelves, checking the spaces beneath the sofas, feeling along the walls.

"What are you looking for?" Mack asked.

"Our next move. Any information about the other Possessors, the binding spell, or even a book of other useful spells you could learn. A hidden passageway to the goddamn Conservatory. Anything."

Mack and Heaton stood up to help.

Ben alone handled the kitchen, sidestepping Braithwaite's corpse to dig around in the cabinets and cupboards, in the fridge, under the sink, and in every drawer. Ben learned nothing except that the old professor had an appetite for both fine scotch and junk food—exorbitantly priced single malts shared shelving space with bags of Doritos and Oreos.

When Ben was satisfied that the kitchen and dining room held no useful secrets, he moved down the hallway to join the others. With the exception of the pentagon-shaped living room they'd entered first, which was carved deeply into the rock and had no windows, nearly every room in the house was filled with bright light pouring in through the glass walls that ran along the sea-facing side. The one-level home unfolded in a zigzagging line, one room leading into the next as the building hugged the rock behind it.

Braithwaite's study wasn't as well appointed as Heaton's, but it had one distinctive feature. Jutting up through the center of the room, rising from beneath the floorboards and disappearing through the ceiling, was a jagged pinnacle of solid rock. Ben ran his hand along its cool surface.

Mack and Heaton were already in the room, flipping through books pulled down from the shelves, rummaging in the drawers of the massive oak desk.

"Any luck?"

Heaton shook her head. She pointed through the open doorway at the opposite end of the study from where Ben had entered. "There's a master bedroom, a guest bedroom, a pair of WCs. Aside from some sort of swing contraption hanging from the bedroom ceiling, there's nothing out of the ordinary in any of them," Heaton concluded.

Mack described the situation more aptly. "He might be some kind of sex freak, but this guy is the most boring super-secret magician ever."

"Then we're definitely missing something," Ben said.

His eyes took in the volumes on the shelves, and the stacks that Mack had made of books she'd already looked through. The titles on the spines marked Braithwaite as an acolyte of magic as much as the symbol on his front door. *Religious Cults of Ancient Mesopotamia. Sorcery, Necromancy, and the Occult in the Roman Empire.* One book in particular caught his eye. *Hiding in Plain Sight: The Secret History of Magic and Those Who Control It.* But it wasn't the title that grabbed Ben's attention; it was the author: Dr. Desdemona Heaton.

"Professor," Ben called. "It looks like Braithwaite was a fan of yours."

Ben held up the book.

Heaton looked touched. "Bless his heart. So he really did value my work."

"Dang," Mack said, "you wrote a book?"

"Of course, my dear," Heaton said with a thin smile. " 'Publish or perish.' Though in the case of that book, I'm afraid it was publish *and* perish. That was the book that so embarrassed the administration at Oxford that they sacked me."

"It's possible it was more than just embarrassing," Ben said. "Maybe you were hitting too close to home, and they were pressured to drop you, to disgrace and discredit you."

"By the Possessors, you mean? Yes, I've wondered that myself."

Ben flipped through Heaton's book, hunting for underlined passages, marginal notes, dog-eared pages, anything to give them a hint of where to turn next. But there was nothing.

If Braithwaite was keeping something important here, he had to have cloaked it in invisibility, or obscured it in some other way . . .

"The new protocols," Ben said to Mack. "The ones Gabe sent over. Did they work last night?"

Mack nodded. "I used the invisibility spell to make my hotel bed disappear," she said with pride, "and one of Gabe's spells worked to make it visible again."

"Try the revealing one now."

Mack reached into her pocket and produced the piece of paper on which she'd scrawled the words Gabe had texted. She squinted at the paper and began reading through Gabe's reworked transliterations. The sounds of the incantations rang alien and uncanny in Ben's ears.

Almost immediately after Mack started reading, something happened.

Ben noticed it first as a trick of the light catching his eye, coming from the wall of the study opposite the windows.

"Keep going," Ben whispered. "Repeat it."

As Mack continued, Ben approached the wall. In the narrow space between one of the bookcases and the desk, a tall, thin rectangle shimmered like a mirage, and gradually solidified. A panel had been cut into the wall. Ben gave it a push, and it swiveled inward on a hinge. Inside was a vault that held stacks and stacks of cash—British pounds sterling, as well as American dollars and Thai baht.

"There must be hundreds of thousands of dollars in here," Mack said.

"And nothing of use to us," Ben replied.

Mack tried the revealing protocol again and again, in every room of the house. Nothing else turned up. Ben was beginning to think that Merlin had swept the place clean of anything useful, until they returned to the kitchen. With Heaton sitting down in the living room—she couldn't bear to set foot in the room with the body of her former friend again—Mack's final attempt revealed a scrap of paper that had been rendered invisible. It was balled-up under the kitchen table.

Ben picked it up and smoothed it out onto the surface of the table while Mack peered over his shoulder. The note, covered in bloody fingerprints, read:

He's going for Leclerc

In his last moments, Braithwaite managed to scribble down and hide an invisible warning, presumably about Merlin's next target. But who—or what—was Leclerc?

Ben's phone buzzed with a message from Gabe:

Novak says run. NOW.

Novak says? He'd found Gabe?

There was no time to reason it out. A thin whining sound drew Ben's attention to the open window. Through it, beyond the strip of pure white sand, bounding over the waves on the glittering turquoise sea beyond, was a jet-black speedboat.

It was aiming right at Braithwaite's island, and it was coming fast.

21

I t's Harris's guys," Ben said, squinting at the boat. He saw the silhouettes of two figures, but it was still too distant to make out more than that. "We've gotta move."

Mack stared out the kitchen window. "How do you know it's the CIA? Maybe it's another Possessor."

As she spoke Ben saw a flash of sunlight reflecting off the lens of a rifle scope. He didn't think, he just grabbed Mack and yanked both of them down to a crouch. They ran, bent double, into the living room where Heaton sat.

"We need to get out of here," Ben said, already heading toward the long stone hallway that led to the dock.

"What happens if they catch us?" Mack asked.

Ben stopped and gave her a hard look. "You go back into a cell while they pick you apart and figure out how to weaponize your power. The professor and I get interrogated by Harris until he gets tired of torturing us, which doesn't happen fast. Then I get tried for treason. That is, unless Harris has decided it would be easier to just get rid of us."

That last scenario was unlikely—but Ben hadn't liked the look of that rifle.

Mack raised her eyebrows. "Well . . . fuck."

"Yeah." Ben jogged down the hallway, calling out behind him, "So let's stop talking."

Ben had already untied their rented boat when Mack and Heaton reached him. He stood with one foot on the dock and the other on the craft. He held out his hand to Heaton.

"Wait!" Heaton said. "What about Carlton? We can't just leave him like that."

"We sure as hell can," Mack said, hopping into the boat.

Heaton looked stricken. Ben took her hand. "The CIA will ID him and make sure his family is notified. They'll take care of it."

As soon as Heaton had allowed herself to be brought onboard and seated, Ben eased the craft out of Braithwaite's rocky inlet and into open water. He idled the boat and listened.

Harris's men were still approaching the opposite side of the island. Ben could hear the growl of their motor getting louder by the second, but he couldn't see them, since the spires of the rock formation hid the rear of the island from view.

Ben threw Mack a look. "Just like in Scotland," he said.

She nodded in understanding. Ben would bring the other boat into view, and Mack would use her power to capsize it so the team could escape. Since they were on the water, no one needed to die this time.

Ben pushed the throttle forward and the powerful engines roared to life. As they came around the island, they saw the black boat of Harris's men a few hundred yards off. Mack raised her hands toward the craft—

There was a loud *crack* and a splash in the water just off the side of Ben's boat. The agent with the rifle had fired on them.

Change of fucking plans.

"*Everybody down!*" Ben ordered, jamming the throttle to the hilt and cranking the steering wheel to turn them around and bring them back behind the island.

Heaton and Mack slid to the boat's plastic floor, bracing their limbs against the seats as Ben completed his on-a-dime turn. The boat doubled back over its own wake. A cascade of water poured in over the front of the craft, splashing Ben and half-soaking the others.

"I can't believe they're trying to kill us!" Mack yelled.

Ben wasn't so sure they were. CIA sharpshooters didn't miss, even from moving vessels. The guy was just signaling that they meant business. Ben would have to show them that he did, too.

The island was once again between Ben and his pursuers, but he couldn't risk setting out on open water. Even if it turned out that Ben was driving the faster boat—far from a certainty—Harris's agents had a scoped rifle. Ben's craft could easily be disabled by a well-grouped volley of shots to their rear. No: they had to stay in close to the island to have a chance.

Which wasn't as easy as it sounded, since Braithwaite's hideaway was surrounded by menacing, jagged rock pillars that could punch a nasty hole in their fiberglass hull.

Ben figured the other boat would try to head them off by going in the opposite direction, so he turned back again the way they'd just come.

It worked. As they emerged in the front of the island, they were now behind the black boat—maybe three hundred yards back. And they hadn't yet been spotted.

Ben drew his gun. He waited until he neared a stretch of deeper water, then he balanced the SIG Sauer's short barrel on the windshield in front of the pilot's wheel.

"I want to help," Mack called from where she was huddled on the floor of the boat.

"Stay down. You're too important to risk while they're still shooting."

Keeping the boat as steady as he could, Ben took aim at the other boat's pair of large outboard motors. He squeezed the trigger three times. *Pop pop pop.*

The first shot went wide. The second appeared to pass harmlessly through the rear hull and seats. The third hit home. A plume of dark smoke rose from one of the engines.

That'll slow you down a bit.

He got both hands back on the wheel just in time to jerk the boat away from a barely submerged finger of rock. He pulled another one-eighty and retreated again to the rear of the island. He heard a burst of rifle fire erupt behind him, but Harris's guys were too slow; Ben was already out of sight.

The game had gotten more interesting, and Ben had drawn first blood. Harris's agents would be more cautious now, knowing their quarry was armed.

He brought his boat as close to the back of the island as he could, idling it alongside a shelf of barnacled rock visible less than two feet beneath the crystal-clear water. Danger lurked everywhere on this island, it seemed. He pointed the boat's nose straight out toward the blue horizon. That way, he'd be prepared no matter which side Harris's agents decided to appear from. He drew his pistol again and waited.

"Okay," Ben said, turning behind him and looking at where Mack and Heaton were still braced on the floor. "Your turn, Mack."

"What are you going to do?" Heaton asked. With her sodden clothes and white hair plastered to her head, she reminded Ben of a miserable poodle condemned to a bath.

Instead of answering, Ben asked Mack, "Are you *sure* you can use the invisibility protocol?"

He heard the buzz of the black boat, fainter now that it was down to one motor. Harris's men were approaching, following the way Ben had come.

"I guess?" Mack said hesitantly. "I mean, I hope . . ." She shook her head roughly, as if to throw off her indecision. "Yes." She stood up next to Ben. "I can."

He smiled. "Good. This whole boat, and us, too, on my signal."

The other boat slowly came into view. Ben raised his gun . . .

"*Now.*"

There was faint whispering next to him, then the gun disappeared. So did the hand that held it. Even the boat was gone—beneath him, instead of legs, feet, and the deck below, Ben saw the flashing rainbow scales of a small school of tropical fish.

The sensation of total body unawareness was similar to being in a pitch-dark room, but the fact that he was outside in the blazing sunshine and still couldn't see himself made Ben's mind reel and his stomach lurch. He wanted to use the opportunity to incapacitate the remaining motor on the other boat, but when he leveled the gun at the approaching craft, he realized he had nothing to sight by. Just because he *thought* he was pointing at the engine didn't mean he really was.

Ben's thumb rubbed at John's Annapolis class ring. He wouldn't risk inadvertently killing other Americans, even if they were after him.

His gun and hands appeared for a split second, then quickly disappeared again, like a reverse blinking. Ben realized the whole boat must have done the same.

"Sorry . . . I can't . . . hold it all . . ." Mack said, her voice strained.

Harris's men had spotted it, too. Now only a hundred or so feet distant, Ben watched the agent with the rifle bring the weapon back up to his shoulder, squinting and waiting for the next flash of visibility.

"Just a little longer," Ben hissed.

Without the boat to obstruct his view, Ben saw that the ledge of rock near them ran much farther out into deeper water than he'd suspected. Ben had only narrowly avoided hitting it as he pulled into position moments before. He could use that to his advantage.

He began to fire again as Mack cried out, exhausted—and their boat and everything in it became fully visible. The driver of the other boat veered hard left to avoid Ben's shots. The man with the rifle, who'd been standing, was knocked back into his seat before he could let off another round.

The deliberately wide shots pushed the driver of the black boat to do exactly what Ben wanted him to do: turn directly into the submerged rock. There was a wrenching sound as the speeding boat's hull crashed hard into the ledge, and both driver and trigger man were launched into the air and sent careening into the water.

"Yes!" Heaton exclaimed, pumping her fist.

Ben gunned his engine and roared toward the disabled boat. The agents were already swimming back toward their craft. Ben leveled his pistol and shot out the remaining motor as he passed.

He opened the throttle and pointed them toward Pattaya City.

22

Novak stood outside the closed door of Director Harris's office, arms folded, waiting to be admitted. No one else was in sight, but there were voices coming from inside, muffled by the solid oak. Judging from the sound, Harris's mood was even worse than usual.

The director's office was at the end of a long carpeted hallway, on a different floor and the opposite side of the building from the Project Merlin command center. Even though Novak was Harris's deputy director, he'd seen the inside of his office only a handful of times. It was not generally considered a privilege to be called for a visit; for many agents, the only time they ever saw Harris's office was the moment they were fired.

Novak wondered now if that was about to be his own fate. His summons had come after the botched operation to pick up Zolstra and the rest of them at Carlton Braithwaite's little island getaway. Except the operation hadn't really been botched. It had been *sabotaged*—by Novak himself. The warning text he had Gabriel Garcia send to Zolstra had given them just enough of a heads-up to successfully evade capture at the hands of the CIA field team. Novak was deep in uncharted territory now, and it chafed against his normal caution. But nothing about these times was normal.

Finding Gabriel Garcia had been a stroke of luck. Back when Zolstra had first fled the safe house with Mack, and Novak's team was still scouring the Annapolis area for anyone that might have assisted the rogue agent, Walters had brought an ex-Marine and occasional forger named Garcia to Novak's attention. At the time, they couldn't make anything stick to Zolstra, and Novak told Walters to keep looking.

By the time Zolstra resurfaced again in Scotland, Garcia had been mostly forgotten—except by Novak, who did a little more digging and had the local PD do a quick drive-by and have a peek in Garcia's garage. Novak knew he'd found Zolstra's contact when the cops reported back that they'd seen a Yamaha motorcycle that matched the description of the one stolen in D.C.

Novak had withheld the information from Harris for the same reason he'd sat on the other info about the G5—because he believed in Zolstra and still thought he was their best chance at finding Merlin and stopping the spread of his protocols.

Inside Harris's office, the voices subsided. The door opened. A small man sporting a bad comb-over and an ill-fitting suit stepped into the hallway. Novak hadn't seen George Torozian, the president's national security advisor, since the Situation Room briefing days before.

Novak nodded. "George."

"Hello, Bill," Torozian said in his perpetually hoarse voice.

"What brings you to Langley?"

"What else? This terrible business about the fucking Merlin protocols," Torozian said, shaking his head. "It's out. It's all out in the open now. Between you and me, aside from urging calm, the president doesn't know what the hell to do next. Do we put soldiers on the streets of every major city? Would that even help?" He lowered his voice to a rasp and put an arm around Novak. "Harris tells me you just lost a big fish."

Novak merely grunted.

"Well, you'd better catch it. Otherwise shit is going to get a lot worse, and I don't just mean for you and me. If we can't stop this, the whole ship goes down." Torozian went ashen. "What happened at that prison in South Carolina is going to look like fucking summer vacation on the Vineyard."

"*Novak!*" Harris's voice boomed through the open office door. "*Get in here!*"

Novak shook Torozian's hand. "Good luck, George."

"I'll settle for a miracle," Torozian croaked. He turned and shuffled up the hallway, seeming almost physically burdened by an endless series of tough choices with no easy answers.

Novak entered Harris's office. The director sat behind a mahogany desk the size of a queen bed. Novak moved toward one of the red leather chairs that faced the desk.

"Don't sit," Harris barked. "You just stand there and answer my question."

Novak froze. "What question is that, sir?"

"How did you do it?"

"Do what?"

"How did you warn Zolstra about the intercept team?"

Novak felt cold needles of anxiety prick at his stomach and arms, but he deflected as well as he could. "I don't appreciate your implication, Director."

Harris smiled, an occurrence so rare it only amplified Novak's discomfort. "I don't know how you got word to him," he said, "or what sort of back channel you've got set up. But I know you helped." Harris's instincts, honed over the years, remained uncanny.

"You're wrong, and you're getting paranoid, sir," Novak responded, surprising even himself with his forceful tone. He sat in one of the leather chairs without being invited. Harris's nostrils flared, but he said nothing. "Ben Zolstra was able to evade capture because he's one of the best field agents either of us has ever seen, and he's working with a girl whose supernatural abilities are frankly beyond description. There's no more to it than that."

Harris leaned forward across the desk, fixing his owlish gaze on Novak. He took a deep breath—full inhale, full exhale—without breaking eye contact.

"We'll see," he finally said. "I'll have Zolstra in hand soon, and I can ask him myself. That, and a whole lot else." His eyes flashed with such intensity at the prospect that Novak felt a flicker of fear on Zolstra's behalf.

"How do you plan on doing that?" Novak asked. "They've completely lost the intercept team."

"Ben Zolstra is not leaving Thailand." Harris spoke with the definitiveness of a judge handing down a sentence. "I don't care if I have to call in every favor, double down on every threat, and bribe every official in the whole of frigging Siam. Zolstra and Mack are not getting out of that country."

Harris sat back in his chair. "You can go."

Novak thanked him and stood to leave. He'd made it to the door when Harris called after him.

"You are . . . of *interest* . . . to me now, Deputy Director Novak," Harris said slowly. "Do you understand what I'm saying to you?"

Novak swallowed the lump in his throat and turned toward the director. "I promise there's nothing interesting about me, sir."

Harris didn't blink. "Leave the door open on your way out," he said.

How far was Novak willing to go to ensure the success of Zolstra's mission? As he felt the director's eyes on him all the way down the corridor, Novak knew he was going to have to decide on an answer to that question, and soon.

23

Constantine raised his freshly poured glass of mint tea from its saucer. His hands shook and some of the scalding liquid spilled over the lip and onto his fingertips. He hissed and set the glass down, unleashing a string of curses in French. He needed to get a hold of himself. He was rattled, yes, but far from helpless.

He stood up from the table. His serving girl, who had been standing near the doorway that led to the main courtyard, rushed to him.

"Is there a problem with your tea, sir?"

"It's fine, Amina," Constantine said. "I have something on my mind."

When he took the call from one of the dozen men that he paid to keep tabs on the affairs of other prominent Possessors worldwide, he had expected a typical report. Perhaps if he were fortunate he would obtain a little unsavory blackmail fodder he could file away to use later, or glean a weakness that could prove useful in gaining some competitive advantage or other. It was, all in all, tedious business.

But the call that came in an hour before from his man in Thailand spoke of darker things altogether. Carlton was dead. No: *had been murdered.* It made Alexavier's death in that Scottish car wreck seem too coincidental to be an accident.

Two days, two prominent Possessors dead. Constantine was determined not to be the third. It had to be this traitor Merlin who was hunting them down—who else but Merlin's fellow Possessors had the power to stop him from his suicidal effort to give magical power to every halfwit and maniac on the planet?

Constantine stepped out of the eating nook but turned back to the girl.

"You should go home, Amina. I won't be needing you for a few days." Why put her in danger?

He brushed past the thin curtain and into the central courtyard around which his centuries-old house had been built. The summer sun beat down on his olive skin. He ignored it, as he ignored the gentle bubbling of the fountain in the courtyard's center and the scent of amber oil wafting on the breeze from the large diffuser set in the corner on the tiled floor.

He walked determinedly up to the head of his guard, who stood near the passage that led to the front door. Remi was wearing the dark sunglasses he favored, and his hands were folded across the compact automatic rifle strapped to his chest. The man straightened up at Constantine's approach.

Constantine spoke to him in French. "Remi, I need you to bring me more men."

The guard frowned. "Sir, I hardly think that's necessary. We now have six men, including myself, on a continuous twenty-four-hour watch. There are always at least three men posted. One out front, one on the roof, and one inside."

"It's not enough," Constantine said, projecting a confidence he could no longer feel. Instead of his default mode of patrician condescension, the noblesse oblige with which he had been brought up, the handsome bachelor felt an unfamiliar and unwelcome emotion: fear.

"Not enough?" Remi cut short a laugh. He must have read the severity in Constantine's face. "This compound is atop a denuded hill, sir, four kilometers from its closest neighbor." He cocked his head toward the front door. "And there's only one way in."

"I'm telling you it's not *enough!*" Constantine threw his arms out wide. Power rushed from him in a gratifying surge. Two of the tall courtyard palms, and the clay pots that held them, burst into white flame and were reduced to piles of smoldering ash.

"For people like me there are always other ways in," Constantine growled. "Or have you forgotten?"

Remi's glasses couldn't mask the fear in his face. "I'm sorry, sir."

Remi had no magic of his own—Possessors did not typically become mercenaries—but he had known about his employer's abilities for some years. The other guards, whose tenures were invariably shorter-lived, had no idea their boss was magical. But it was important to Constantine that the head of his guard knew what he was capable of; it would keep the man from getting any unhelpful ideas about rising above his station.

Remi went on, suitably subdued. "It's just that it's hard enough to get good men to agree to a posting like this."

"A posting like this?" Constantine repeated incredulously. "I pay you all well enough, don't I?"

"It's not that. It's remote out here, quiet. There's not a lot of action for guys like us."

"There's about to be." Constantine felt his stomach lurch at the thought. "I want the shifts doubled by tomorrow."

"If you want reliable people, ex–French Special Forces like me, it's going to take a bit longer than that."

"Tomorrow. Convince them. I don't care what it costs."

Constantine moved down the corridor to the heavy wooden front door. He drew back the bolt and opened it, then hesitated. He turned around and motioned to Remi.

"Give me your gun," he said as the guard approached.

"What?"

"You have another, haven't you?"

"Of course."

Constantine held his hand out. Remi reluctantly unlatched the weapon from its strap and passed it to his boss.

Constantine went out, gripping the submachine gun in his hand. He stalked past the front guard on patrol without looking at him.

Merlin. Who was this bastard who was coming for him, and how powerful would he be when he arrived?

Constantine marched across the dust and gravel expanse in front of his home, stopping fifty yards out, near a chest-high mound of rocks. He turned around. The guards, at the door and on the roof, studiously avoided looking in his direction. Even if they were concerned about their employer's strange behavior and the fact that he was toting a gun, they didn't want to earn his ire.

He braced the rifle, with its barrel aiming directly at the front door of the house, in the space between two large rocks. With barely a breath of effort, he made the weapon disappear. After a slightly more laborious few phrases spoken aloud, he had enchanted the gun to fire on its own at anyone who possessed substantial magical ability. It was a start. He had more in store.

Constantine stepped back and surveyed the compound that comprised his dominion. With his power—along with another handful of guards and a few more well-placed magical surprises he was busy thinking up—he would defend his home against this disgusting turncoat.

His cell phone rang. His senior financial manager was calling.

"Yes, Symone? What is it? I'm quite occupied at the moment."

"I . . . I don't know how to tell you this . . ." The woman's choked whisper was a far cry from her usual no-nonsense brassiness. Constantine's heart double-timed. *Putain de merde, what now?*

"Out with it, please," he said. "What happened?"

"I don't know how it's possible, sir. I've been poring over the records of the meeting and there was no proper authorization or documentation . . . they had no right to . . . but the board signed off on—"

"The *point*, Symone."

"Your family foundation has been dissolved," she said in a rush. "The funds were appropriated by the board."

"Impossible," Constantine said. "They couldn't do that without my approval. I am the heir. It's *my* family's foundation."

"All eight members voted last night to declare you unfit and profligate in absentia, which rendered your approval unnecessary under article H of the bylaws."

Constantine's mouth fell open. "Well . . . we'll contest it. My lawyers will destroy those ingrates. Don't worry, they won't get away with this."

"They already have, that's what I'm trying to tell you. They're gone. They're unreachable. Their homes are empty. Their children didn't report for school today. They robbed you, and then disappeared."

All the members of the board were fellow Possessors. They were men and women his father had trusted, or their descendants. And they had betrayed him. Were they running scared from Merlin as well?

His financial manager was breathing rapidly into the phone.

"Symone, calm down," he said. "How bad is it? How much is gone?"

"How *much*? All of it, sir. They left you nothing. Nothing at all."

"*All* of it . . ."

His living allowance was provided for out of the foundation's coffers. Constantine was completely broke. First Merlin and now this? The old order was utterly dead then. It was every Possessor for himself.

24

They couldn't return to the rental car; it was compromised. Harris's men had obviously tracked it from Bangkok. Ben flagged down a taxi to the train station instead.

Pattaya City's main station ended up being little more than a long, shaded platform, open to the warm tropical air. Ben and Mack helped Heaton up the steep steps of the train bound for Bangkok. The metal behemoth wasn't air-conditioned.

"God," Mack groaned, "it's roasting in here."

Ben stashed their bags on the racks above the seats. They sat down on the hard wooden benches, Mack and Heaton facing Ben. With a jerk, the train started to move, then rattled from the station. It only got hotter once they left the shade of the platform. Every window in their car had been pulled open, but the chugging train seemed unlikely to pick up enough speed to generate a decent cooling breeze.

Once they had put some additional miles between themselves and Harris's men, Ben could finally try to figure out what the hell had happened, and what they were going to do next.

He couldn't stop thinking about that warning text, where Gabe dropped Novak's name. The only conclusion Ben could reach—as unlikely as it seemed—was that Novak was actively undermining

Harris's pursuit of Ben. Somehow Novak had determined that Gabe was Ben's asset Stateside, but instead of turning that information over to his boss, Novak had decided to use Gabe in order to back-channel communication with Ben. The yes-man deputy director had never seemed to have even a hint of subversion in him, but the heads-up he had sent to Gabe had bought Ben and his team the precious minutes that meant the difference between freedom and capture.

Ben took out his phone and tried to call Gabe, but the between-city service was spotty and the call wouldn't go through, so he turned his attention to the note he and Mack had discovered: *He's going for Leclerc.* Ben removed the crumpled piece of paper from his pocket and passed it across to Heaton.

"Before we had to run, we found this in Braithwaite's kitchen."

Heaton took the scrap and held it gently in both hands, studying it like it was an unearthed ancient papyrus.

She closed her eyes and whispered. "*Leclerc . . . Leclerc . . .*"

Ben knew Heaton's powerful mind was racing through the vast database she'd internalized over decades of dedicated research—cross-referencing names, dates, places.

There was a loud rumbling as a train lumbered past them in the opposite direction. Mack was staring out the other window, watching the fields and palms roll by at barely more than walking speed.

"Well, there *is* a Leclerc family," Heaton finally said, her eyes opening. "They were French nobility for centuries until they fled to the colonies of North Africa after the First World War."

"Are they Possessors?" Mack asked.

Heaton pursed her lips. "They are in the tier of candidates I'd consider 'very likely,'" she replied. "My research indicated that they moved because the French government was beginning to look a bit too closely at their financial transactions during the war. The Leclercs were not exactly models of patriotism."

"You mean they were traitors?" Ben said.

Heaton smirked. "If I've learned anything in my years it's that a Possessor's first loyalty is always to himself. In this case, the evidence shows that it proved quite lucrative to the family to provide Kaiser Wilhelm with certain desired information."

"They sold out their own country to the Germans?" Mack said, looking disgusted.

"Where are the Leclercs now?" Ben asked.

"I believe those that survive still live in Morocco," Heaton said.

"Why would Merlin be going after this particular family next?"

"I haven't the faintest idea why this person is doing any of this," Heaton admitted. "Betraying centuries of secrecy, murdering other Possessors." Her voice dropped to a near-whisper. "What is it for? What is the endgame?"

Ben scratched at his unshaven chin. "Back in Scotland, you said that you believed that Possessors have organized themselves into re-gional sects, with each having a leader."

Heaton waved her hand. "It's merely a working theory based on patterns of interaction . . ."

"But if you're right," Ben said, "then maybe the head of the Leclerc family is one of these leaders. Someone who might know the binding protocol. Could that be why Merlin's after him, to prevent him from using it?"

"But if Merlin was really going to Leclerc's next," Mack said, "it's got to be too late to stop him, right? You said Braithwaite was killed days ago."

Heaton lowered her eyes at the mention of her dead friend.

"Maybe Merlin got to him already," Ben said, "but maybe not. It's a long way from Thailand to Morocco. Merlin might have had other affairs to get in order. Or Braithwaite was wrong, and Merlin isn't after Leclerc at all. Either way . . ."

"Either way it's worth following up," Mack said, continuing Ben's line of thinking. "We have a lead on another Possessor, and we might even be able to catch Merlin in the act."

Ben grinned at Mack. "Now you're thinking like a spy."

"I've had quite a crash course lately."

Getting to Morocco wouldn't be easy. The international airport was out. Now that Harris knew they were in country it would be locked up tight, even with the high-quality fake documents they still had.

Ben did know someone in Bangkok who might be able to help—if the asset he'd cultivated five years before was still operating. Kovit was as shady a motherfucker as there was, but Ben knew just the lever to use to push him.

"Even *if* the binding spell actually exists," Heaton scoffed, "you can't seriously expect to walk into a Possessor's house and demand that he help you end magic."

"You're right," Ben admitted. "But it's reasonable that the Possessors might want to stop Merlin as much as we do, if only to save their own asses. Imagine if you were in their position. This secret your family has been guarding for centuries has been released into the open, and the one who did it is coming to kill you so you can't impede him."

"The enemy of my enemy . . . ," Heaton said, a smile playing on the corners of her lips. "You know, I *have* always wanted to visit Morocco."

Ben looked to Mack. "What do you say?"

Mack buzzed her lips. "I don't know. It seems like the only way forward, but part of me says that going off to find another Possessor is crazy. Two days ago one of them tried to kill us, and two hours ago we were getting shot at by the CIA outside a different Possessor's house." She folded her arms, leaning back into the bench.

Ben inclined toward her. "I hear you. But we're getting somewhere. And we have something that Merlin, the CIA, and even the Possessors don't have."

"What's that?"

"We have *you*." Ben forced his warmest smile. "Look how you stopped that car in Scotland. Or what you just did out there on the water, making our boat invisible. We can do this. We *have* to do this."

Mack sighed, nodded, slouched farther into her seat, and said nothing.

Hours later, as the sticky, humid midday gave way to the even stickier late afternoon, their train limped into Hua Lamphong station.

The first sign for Ben that things had changed in Bangkok was the lack of drivers. On a normal day, any foreigner arriving by train would be immediately overrun with offers for rides, most of them ludicrously overpriced. But that day there were only a handful of taxis outside the station, and the drivers weren't hustling around trying to drum up business. Instead, they sat inside their cars, smoking nervously.

Two taxi drivers waved Ben off before he was able to cajole a third into taking him to his destination. No one was anxious to go near the Khlong Toei slum.

They navigated through streets dotted with abandoned cars and smashed glass. The taxi sometimes had to crawl up onto the sidewalks to get around the debris. There were still people out, and some of the food vendors went about their business unfazed, but the atmosphere of the city was quietly edgy.

"What happened here?" Ben asked the driver.

"Protesters," he spat out the word. "They are using this . . . magic to help them."

Ben gritted his teeth. He, Mack, and Heaton exchanged a look. It had finally happened: knowledge of magic had gone fully public.

"Military took care of them, for now," the driver continued with satisfaction as they passed a street that had been completely blocked, overturned cars turned into a makeshift barricade. "But with this magic they have? The shits will be back out tonight."

"God," Heaton said softly, "I wonder what's happening in London."

"Or Washington," Mack said.

The driver shrugged.

They approached Khlong Toei. Ben watched Heaton's and Mack's shocked faces as the car neared the dense rows of rusting tin shacks propped up on wooden stilts that disappeared into a canal of gray, fetid water littered with trash. A freeway, its damp concrete sides green with mold, was built a few feet above the corrugated roofs of the highest dwellings.

They got out and paid the driver, who looked relieved to be released.

Mack surveyed the area skeptically. "The guy that's going to get us a plane to Morocco lives *here*?"

"Actually, he lives in a gilded high-rise on the other side of town, but he grew up here, and does business here," Ben said. "He flatters himself that he's a man of the people."

Ben didn't say, *and he likes to intimidate his millionaire partners and customers by forcing them to trudge through the slum muck in their thousand-dollar shoes to meet him.* It also didn't hurt that the area was so densely packed with elevated, half-built structures and forked pathways that Kovit's men could always keep an unseen eye—and more than a few ready gun barrels—on any visitors.

Ben led them by memory along a path he'd trod many times when he was first trying to prove himself reliable to the arms dealer.

They were surrounded by the smoke of cooking fires and the chittering sounds of a dozen domestic conversations in Thai—but aside from some curious children who poked their heads around corners to ogle the visitors and then ran away giggling, they saw few people, and no further signs of magic's spread.

A voice shouted at them in Thai from somewhere inside one of the shacks above and behind them. Ben turned around. He could feel eyes on him, but saw no one.

The harsh voice switched to English. "Why you here? What you looking for?"

"Kovit," Ben said.

"Nobody name that here," the voice barked. Ben heard a shuffling sound in one of the shacks in front of him. Another guard getting into position? "You go," the voice insisted. "Or you die."

"Tell him Ben Zolstra wants to see him."

All Ben could do was hope that Kovit would remember what Ben had done for him—and what he could still undo, if he wanted.

"Don't move," the voice said.

Squawks of static and the hiss of clipped walkie-talkie exchanges fired off in little bursts all around them.

Heaton looked warily at Ben. "Are you sure about this?"

A bored-looking young man soon appeared in front of them, cigarette dangling from his lower lip, one hand resting on the Thai army–issue MP5 slung across his shoulder. He jerked his head to the side with little enthusiasm, directing Ben and the others to follow him.

After they'd turned another few corners in the corrugated metal labyrinth, Mack elbowed Ben to get his attention. He followed her insistent gaze to the two other armed guards who had taken up position behind them. Carbon copies of the kid they were following—tight jeans, sandals, cigarettes, and submachine guns—trailed them as they walked.

Ben and the others mounted a set of creaky wooden steps and entered one of the shacks, while the guards who had led them there waited on the landing outside.

Kovit's "office" was more or less as Ben remembered it. Much better appointed than it would have seemed from the outside, the room they now entered looked more like a slick studio apartment than a desperate hovel. There was a plush couch with matching love seat, and a wall-mounted wide-screen television currently showing a muted Thai music video. At a teak table in the back corner, another trio of young men sat smoking and wordlessly swiping through their smartphones, their weapons propped against the wall.

Reclined in a corner of the couch was a Thai man in his fifties. Though he wore sweatpants and a white T-shirt, Ben knew each item was a designer brand and probably cost more than the combined monthly income of all the residents of the slum he presided over.

"Would you take your shoes off, please?" Kovit said, motioning toward the thick-pile, cream-colored carpet. "This is new."

It wasn't a request. They removed their shoes and placed them on a rack next to the door. Kovit invited them to sit.

"I didn't expect to ever see you again, Zolstra," he said. Ben knew he considered his barely accented English a point of pride. "And you've brought friends." His tone darkened. "To my place of business."

"We need your help," Ben said.

Kovit laughed. "Is that how I'm known these days at your CIA? As a helper?"

"No," Ben said. "At the CIA you're still pretty much known as an amoral piece of shit who sells weapons to the highest bidder and doesn't lose sleep over who gets killed."

Ben felt the energy in the room shift as the guards at the back table snapped to attention. Mack and Heaton looked at Ben like he'd lost his mind.

Kovit's face split the difference between a smile and a sneer. "That honesty of yours," he said, "it'll get you killed."

"But not today. Today you're going to do me a favor."

"Oh? Lucky me." Kovit crossed his legs. "What am I going to do for you?"

"You're going to have one of your planes fly us to Morocco."

"How sad that the U.S. government is so hard up for cash that they can't afford to buy their agents plane tickets anymore." Something on the TV caught Kovit's eye. "I *love* this song!" He unmuted the video, and the rubbery bass and bubblegum vocals of a Thai pop song thundered out from speakers installed in the corners of the room. Kovit began to sing along.

Ben stood up, grabbed the remote control from the glass coffee table, and flipped the TV off. The guards in the back also stood. They picked up their guns.

Mack gave Ben a questioning look: *Do I need to do something about those guys?* Ben gave her a subtle shake of his head. They didn't need to magic their way out of this one.

Ben towered over the still-seated, red-faced Kovit. "Lawan," Ben said.

All the anger in Kovit's face drained away at the mention of his daughter's name. "What about her? Has something happened to her?"

"Not yet," Ben said.

"What . . . what do you mean?"

"Tell your men to stand down."

Kovit snapped at the guards in Thai, and the men reluctantly exited the room.

"Have you forgotten what I did for you?" Ben demanded.

Kovit, seeing where this was going, regained his composure somewhat. "Of course not. It's the only reason you're still alive."

"Lawan must be a senior by now. Is that right?"

Kovit merely glared at Ben.

"Stanford," Ben continued. "A good school. It's amazing she was able to get a student visa, seeing as her father's a notorious arms dealer. Somebody must have risked a lot to help her obtain the proper documents."

"You don't think *I* risked a lot!?" Kovit exploded. "I gave you *names*! Names of men who would burn me alive if they found me! That was our fucking deal!"

Ben had to laugh. "Am I supposed to feel sorry for you because you got into bed with terrorists?"

"I don't give a fuck how you feel," Kovit spat. "We're even. I gave you my clients, you helped Lawan. It's done."

"Nothing's done." Ben leaned toward Kovit. "Our little deal? That was just between you and me. The CIA would never have approved it. If they knew your daughter was studying in their own backyard? Boy would they love to get their hands on her. The things she must know about you . . ." Ben clucked his tongue. "They might hold her just for spite."

"You motherfucker," Kovit whispered. "I should have killed you when I first met you."

"It's a shame you hesitated," Ben said. "Now let's talk about how you're going to get us to Morocco."

25

Kovit's plane was a former Thai Airways commercial jet. A far cry from the luxury of the G5, the small plane looked like what it was: an old regional carrier with nearly all the rows of seats removed to make space for additional cargo. It was barely insulated, and the pilot was a furtive Thai man who communicated solely in orders and scowls. Ben was sure Kovit had chosen this one of his many planes especially for him.

He had to admit though that the man had come through. Ben knew he would, with his daughter's fate hanging in the balance. Despite cursing the three of them and their mothers unceasingly, the arms dealer had secured passage for Ben's team on this jet out of Bangkok. They'd be stopping in a few hours in Qatar to refuel, then on to Marrakesh.

The plane did have a few things going for it. It had Wi-Fi and two internet-connected TVs mounted near the front bulkhead. Ben was on his feet trying to make them work, navigating the on-screen menus written only in Thai, a language he hadn't spoken or read in years. Mack was half-dozing on a sweater balled up against a window, her goose-bumped legs curled onto the seat next to her.

The jet also sported a cheesy, bamboo-sided wet bar that had been inexpertly fixed to the fuselage with nylon straps. Heaton was the only one using it. She poured herself a tall glass of cheap scotch and dropped into the seat next to the two Mack was taking up.

"I keep seeing Carlton's body in my mind," she said to no one in particular, taking a big sip of her drink. "What a ghastly way to go."

Ben looked back from the TVs. "Let's hope we make it to Leclerc before Merlin does. As long as other Possessors exist, especially the sect leaders, their power remains a threat to him."

"Also Merlin hates all of their guts," Mack said, shifting position on the seat. "Don't forget his manifesto. This guy wants a revolution."

"And a revolution means heads roll," Heaton said. "You're right. History has taught us that."

Mack sat up. "You know, speaking of history, Professor, you never told us how you became interested in magic in the first place. As a field of academic study it just seems so . . ."

"Disreputable?" Heaton offered cheerfully.

"I was going to say *unusual.*"

"I come by my interest honestly," Heaton began as Ben brought the TVs online. "When I was a little girl, my father used to take me to a sweets shop as a reward for sitting through interminable church services on Sunday mornings. I was allowed to pick out a single candy— any more than one might send the wrong message about the relative importance of God versus sugar, you see." She chuckled.

"Once when I was six years old, my father sent me inside alone and waited for me on a bench outside. There was another girl about my age in the shop, and as her mother dropped her coins on the counter to pay, I caught the girl whispering to herself. And then something happened that I have never been able to forget. Two candies leaped off the shelf and flew directly into the girl's pocket. I must have gasped out loud, because the girl turned to me, and so did her mother. The mother knew immediately what had happened—perhaps her daughter's kleptomaniacal tendencies were well established. The mother looked at me then, and the severity of the threat in her eyes frightened me to my very bones."

Ben, who had opened a browser window on the smart TV screen, turned back in time to see Heaton shudder at the memory of the woman's stare.

"She put a single gloved finger up to her lips." Heaton copied the motion. "*Shhh.* I knew in that moment that I had seen something I wasn't meant to see. Something that I was never to tell, not to a single soul, or the consequences would be more dire than I could even imagine. I understood this in an instant, though the mother said nothing."

"So what did you do?" Mack asked.

"I told everyone I knew, of course!" Heaton said with a burst of laughter. "No one believed me. Not my friends, not my siblings. *Certainly* not my father, who did not spare me the rod for telling such a frivolous lie. But I was convinced that what I'd seen really happened, and I wouldn't rest until I learned as much as I could about it."

"But in all these years you've studied, you never had any doubt?" Mack asked. "You never questioned your six-year-old memory of those events and wondered if you were spending your whole life chasing something that wasn't real?"

"My dear," Heaton said with a sad smile, "I doubted all the time. I'd be lying if I said that seeing my work proving itself to be true wasn't intensely validating."

"Your work is proving true, all right," Ben said, using the remote to navigate to CNN's website. "Take a look."

Mack's breath caught in her throat as the home screen loaded up. "It's worse than we thought," she said.

The banner headline set the tone in red block letters:

MAGIC GOES VIRAL. THE WORLD REELS.

For the next half hour, as the others followed along on the bulk-head-mounted screens, Ben clicked on links, scanned articles, played videos—getting a visceral sense of how much the world had already changed.

It seemed a few of the more popular YouTubers had gotten wind of the protocols and were the first to put them on most people's radar. "How to levitate your stuff (or someone else's!!)!" and "How to become invisible (REALLY!!!)" had spread faster than any other videos in the site's history. They were poorly edited webcam vlogs, but they still showed the teen web stars reciting the protocols, subtitled with helpful transliterations, and performing clumsy acts of rudimentary magic.

Ben kept clicking. One story revealed that a massive heist at the Prado museum, led by a team of invisible burglars, had taken the institution for over three-hundred-million dollars' worth of artwork. In its wake, many major museums, among them Paris's Louvre and New York's Met, had decided to close their doors to the public indefinitely, and substantially beef up security.

Another video reported that the Chinese government, fearing popular uprising, had officially banned all public gatherings of more than ten people, "to ensure the safety of our citizens in the wake of recently revealed threats." They had also begun conducting arrests of suspected "unnatural dissidents" on a massive scale.

More clicks, more outrages. A man had invisibly entered a house party in San Diego and shot over thirty college students with his two equally invisible assault rifles. An unknown person or persons had used the levitation protocol to derail a Chicago El train in the heart of the downtown Loop. The images showed the fallen train car completely vertical, its front end smashed into the sidewalk while its back end was still barely coupled to the car on the tracks above it. Three riders and two pedestrians were killed.

There was more, pages and pages full of it, and all from the last twenty-four hours.

Ben let out a long sigh and sat back in his chair. Heaton rubbed at her face. Mack hugged her arms across her chest. For a while, no one spoke.

"Okay, everything on the table," Ben said to his team. "What do we know right now? I'll start with the obvious: magic is fully out in the world."

"The next protocol could drop any minute," Mack added. "I mean, there's no reason to think it stops with levitation and invisibility, is there, Professor?"

"No," Heaton acknowledged.

"What else?" Ben asked.

"Merlin is hunting down Possessors," said Mack. "Which makes it harder and more dangerous for us to get the binding spell."

"True," Ben said. "Also, Harris is still only a step behind us."

A patch of turbulence shook the plane. Heaton took a nervous sip of her drink.

"What about Leclerc?" Ben asked. "What do we know?"

"I'm afraid I don't know anything more about that family than what I've told you," Heaton said.

"Okay, let's see what we can find."

Ben started searching online. Any details they gleaned would help reduce the giant unknowns they were walking into.

It turned out to be easy to find public information about Constantine Leclerc. Pictures of the dapper, dark-haired man had graced a number of European society pages over the years. Leclerc was the forty-something chairman of a decades-old family foundation that claimed to provide educational opportunities for young people of limited means in North Africa. His actual role, in practice, seemed mostly to involve attending elaborate social functions both in Africa and on the Continent. He was single, no children, both parents dead. The man was one of Ben's least-respected types: a playboy bachelor living large off the family fortune.

"Okay," Ben said, thinking ahead to their next move. "It's pretty clear we don't know what the situation is going to be on the ground in Morocco. We'll have to be ready for anything. Even the airport could be in chaos. So everybody be ready to run, or to shoot, or"—he nodded toward Mack—"to do your thing."

Mack smiled. A glint in her eye told him that she was thirsty for some trouble.

The pilot yelled back to them from the open cockpit. He'd apparently been listening in. "Airport no problem," he said. "We have a guy."

Of course you do, Ben thought. Kovit's operations reached their tentacles into many countries. Dirty money spoke every language.

Ben thought the pilot's first words all flight would also be his last, but then the man added, "This magic, very bad for business."

"What do you mean?" Ben shouted back.

"Now, no one gonna need guns anymore. Just point a finger. *Bang*. You dead. *Bang*. You dead, too." The man cracked himself up with laughter.

Ben didn't find the situation nearly so amusing.

26

Fuck Abkhazia. Fuck every square fucking inch of this Devil's anus.

Demyan pulled down the last drag of his shitty Georgian cigarette and crushed the butt under his heel. Three more months. That was all he had to wait until his deployment was over. Then he would return to Moscow, where he could eat blini and pelmeni until his stomach burst, smoke cigarettes that didn't taste like they'd been rolled in dung, and fuck Svetlana until his dick fell off.

He adjusted the rifle on his shoulder and spat onto the ground. He continued making his rounds on the inner perimeter of the base's barbed wire fence. At least it was a cool, clear night. Two days ago he'd patrolled in a summer storm that came down so hard he couldn't even light up a smoke.

The worst part was it occurred the same night they'd brought in the shipment from Siberia. His superiors were being even more up-tight assholes than usual the whole time, even as everyone stood there soaked to the balls. Whatever had been in those crates that they'd unloaded, the officers certainly seemed to think it was a Big Fucking Deal.

The rumor going around the base was that the crates were filled with radioactive junk they'd salvaged from some warheads deactivated in the days of the Glorious Soviet Empire. Demyan was sure it would all be gone just as suddenly as it arrived, sold off to some semifriendly Ukrainian militia to line the pockets of the officers. It wasn't as though this ass-freezing mountain outpost was some sort of well-defended military depot.

As he neared the rear of the base, Demyan saw three dark figures approach the fence from the opposite side. *Great,* he thought, *another useless preparedness drill.*

Then he heard the snipping of the metal links of the fence as they were cut through. The higher-ups were way too cheap to destroy army property for a drill.

Shit. Demyan quickly ducked around the concrete blocks of the nearest barracks. He didn't think he'd been seen. Maybe it wasn't too late to walk away, pretend he hadn't seen them either?

Demyan peeked his head around the corner. The three men had finished their cutting and were moving inside the perimeter. They were headed straight for the warehouse that held the Siberian crates. One of the trespassers towered over the others—he was well over two meters tall, and built like a horse.

Demyan's mind started screaming at him—as usual, in the voice of his mother. *You're guarding this place, aren't you, you worthless coward? Get out there and shoot the bastards.*

Right. Demyan gave a pig's fart about protecting Mother Russia's precious mystery crates, but he wasn't about to let the senior officers haul him in front of a tribunal for dereliction of duty.

He stepped out from behind the barracks and crept along the wall, following the intruders, trying to get close enough to shoot without missing. He'd always been a lousy shot.

The men were nearly to the roll-up metal door of the warehouse when Vitaly, another of the guards on Demyan's patrol shift, stumbled into view maybe twelve meters from the criminal trio. The joker had been hitting the vodka—and not sharing—that much was obvious from the sway in his steps. Vitaly and the gate-crashers noticed each other at the same instant. Instead of raising his rifle, the drunk son of a bitch raised his hands.

But it wasn't a surrender. Vitaly shouted something. Something strange. It had to be those magic words everyone was trying out—and they worked! Vitaly's words knocked one of the intruders clean off his feet and sent him sprawling and tumbling onto the grass. Crouched in the shadows, Demyan felt himself smiling.

Then one of the trespassers, the giant, lifted his own arms. In a split-second movement, before Demyan could aim his gun, the man growled out the same words and sent Vitaly catapulting through the air. The small guard's body hit the concrete wall of the warehouse with such a sickening crack that Demyan didn't have to see Vitaly's broken neck to know he'd been killed instantly.

The scream tore from Demyan's throat without his permission. Not a battle cry, but a yelp of fear. Loud enough to get him noticed.

The man who had murdered Vitaly spotted Demyan huddled in the shadow of the barracks, and stomped across the grass in his direction.

Demyan's shaking hands fumbled with his rifle. The barrel stuck on his belt as he tried to raise it and *oh, shit it was too dark to see and where was the motherfucking trigger and why were his fingers fat clumsy sausages and—*

There it was. Demyan's finger found the trigger. But the man was only a few meters away now, and with another swipe of his hand through the air Demyan's gun was out of his hands, flying, gone.

Then the murderer was on top of him. Demyan wanted to scream again, but the man was enormous, heavy like a truck, and squeezing the air from his body. They were face-to-face, the giant on top of him.

The man's beard was a black forest, the mole on the side of his nose was a boulder on a mountain.

Demyan didn't see the knife—but the last thing he heard was the soft *pop* of his own windpipe being penetrated with the single plunge of a blade.

27

The plane touched down on the tarmac, but instead of taking them up to a gate, the pilot taxied Ben and his team to an area far from the main terminal, stopping near a handful of administrative trailers lined up against a high fence.

"We're here," the pilot said, powering down the engines.

He unbuckled himself and opened the cabin door, lowering the stairs and letting the hot, dry air of Marrakesh waft into the small plane. The pilot didn't wait for his passengers before exiting. Ben, Mack, and Heaton gathered their bags and followed him.

A suited, mustachioed official emerged from one of the trailers and approached the pilot, greeting Kovit's man with a bear hug followed by a long, friendly exchange that Ben wished hadn't been out of earshot. The pilot then handed the man a thick envelope, which immediately disappeared into a pocket inside the man's coat.

Business concluded, the official now took notice of Ben and the others. "Ah! You brought friends!" he said, his paunch jiggling a little with the exclamation. "Welcome to Marrakesh!"

Any friends of Kovit's, the official quickly assured them with a wide smile, surely didn't need to bother with the hassle of passport control, customs, or other such headaches. He hurried them through a gate in the fence and up to a waiting car. Kovit's pilot had already returned to the jet and closed the cabin door.

Ben was somewhat surprised when the VIP treatment didn't extend to the car. It was the same model of dusky-yellow Dacia that made up much of the city's taxi fleet.

"No unnecessary attention this way," the official whispered to Ben with a wink while simultaneously slipping a sizable handful of bills into the driver's palm.

"Now," he added, "I don't know where you're going, and I don't want to." He held up his hands to his ears to drive home the point. "But just so you are aware, I might suggest you stay *out* of the center of town if possible, eh?" The man's mustache twitched. "Recent developments have made it . . . unsafe."

"Recent developments?" Mack said.

"I'm afraid to say our lovely city has not escaped the curse of this new magic," he said to Mack apologetically. "The people are worked up, the thieves have grown quite brazen, and at night especially a woman like yourself, walking alone—"

"You don't know anything about a woman like myself."

Mack slid into the rear seat of the taxi without another word. Ben and Heaton followed.

They rode off under the blazing Moroccan sun. Finally back on the ground, they were now only an hour from Leclerc's residence in the mountainous outskirts of the ancient city.

The air-conditioning in the old car didn't work, but that didn't matter. All the windows were down, and Ben breathed in deeply, catching the acrid tang of engine oil and the dry dust of the desert, familiar smells from his years in the region.

"You're sure about this address?" Ben confirmed with Heaton, shouting to be heard over the open windows.

"Lucas did all the legwork," Heaton said, nodding, "and he's spent so much time organizing my books and files that he knows them almost as well as I do at this point."

Heaton had called her research assistant before they'd left Thailand and told him to dig up everything she'd ever looked into related to the Leclercs. By the time they hit Qatar, Lucas had come through with an address.

Heaton continued with growing pride in her voice. "He even tracked down old maps and colonial records of transfer and titles, and cross-referenced them with the current maps of the city. Though I daresay it doesn't look like things have changed much around here in a hundred years."

Lucas had also taken Ben up on his offer to investigate the Possessor who tried to run them down in Scotland. According to him, the car was unregistered and untraceable, and the body that the authorities pulled from the wreck was so badly burned that it couldn't be identified; the dental records had either not come in yet or were not being made publicly available. Lucas suspected a Possessor cover-up, which Heaton concurred was likely. It appeared to be another dead end.

As they passed through a stone arch to enter the medina—the ancient, walled part of the city—the streets narrowed. Some looked hardly wider than sidewalks back in the States, their rose-colored, clay-daubed walls almost entirely in shadow despite the midday sun overhead.

People swirled around their car—women in colorful wraps, men in flowing kaftans. Shops beckoned to them, overflowing with bright fabrics, clay dishes, metal lamps wrought in ornate shapes. A donkey squeezed by their cab, pulling a long cart in the opposite direction. Riding high on the cart, a tired old man whipped passionlessly at the fly-swarmed beast. At least in this district of Marrakesh, it seemed to be business as usual.

Then they passed the Djemaa el-Fna, a huge public square, and caught sight of the crowd.

Or, more accurately, *crowds*. There were three massive groups, many hundreds strong, each surrounding a different speaker on an elevated platform.

"More demonstrations?" Heaton asked.

"Looks like it."

One contingent appeared to be government loyalists. They waved the flag and held up pictures of the Moroccan king. Their speaker, Ben gathered from his proficient Arabic, urged people to stick with their leader through "this unprecedented and challenging time." Another, visibly angrier group must have been the opposition party. Their red banners demanded an end to the monarchy and the establishment of a socialist government. WITH MAGIC ON OUR SIDE, one banner read in French, WE WILL FINALLY WIN THE CLASS WAR.

The third congregation, angrier still, surrounded an imam who was denouncing the rise of the "ungodly dark arts," raving that the end was nigh and the only thing to do was immediately appoint a devout, religious government that would court God's favor instead of His wrath.

The borders between the various groups undulated—the people surging toward one another, shouting, threatening, then pulling back. Violence was brewing.

"This looks like it could get ugly," Mack said.

"Let's not be around when it does," Ben responded.

They drove on, up into the dusty hills outside the city. About thirty-five minutes after they'd left the medina walls behind, the taxi came to an abrupt stop.

The driver craned his neck to turn around and face his passengers. He pointed off to the right side of the car, the jabs of his finger punctuating a long blast of gruff Arabic.

"What's he saying?" Mack asked Ben.

"This is as far as he goes," Ben said. His eyes followed the direction in which the driver was pointing. "He says the place we're looking for is up this dirt trail on the other side of the ridge, but he doesn't want to go any closer because the compound is surrounded by armed guards who are none too friendly. He dropped a few men off there early this morning, and they insisted on searching his whole vehicle."

"He dropped people off there this morning?" Heaton said with concern. "Could one of them have been Merlin?"

Ben asked the man a few questions, his Arabic returning easily though it had been nearly two years since it had last passed his lips. The driver's answers were chilly at first but warmed as Ben continued to press bills into the man's hand.

Ben turned to Heaton and Mack. "He says it was three big guys, built like soldiers. He took them right from the airport, like us. He picked up one of their bags to put it in the trunk and could barely lift it. That was before they yelled at him and told him not to touch anything else. It doesn't sound like Merlin to me. It sounds like Leclerc got himself reinforcements."

Ben asked the driver a few more questions, then they stepped out of the taxi, which sped away in a cloud of dust. He shouldered their bags and they started up the rocky trail.

"Did he say how many guards there were?" Mack asked.

"Two guys stopped him and searched the car, and he saw another one or two on the roof. He wasn't sure."

"So there are potentially seven guys or more up there, plus a powerful Possessor?" Mack said. "How the fuck are we going to do this?"

"The way I see it, we've got two major things working in our favor."

"And they are?"

Ben pointed to himself, then he pointed to Mack.

Mack rolled her eyes. "Oh, Jesus."

They scrambled up the trail. After twenty minutes, they neared the ridge. The roof of a large square structure came into view. Ben immediately crouched down and signaled the others to do the same. He stashed their bags as well as he could under a scrubby bush nearby. Then he dropped to the ground and crawled forward to get a decent look at the place. Mack wriggled up next to him.

The building was a four-story mansion constructed in the *riad* style. The outside was a practically windowless fortress, but Ben knew each floor inside was built around a large central courtyard that was open to the sky. It was a brilliantly simple design. With only a few guards on the roof, a *riad* was fairly easy to defend. Ben counted three of them on this roof. Another two stood inside a small, open foyer fronted by a keyhole-shaped arch cut into the stone. Behind them a set of imposing wooden doors comprised the main entrance. If there were any more guards, they had to be inside.

"This guy *must* be a sect leader," Mack whispered excitedly. "Why else would he need so much security?"

"He's definitely got something worth protecting," Ben agreed.

They crept back out of sight behind the ridge.

"So what's the plan?" Heaton asked.

"You stay here until we give you the all clear, Professor," Ben said.

"I beg your pardon," she answered indignantly, "but I'm not dead yet!"

"Not a debate," Ben said simply. He reached into his bag and took out his pistol, then tucked the gun into his waistband. He turned to Mack. "Can you make us invisible? Best if we can avoid the guards altogether."

Mack nodded and whispered the incantation that caused both her and Ben to vanish from view.

"Heavens!" Heaton exclaimed, shaking her head. "I don't think I'll ever get used to that."

"Stay close," Ben said softly to Mack. He put a guiding hand on her back as they stood and walked over the ridge in the direction of the front entrance.

They had gone no more than twenty feet when the cover of invisibility fell away, leaving them exposed. They froze.

"What happened?" Ben hissed.

"I don't know!"

The guards spotted them easily in the deserted landscape. Their heads snapped toward Ben and Mack.

"Put us back under."

Mack frantically repeated the protocol.

"I . . . I can't." She took a step backward, winked out of sight, then stepped forward into visibility once again. "I think we crossed a threshold that had a revealing spell woven into it."

Ben saw the guards tense up, saw their guns raise and take aim. "All right," he said, "new plan. Follow my lead."

They started moving briskly toward the *riad*.

"*Hey!*" Ben shouted at the guards. He waved both empty hands in the air. "We don't want any trouble! *Nous ne voulons pas de problèmes!* We're here to talk to your boss, just talk!"

The guards on the roof gesticulated in apparent disagreement about their course of action, while the two posted in the open foyer kept their guns leveled at Ben with a steely calm.

Ben continued moving toward the doors. "We're only here to talk!" Ben repeated. "Leclerc is expecting us!"

They were maybe fifty feet from the front of the house. The bluster appeared to be working.

Then one of the rooftop guards tilted his head slightly, squinting down his sights.

The pistol was in Ben's hands before he realized he'd reached for it. He and the guard fired at the same time, Ben diving to the side as he did. He squeezed the trigger twice before hitting the ground, dropping two of the roof guards, while the round that had been aimed at Ben dug into the earth. The remaining man on the roof retreated out of sight.

The door guards ducked behind the stone arch, spraying cover fire as they ran.

Bullets bit into the red dirt around Ben and Mack. Ben scanned the area for cover of his own. They were in the middle of a scrubby open expanse. A small pile of rocks on the opposite side of the clearing was too low to be of much help, and they'd be gunned down long before they could make it back to the ridge.

"You okay?" Ben asked.

Mack's eyes were wide with fear, and her pulse visibly throbbed in her neck—but she nodded. "I'm good."

Ben pulled them both down to a crouch. He braced his gun on a knee, aiming halfway between the roof and the entrance, ready to open fire on whatever moved next. It was a shit position: the split second it would take him to raise or lower the barrel could get him killed.

Mack sensed it. "I'll watch the roof," she said.

"Are you sure you can—?"

One of the guards in the foyer leaned into view from around the arch, sighting down the barrel of his rifle. Ben popped off two shots that hit the man square in the chest and put him down. Ben kept his gun fixed on the arch, but the second door guard wisely kept himself hidden.

"We need to get in closer," he said. "We're sitting ducks from above."

He took Mack's arm and they rushed toward the entrance, clearing half the distance before the remaining guard from the roof reappeared. Ben aimed in the man's direction as they ran, but before he could pull the trigger his vision began to swim. A wave of vertigo overtook him, and he stumbled and dropped to one knee. He held his head in his hands, but the faintness and nausea continued. What was happening?

Out of the corner of his eye he saw Mack wave her hand toward the roof. She plucked the guard from the rooftop and let him drop the nearly fifty feet to the ground. He screamed and flailed as he fell, and landed with a thud a dozen feet from them, his limbs at an un-natural angle.

Mack put a hand on Ben's shoulder. "I feel it, too," she said. "Some kind of disorientation spell or something. It must not be hitting me as hard as you."

The second door guard reappeared. He had lowered himself to the ground. He log-rolled out from behind the arch and stopped, prone on his stomach, rifle extended in front of him. Ben raised his gun, but his vision lurched as he fired and his shots went wildly astray.

He saw the flash of the man's rifle barrel and heard the shots. They were dead.

Except . . . there was no pain, no shattering impact of bullets rend-ing into flesh and splintering bones. Ben looked at Mack, who had her eyes closed and her hands outstretched toward the guard.

"Come on, *shoot* him!" Mack yelled.

He lined up his shot, squinting hard, and managed to put two rounds into the befuddled guard as he attempted to roll back to safety.

"What did you do?" Ben asked. "How did you stop the bullets?"

"I didn't, I just sorta . . . deflected them. It was like instinct. I don't think I could do it again if I tried."

"That was . . ." Ben's words failed him.

He and Mack scrambled through the keyhole arch and into the foyer, both breathless. The disorientation, whatever it had been, was fading.

A volley of shots came in quick succession from somewhere in front of the house. Mack screamed as Ben grabbed her and threw both of them to the ground. Round after round of automatic fire struck the solid wooden doors above them, covering them in a shower of splinters. Just as suddenly as it had begun, the fusillade ended with the telltale clicking of an empty ammo magazine. Ben scanned the area but saw no sign of any more guards or mounted weaponry. It had to be one more fucking magic trick.

He scrambled to his feet, and helped Mack up.

Just then Heaton came running toward them across the wide expanse of scrubland that separated the mansion from the ridgeline. She made it through the arch and into the foyer, then doubled over, panting for breath.

Ben was livid. "What the hell are you doing here?" he demanded. "We're not in the clear yet, there must be more guards inside!"

"I'm not waiting outside while you two meet a living Possessor," Heaton huffed. "Oh!" She seemed to suddenly notice that they were standing among the bodies of the two slain door guards. "Terrible, just terrible."

Ben tried to avoid looking at the young guards as they approached the double doors. He didn't need one more face that could appear out of the darkness on a sleepless night.

"Hey," Mack said, "look."

The knockers set into the center of each door were identical to the one they'd seen at Braithwaite's island hideaway—the same thin, right-pointing triangle, with four straight bars running vertically through it. *It means to fetter, or to shackle.* Now the fate of the whole world was riding on whether someone inside could be convinced—or forced—to help them put the shackles back on magic.

Ben looked at Mack, who nodded, ready. He reached through a jagged hole that the bullets had ripped in the wood and drew back the bolt. He pushed at one of the heavy doors, and it swung slowly inward. He kept his gun out—if the taxi driver was right they still had more guards to contend with, not to mention the powerful Possessor himself.

28

The long, dark hallway that led away from the door opened into a spacious, sun-drenched courtyard. Mosaic tiles of blue, yellow, green, and red formed complex, interlocking patterns on the walls and floor. In the center stood a shallow pool in the shape of an eight-pointed star, with a bubbling fountain on an ornate pillar sticking up from it.

If there were other guards, they were staying hidden.

There was a sound of footsteps approaching from the other side of the courtyard. Ben whipped around to find his pistol pointed at a tall, raven-haired man in a violet silk shirt. Even now, the perfectly coiffed Leclerc looked like he was ready for a magazine photo shoot.

"Are you here to try to kill me?" Leclerc asked. "Are you the one who calls himself Merlin?" He inspected Ben for a moment, then concluded, "No, you are not him. I would already be dead. So who are you and what is the meaning of this intrusion? You have thirty seconds to explain yourselves before I order my guards to fire."

The guards were still out of sight, maybe even invisible . . . unless Leclerc was bluffing and all his sentries had already been dispatched.

"We have a common enemy," Ben said by way of introduction. "Merlin is the reason we're here. We can help each other."

"That's funny. It seems to me you killed five of my men."

"It was self-defense—not that you cared about them," Ben said. "Tell us what you know about Merlin."

"I know he is a madman." Leclerc's eyes blazed. "I know he hates us all."

"All Possessors, you mean?" Mack said. "But he is one himself, isn't he?"

Leclerc flinched, evidently taken aback by the fact that this woman knew about his ancient secret, but he quickly regained his composure and nodded. "He is our Judas, yes."

"Is that supposed to make you Christ?" Ben said. "Please, we know who you are, who your family is. Traitors to your country."

"My *country*?" Leclerc scoffed at the word. "There was no such thing as France when we started this. There was no Europe, there was not even Rome or Greece. We have never betrayed our first loyalty."

"Your first loyalty . . . to the original families," Heaton ventured.

"Well, aren't you people clever?" Leclerc said, looking around at his uninvited guests with evident amusement. "Knowing so much about me, when I have not the slightest clue who any of you are. Your time is up by the way, so unless there's anything else . . ."

"There is," Ben said. He fired a single shot, intended to wound the Possessor in the leg, but it passed right through as though his body were no more substantial than smoke. Was the figure some sort of projection?

Leclerc—his image—smiled broadly, then barked a command in French. Four armed men appeared. Two emerged from rooms on either side of the courtyard, two on the landing one floor above them. They took aim at the intruders.

"*Wait!*" Mack shouted. "If you shoot us you'll never stop Merlin! He'll kill you just like he killed Carlton Braithwaite!"

Leclerc raised a hand and the guards held their fire. "You know about Carlton?"

"He was my friend," Heaton said.

"We were the ones who found his body," Ben added. "Like you said, Merlin's a madman."

"What makes you think I would need you to stop him?"

"He's already shown how powerful he is by getting to Braithwaite," Ben said. "And the extra guards you brought up here this morning tell me that you know it. He scares you."

Leclerc wore a smug look. "Do I look scared?"

Next to Ben, Mack quickly recited an incantation, then another in rapid succession. The projection of Leclerc, which was like a hologram of outstanding quality, dimmed, and the man's face wrinkled in consternation. The guards looked at one another in bafflement.

"What are you—?" Leclerc began, then his figure went rigid and the projection disappeared.

"I'm holding him," Mack said to Ben through gritted teeth. "I did the revealing spell and sensed him in the room on the right. He's trying to fight, but I caught him by surprise and—" Mack cried out and took a step backward. "Hurry!"

Ben needed no more prompting. In a flash of movement he lunged forward and smashed his gun into the face of the guard nearest to him. The guard dropped his weapon and his hands flew to his broken nose. Ben slid behind him, grabbing the man and pinning him tightly against his chest with one arm, using the other to press his gun against the guard's temple.

"I'm going to let all of you walk out of here alive if you don't do anything stupid," Ben shouted to the other sentries. "Now move into the middle of the courtyard and drop your weapons to the ground." When they hesitated, Ben added, "It's too late for the others, but you have a choice. Whatever he's paying you, it's not worth dying for this rich asshole."

When the guards grudgingly did as Ben asked, he knew he'd correctly deduced that they were mercenaries with no particular loyalty to their patron. They set their rifles onto the tile floor and stood warily in the center of the courtyard, squinting in the sun. Ben released the guard he held and shoved him toward the others.

Next to Ben, Mack groaned. "Hurry, he's fighting."

"Take off your boots and your shirts," Ben ordered the guards, knowing that the less equipped they were for the rugged desert landscape outside, the less likely they would be to try any heroics. When the men complied, Ben said, "Now get the fuck out of here and don't come back. And you better forget you ever saw us."

When the last guard had trudged down the hallway, and Heaton had bolted the heavy wooden doors behind them, Ben raced toward the room Mack had indicated. A sheer white curtain was pulled across the open doorway, fluttering in the breeze. He parted it and entered a large room dominated by a U-shaped sofa that ran almost the entire length of three walls. It was low, strewn with dozens of pillows and cushions in deep reds and purples. Metal lamps dangled from the ceiling, casting circles of dim, orange light around the room.

In the middle of the room stood Leclerc, stock still as though paralyzed. Ben tore the curtain from the doorway and ripped it into strips that he used to bind the Possessor's hands and feet. Then he pushed Leclerc down onto the sofa, and stood across from him, his gun pointed at the Possessor's chest.

Mack and Heaton came into the room.

"Okay," Ben said to Mack, "let him talk."

Mack relaxed visibly, and Leclerc began to buck against his restraints. Ben cocked his pistol and the Possessor went still.

Leclerc's eyes burned into Ben. "What do you want?"

"Everything you know about magic," Heaton said.

"And how to stop it," Ben added.

"Oh, is that all?"

"One more thing," Ben said. "Any hint that you're using magic and I shoot, understood?"

"Yes, yes, I see your gun," Leclerc said with a sneer. "You Americans do love those things. But you should know that your pretty friend here"—he winked at Mack—"is far more formidable than your little pistol."

Mack shuffled her feet, seeming not to know if she should be offended or proud.

"It was amusing to see you when my vertigo spell went to work," Leclerc continued. "I was projecting, watching you from above. It was so easy to undo all your . . . machismo."

"Projection," Heaton said in wonder. "It's just incredible."

"We may be here a while," Ben said to her. "Why don't you have a seat, Professor?"

Heaton and Mack moved to the sofa, stepping across an elaborate pattern set in pearlescent stone in the center of the floor. It was a spiral of marble slabs reminiscent of the inside of a chambered nautilus.

Heaton and Mack sat on the end of the long sofa. Ben remained standing.

"I'm not interested in anything but answers right now," Ben said. "The binding spell. Give it to us, or give us someone who can."

"I'm afraid I don't know what you're talking about."

"Bullshit."

Leclerc shrugged.

"It's a spell," Heaton tried, "for ending magic. You might have heard of 'the finishing words,' or 'the words-never-to-be-said'?"

A long pause. "I've heard of it. Assuming it exists, why would you want this . . . binding spell, as you call it?"

"*Why?*" Ben repeated. "So we can *use* it. People are dying. Societies are coming apart. Outside the walls of your safe little compound here, governments are losing control and we're beginning to see what real anarchy looks like. Does any of that matter to you?"

"You're quite concerned with things being under control." Leclerc scrutinized Ben's face. "You're a government agent, aren't you?"

When Ben didn't answer, he went on, "Have you ever asked yourself why our ancestors would have even created a binding spell in the first place? It exists for the same reason the nuclear bomb exists. To maintain the balance of power, the very law and order you love so much."

"Of course," Heaton said, understanding dawning on her face. "To ensure parity among the leaders of the different Possessor sects."

"Exactly," Leclerc said, again seeming surprised at how much they already knew about Possessors. "We live fairly comfortably within our own spheres. But for some people, that may not be enough. If my counterparts in New York or Tokyo, for example—"

"I doubt any sect leader would stay in New York City now," Ben cut in. "Some maniac is bound to blow it up soon."

Leclerc smiled. "He'll know when the time comes to leave, I'm sure. To my point, if a sect leader wanted more power, if he started to get too dominant or aggressive, the other leaders have always been able to rein in such excesses by threatening to use the binding spell and end the game for everyone."

"Mutually assured destruction," Heaton said.

"Quite."

Ben was growing restless. They were wasting time. As he was about to lay into Leclerc again, Mack jumped in with her own line of questioning.

"What other spells are there?" she asked, unable to keep the excitement from her face. "I knew about levitation and invisibility from Merlin. Then I learned a revealing spell. And now I see the projection and vertigo that you've used today. Are there a lot more?"

"My girl," Leclerc began, trying to lean closer to her. Because of his bindings, he succeeded only in listing sideways on the sofa. "We can do more than you could ever imagine. Of course, the majority of our abilities can only be performed by the best and strongest among us— and even then their use is extremely limited. The risk of being discovered using most spells often outweighs their benefit. Our secrecy has always been paramount. Until now, that is."

"Which brings us back to the binding spell," Ben said. "Give it to us."

For the first time, Leclerc appeared to consider it. With some wriggling, he set himself back upright. "And if I do?" he asked. "What do I get? I betray centuries, millennia, of sacred trust. I even lose my own power. What do I receive in return?"

"You'd be a hero," Ben said, hoping to play to Leclerc's substantial ego. "You'd be the man who kept the world from tearing itself apart."

A gleam in the Possessor's eye told Ben that his vanity liked that idea very much. "What else?"

"Aside from the fact that it would save your ass because ending magic would eliminate the reason for Merlin to hunt you down and kill you? What do you mean, *money*?" Ben laughed. He spread his arms wide to encompass the opulent space. "I'm sure you don't need more of that."

Leclerc raised his eyebrows. "As it happens, I've recently experienced a . . . setback in that department."

"The U.S. government will give you whatever you want. That's easy."

The clandestine services were awash in black money that could be tapped for informant payoffs and the like. It was the cost of doing dark business.

"Very well, I will do what you ask." Before Ben could even mentally celebrate, Leclerc added, "*but* this spell is far too long and complicated to simply memorize. I don't know it, but I know where to find it. You'll need to untie me."

"If you try anything—"

Leclerc rolled his eyes. "You'll shoot me and your pretty associate will tear me limb from limb. Understood."

Ben released Leclerc from his restraints. The Possessor, rubbing his chafed wrists, walked over to a small table. He slid open a thin drawer hidden in the table's side, then reached inside. There was a clicking sound, like a flipped switch.

A series of noises answered from somewhere beneath them—the cough of a motor coming to life, the clank of metal on metal, the whine of a machine exerting itself. Ben felt rumbling through his boots.

Mack spoke for all of them: "What the hell's going on?"

The nautilus pattern in the center of the floor was dropping, marble slab by marble slab, leaving a large, circular hole in the middle of the room. Each stone sank just a little farther down than the one that came before it.

A spiral staircase was descending before their eyes.

In another ten seconds, the operation was finished, and the racket the contraption had made was replaced by a stunned silence.

Mack let out a burst of laughter. "That. Is. *Awesome.*"

Ben peered over the edge but couldn't make out wherever the stairs led to. "The binding spell is down there?"

"It is." Leclerc nodded toward the stairwell, which quickly disappeared into inky darkness. "Shall we?"

Ben motioned with his gun. "You first."

29

Ben followed Leclerc, with Mack assisting Heaton down the steep steps that fanned out from a central column. As they descended and passed below the floor, the darkness became nearly all-encompassing. Just as Ben was about to shout to Leclerc about the lights, they clicked on automatically. From his elevated vantage point, still ten or so stairs from the bottom, Ben surveyed the space.

This was no trap, that much was immediately clear. This was . . . the mother lode. A vast subterranean library stretched out before them, with jam-packed shelves stacked from the floor to the surprisingly high ceiling. But it wasn't just books. Everywhere there were tables, ledges, and counters—some freestanding, others built into the walls. Displayed on their surfaces were all kinds of quasi-scientific-looking instruments. Most of them Ben guessed were medieval or Renaissance-era, with lots of burnished wood, bronze, glass, and copper tubing. Some seemed to be surprisingly modern, elaborate plastic contraptions bristling with wires and cables.

On the far side of the room, away from the stairs, stood a round wooden table at least fifteen feet in diameter. A heap of vintage maps and crumbling charts, laid flat and weighted down with heavy hunks of rounded glass, covered the table's surface. Ben didn't know what anything in this chamber meant or did, but he was sure Heaton would.

Sure enough, he soon heard the pure joy in her voice as she reached the bottom and cried out, "This is incredible!"

Heaton didn't wait for permission to begin exploring. Her face beamed as she took in the space, running her fingers along the spines of books, examining the instruments. She murmured to herself excitedly.

"My God," she exclaimed, "this is like the Library of Alexandria for magic!"

Ben had to smile. This, here and now, was the pinnacle of the old professor's life. After decades of study, she'd finally arrived at the culmination of all her research.

"So where is it?" Ben asked Leclerc, who was hugging his arms to his chest in the cold underground chamber.

"How should I know?" Leclerc retorted. "This was my father's library. I never come down here."

"You lying bastard."

"What you seek is here," Leclerc insisted. "My father told me it was here, but no more than that. How could I ever think I'd have need of it?"

"You sit," Ben said, pushing the Possessor into a dusty wood-and-leather chair. "Move and you die." He turned to Heaton. "Okay, Professor, this is your area. Where do we start?"

Heaton started giving orders to them like a general on the march—which books to pull down, which charts and maps to seek out, which scraps of decaying paper in which rusting file cabinets to bother with.

It was going to be slow work. There were miles of books in the place—and enough journals, obscure graphs, cryptic illustrations, and bizarre instruments to keep a team of scholars busy for years.

Ben kept one eye on Leclerc the whole time, but the Possessor simply stared back at him with discomfiting amusement.

"Remember," Heaton said, "anything as important as the binding spell is probably not going to be clearly marked, bolded, and underlined. 'Here it is,' " she said mockingly, " 'the spell to end all magic. Do be careful with it.' "

"What are you saying?" Mack asked, turning to her. "It'll be written in some kind of code?"

Heaton shrugged noncommittally. "A riddle or puzzle, perhaps. Possibly scrawled in a margin somewhere. Or concealed in an image. We really have no idea!"

She seemed completely at ease with that, like she could spend the rest of her life in this room. Unfortunately they didn't have that kind of time. They needed the goddamn spell.

While climbing a wooden step stool in an attempt to free a heavy tome from a high shelf, Heaton stumbled backward. Ben rushed over to steady her, only to be overtaken by another strong surge of disorientation. He managed to stop Heaton from falling, but then they both careened into one of the unusual instruments and sent it crashing to the floor. Ben looked for Leclerc through his blurred vision. The Possessor had vanished.

"Fuck!" Ben shouted. "He's gone!"

"What? How?" Mack said.

"I don't know. But we should get out of here."

Just then, Leclerc's voice boomed from the top of the stairs, though the man himself was still invisible. "I would never have given you what you asked," he said, "not for all your American dollars. The Leclercs remain loyal. I cannot let you end magic. Too many men have died to keep these secrets—which you will now take with you to your graves."

Leclerc momentarily reappeared at the top of the stairs, his hands raised above his head. He clapped them together, and a halo of blinding white flame appeared, encircling his palms.

"*Fire* magic?" Heaton gasped.

Ben wasted no time in firing his gun at Leclerc—three shots that in his dizziness he could only hope hit home—at the same time that the Possessor sent a bolt of crackling fire down into the subterranean chamber. The flames swept around the ancient library like a jet of scorching wind. Within seconds, the shelves that lined the walls were alight.

"*Oh, God!*" Heaton shrieked. "*We're going to lose everything!*"

Ben could see Leclerc crawling on all fours up the final steps and out of sight. So the Possessor had been hit—but how seriously?

Then once again came the chugging noise of a motor and the clanking of chains. Leclerc was pulling the staircase back up, stranding them below.

"We need to get up those stairs!" Ben shouted.

The flames had swallowed the bookcases behind them and were still hungry, leaping eagerly to the chart table and devouring the neighboring countertops. Black smoke was filling the air, making Ben's eyes water.

With faltering steps he pushed Mack and Heaton forward toward the stairs.

They raced away from an advancing wall of fire. Only a few seconds had passed and already half of the chamber was engulfed in blazing white flames as the ancient documents proved ready kindling. The steps had started to retract when they reached the staircase, the bottom one already a few feet off the ground.

Ben hoisted Mack onto the step.

"Use your magic for the professor," Ben shouted to Mack over the roar of the flames. He coughed, the smoke poisoning his lungs.

Ben took his own running leap at the staircase. It was ascending so rapidly he just managed to catch hold of the bottom step in his hands. He pulled himself up onto it.

Mack was focusing on levitating Heaton.

"What has he done?" Heaton whimpered. Even as she flew upward, her eyes were on the ancient library below. "All these spells . . . all this history . . . what will we do now?"

The conflagration reached the floor beneath the stairs themselves.

The heat was sharp, savage. Ben could hear beneath him the creaking and pinging of metal under stress as the file cabinets and instruments bent and warped. It was going to be close.

Heaton drew near enough that Ben could grab her. He caught hold of her wrists in his hands. "Gotcha."

They were both sweating profusely in the heat. Heaton slipped a bit in Ben's grip. He leaned back to try to pull her up onto the stair.

They were only ten feet from the ceiling, from the complete closure of the staircase. All at once Heaton started screaming and kicking wildly. Her clothing was on fire.

"Don't struggle, Professor," Ben said through gritted teeth, holding on with all his strength. "We're almost there."

Yet the fire had engulfed her. Heaton flailed and screamed again—a horrible, animal sound—then slipped from Ben's hold.

She was suspended in the air for a moment as Mack tried to use magic to pull her back up. Then the staircase closed completely, sealing off Ben and Mack from the underground chamber.

Heaton was lost to the inferno.

30

Leclerc was sprawled motionless on the sofa, dark blood spreading out from the ragged wound in his stomach, soaking his silk shirt and seeping into the fabric on either side of him. He wasn't dead, but the sheen of sweat on his face, and the distant, glassy look in his eyes told Ben he soon would be.

Mack ran to the small end table that hid the switch for the staircase and attempted to open it back up. She flipped the switch again and again, shaking in frustration and anger.

"Why the fuck won't it open?!" she screamed.

Beneath them, Ben could hear the continued wrenching and popping of the metal substructure under extreme heat.

"The mechanism is destroyed," Ben said.

"But the professor! We can't just leave her down there!"

Ben shook his head. Mack knew as well as he did that the professor was already gone.

Mack let out a gasping sob and Ben put his arms around her. Whatever words of condolence he might have offered were cut short as the staircase buckled, cracked, and fell away, and the fire rushed up through the hole in the floor as though stoked by a giant bellows.

Greedy tongues of flame swarmed onto the couch and the cushions, licking toward Leclerc.

Ben grabbed Mack's hand. Pursued by fire, they ran through the open courtyard and back out onto the *riad*'s stony grounds.

When they reached the ridge, they stopped to catch their breath. Ben looked back at Leclerc's house. A tower of white fire was laying waste to the entire structure. Even from this distance, the heat was searing.

Ben tossed their bags over his shoulder, then took Mack's hand again, more gently this time. Tears rolled from her eyes as he led them down the path that took them, after twenty-five minutes of scrambling over loose rock in the dark, to the main road.

He flagged down a driver in a rusted pickup. For a few dirhams, the man gave them a lift to a chain hotel on the outskirts of town.

A half hour later, Ben was closing the door to one of two tiny hotel rooms for which he'd paid cash up front. He leaned back against the door and rubbed at his smoke-bleary eyes. For the first time since this had all begun, he was completely unsure of what to do next.

How had everything fallen apart so fast? Heaton was dead. The same fire that killed her and finished off Leclerc had also destroyed any possibility of finding the binding protocol in the Possessor's vast library. They still had no idea who Merlin was or when his next protocol would be unleashed. Even with Novak running interference, Harris had probably made the connection to Kovit in Thailand by now. Ben and Mack needed to keep moving, but to where? In pursuit of what? There were no leads left to chase down.

They were back at square one, but even worse off. When they'd flown to Scotland, they were still ahead of the protocols, racing to keep magic from getting out into the world. At this point, they'd already failed: the protocols were out and wreaking all kinds of havoc. If the next one to be released was *fire*? Good-bye, civilization.

Ben shook himself from his stupor and turned on the shower. He peeled off the clothes he'd worn since leaving Bangkok—clothes now caked with sweat and blood, now stained brown with dirt and charred black with flame. Stepping into the steaming shower, he let the hot water ease the tension from his muscles, and the warm vapor relieve his parched throat. A sliver of soap shaved off the bar and got stuck under John's ring. Ben twisted it free.

I swear I'm not giving up, John. I just don't know what to do.

Ben got out of the shower and dried off. He wrapped the towel around his waist and picked up the remote to turn on the news and see just how bad things had gotten.

A knock at the door stopped him. Ben's pulse spiked and he reached toward where his SIG Sauer lay on the nightstand.

"You don't need your gun," said Mack, her voice muffled by the door, "it's just me."

"Give me a sec."

He pulled on a gray T-shirt and a pair of athletic shorts, then opened the door. Mack stood in the hallway. She'd also washed up, and now wore an outfit nearly identical to Ben's, except her shirt was oversize and hung down to her thighs.

"You gonna invite me in?"

Ben pulled the door open wider.

Mack sat down on the edge of the bed. He sat next to her.

"So, we're fucked, right?" she asked.

Despite everything, Ben had to smile. "You like to get right to the point, huh, Eila?"

"No sense wasting time," she said. "I've done enough of that."

Ben nodded. "We'll think of something," he said, hardly believing it himself. "Maybe Gabe will come up with other useable counterspells. Or maybe there's something back at Heaton's that she overlooked . . ."

Heaton.

"I can't believe she's gone." Mack shook her head. "She was so kind. But fierce, too, you know?"

"Yeah, I know."

"I feel like it's our fault. We never should have let her come." She squeezed her eyes shut.

"Don't forget that she wouldn't have missed coming on this mission with us for anything," Ben said gently. "She was happy to be along for this ride, to finally be in on the action after only reading about it her whole life."

"I guess."

Ben wondered if he should touch Mack, comfort her. She'd come to his room, she was on his bed.

"What about you?" he asked. "Are you glad to be in on the action?"

"I don't know." Mack's eyes were still rimmed in red. "I love being able to do magic, but it kinda means the world's ending at the same time, so . . ." She threw up her hands and let them fall into her lap.

A long silence followed.

"Is this over?" Mack finally asked.

"Is what over?"

"This whole . . . adventure. Is it time to go back? Can't we just go to the CIA, tell them what we've learned, beg for mercy?"

How many cries for mercy had Ben ignored as an agent? How many interrogations that went on and on?

"The CIA doesn't do mercy," Ben said. "Harris certainly doesn't. If we go back without completing this mission, neither of us has got a chance of seeing anything but the inside of a cell for years."

Mack flung herself back onto the bed with a groan. "Well, that's depressing."

"Do you want a drink?" Ben offered. The minibar wasn't much, but it did include a trio of minuscule, overpriced bottles of Jack Daniel's.

"I don't drink anymore," Mack said.

Ben winced; he knew that.

"But I'll take a soda."

"They sold some in the lobby," Ben said, slipping on his shoes.

"What do you want? Don't hold back now"—he smiled—"I'm buying."

"Anything with lots of sugar and lots of caffeine," she announced, still staring up at the ceiling.

"Don't go anywhere."

"Where am I gonna go?"

Lots of levels to that question, Ben thought as he stepped through the door and into the hallway.

Halfway to the elevator he realized something was wrong. It was too quiet somehow—a loaded silence. He turned back toward the room, not entirely sure why he was doing it.

There was a spit of sound from somewhere—the stairwell on the right?—and Ben felt a pinch in his neck. He reached up to touch the area and felt the feathered end of a small dart. A tranq. *Fuck.* He had mere seconds before losing consciousness.

He yelled at the top of his lungs as he stumbled toward the room. *"Mack! Get out of here! Get back to the States and find . . . my friend . . ."* The hallway twisted and lurched like an Escher drawing. *Fuckfuckfuck.* Had she heard him? He got his hand on the doorknob. "Don't use your . . . passport. Just . . . use your . . . abilities . . ."

The floor rushed up to meet Ben's face, its nauseating maroon pattern coming closer and closer until he was right up against it. He felt a knee in his back.

A triumphant voice he didn't recognize: "Director Harris says hello."

31

When her national security team was announced and admitted into the Oval Office the president had been staring out the windows onto the White House's South Lawn, wondering why exactly it had been her fate to suffer the singular misery of being the sitting commander in chief when *magic* was unleashed upon her country.

The president invited them to sit on the facing sofas, then opted as usual to stay standing herself, leaning slightly against her desk.

She folded her arms and looked at the grim faces before her. She already saw there was no shred of good news to be had. The thought occurred to her, not for the first time since this crisis blew up, that if things kept on the way they were, she might end up being the last president her country would ever have. It was *someone's* lot to be the captain of the *Titanic*.

She spread her arms. "Well?" She trusted that there was no more she needed to say.

They all checked in. Torozian, her perpetually rumpled national security advisor, led off, telling her nothing she hadn't been perfectly able to glean from the wall-to-wall TV coverage. Predictably, all the worst people wanted a piece of these new abilities. The increase of both run-of-the-mill criminality and outbursts of terrorist violence had hit major metro areas hard and fast, and a number of people in cities from coast to coast were starting to skip work, refusing in particular to board public transportation. Many residents of rural areas, meanwhile, had taken to stockpiling—foodstuffs as well as weapons.

"That's just wonderful," the president said. An uncomfortable, cold wetness seeped into her armpits. And why *wouldn't* she be sweating? "Meg?"

NSA Director Byrne spoke next, detailing her agency's attempts to intercept and flag potentially dangerous communications about magical attacks. That effort was proving nearly impossible, since all anyone in the entire world was talking about was magic. Separating the signal from the noise required more time, agents, and computing power than they were even able to accurately estimate. Every minute, they fell further behind.

The president turned to her CIA director. "What about your team, Bill? Any progress at all?"

"Actually, things on our end just took a turn for the better, Madame President," Harris said, with an uncharacteristic, and unsettling, half-smile.

But before Harris could elaborate, a door opened and a trio of Secret Service agents rushed into the room.

"What's going on?"

"Madame President," one of the agents said, "we have orders from the director of the Secret Service to remove you to a secure location immediately."

"Based on what, exactly?" the president demanded.

"Our own intelligence assessment of the current level of instability," he answered. "We can no longer ensure your safety on the outside."

Torozian spoke again. "I concur with their assessment," he said gravely. "The raising of the NORAD threat level alone should have been enough. I know you don't want to leave, Madame President, but I'm afraid it's time."

"Very well," she said. "I assume Marine One is waiting?"

A different agent spoke. "A helicopter is out of the question. Given the nature of the, ah, magical threat, putting you into the air is . . . ill-advised."

"We'll take you out through the tunnels," the third agent concluded.

The president saw it all unfold in an instant. Racing through the hidden tunnels under the White House. Being hustled into an unmarked car. A long trip to a secret bunker whose location even she didn't know. And then waiting and watching on a wall of monitors as the country she'd been chosen to lead fell to pieces in real time. *Funny, at first the iceberg hadn't even seemed that large* . . .

"Let's go," she said to the agents.

As she was leaving, the president stopped to put a hand on Harris's shoulder. "Bill," she said.

"Yes, Madame President?"

"Whatever you've got going on, don't fuck it up."

"I don't intend to."

Without another word, the president and her agents rushed out of the room.

32

Taganskaya Metro Station was one of Moscow's busiest, a transfer hub where three lines met. During morning rush hour it was thronged with people, shoving their way on and off crowded trains, up and down narrow stairs.

It was an ideal target.

The man known to his associates and enemies alike only as Nezh crossed the street toward the station entrance, dragging his unnaturally heavy wheeled suitcase, his broad shoulders hunched against the predawn drizzle.

"*Bismillah*," he whispered as he pulled open the glass door and stepped inside. A single word of prayer was all he had time for. It would be enough; Allah was on his side.

He pulled a few rubles from the pocket of his trousers and purchased a ticket at the machine. The bored guard raised an eyebrow at the giant Chechen as he squeezed his bulk through the turnstile, but said nothing.

Russian coward.

Nezh stepped onto the escalator with his suitcase, joining the horde of grim-faced commuters. There were maybe not so many as there would have been a few days before. Some people were beginning to be afraid to go to work, not knowing what might happen with magic in the world.

The fearful ones were going to get lucky. The contents of Nezh's suitcase had been painstakingly tracked down and assembled for maximum impact. He'd only just secured the last, most vital piece—the radioactive material—from a remote outpost in the Abkhazian mountains. If he were blessed today, thousands would die in the initial blast, and, God willing, many thousands more from highly radioactive fallout in the days and weeks to come. Once the dust settled and the corpses were laid to rest, the Russian bear would finally learn to leave Chechnya to the Chechens.

The escalator deposited him onto the station floor. The grand central hall stretched out before him—its graceful white ceiling vaults coming together above domed-glass chandeliers, its dozens of blue majolica panels celebrating in noble bas-relief the brave servicemen of the Red Army. Nezh wanted to vomit.

Propaganda, misinformation, shiny illusions of unattainable grandeur. These were the Russian lifeblood: a glossy picture of fresh-baked bread when there was no bread to be had, sweet words about noble sacrifice while desperate fools were marched into the meat grinder of war. For what? What had Mother Russia ever done for any of them?

Nezh moved through the central hall. The heat down here at the peak of summer's fury was thick and close, compounded by the swarm of city dwellers jostling one another to board the heavy metal trains that rattled into the station seemingly every minute. No sooner did a wave of people roll out of each train, than an undertow of passengers swept back against them to fill the cars up again.

People got out of his way—they always did—as Nezh strode up the length of the cavernous central hall. Through the marble arches on either side, the blue trains continued to arrive and depart, spewing out their occupants and swallowing more down. Somewhere a musician was torturing a violin. *A fitting elegy,* Nezh thought. *Let them die listening to their shitty, saccharine music.*

He approached the end of the hall, where the stink of homeless piss meant there were fewer passengers and fewer eyes. He lay the suitcase flat on the ground, flush against one of the thick columns. He unzipped the case, examining the three long, metal canisters bound to a half-dozen fat bricks of plastic explosive. The plastique was wired to a cell phone detonator. It was a pleasing model of brutal efficiency. Nezh reached into the case to arm the device.

The sound of rushing footsteps came from the end of platform— the end where no one stood. Nezh only had time to register the disconnect before he was slammed backward into the pillar behind him with so much force it knocked the wind out of him. Something— some*body*—kept him pinned there by magic. He gasped for breath. His feet dangled uselessly, inches off the ground.

Nezh fought against the hold as hard as he could, but he could barely do more than wiggle his goddamn fingers and toes. He wanted to use what he'd learned, the magic, but he couldn't think straight, couldn't remember the fucking words.

He also couldn't get enough air. Blackness began to appear at the edges of Nezh's vision. He would pass out soon.

Who was doing this? Who would betray him? *Who had this kind of power?*

Nezh's mind howled and his stomach burned in acid rage at how easily he'd been incapacitated by his assailant. His fingers grasped futilely at the smooth marble cladding of the column.

Moments later, still suspended immobile in the air, strangled and choking, Nezh heard the sirens. Then followed the shouts of police as they closed in on him, guns drawn, ugly smiles on their cursed faces.

33

The iron tang of blood in his mouth was the first thing Ben noticed when he regained consciousness. His tongue explored the damage—the inside of his cheeks were shredded and pulpy, and there was a hole where one of the teeth on the upper left side of his mouth had been knocked out.

Harris's guys had worked him over pretty well on the three different planes they'd taken since Marrakesh. No questions, no interrogation. Just softening him up for the boss. Now, after however many blindfolded, half-drugged hours, they were letting Ben sweat it out.

He knew the playbook. He'd run it himself on countless suspected terrorists—though he didn't much enjoy being on the receiving end.

Ben opened his eyes, or tried to. The left one was stuck shut, whether swollen or caked with blood he didn't know. His hands were bound and he couldn't touch it to find out. Through his right eye he took in the room.

It hadn't originally been designed for interrogations, that much was clear. Like the NSA safe house where Ben had first seen Mack, the space obviously had once been used for more pedestrian purposes. Now there was a metal table in the center, in front of the cold metal chair he was chained to. A two-way mirror was set into one wall, and there were two long fluorescent bulbs that shone their glaring light directly down onto the center of the room. But there were little touches—the molding on the ceiling, the dark wooden frame around the blacked-out window—that hinted at the room's former life.

Ben guessed he was in some mid-twentieth-century house, similar to the one they'd been holding Mack in. He bet he was back in Washington, or nearby. Harris would want him close.

The bolt in the door retracted with a metallic *chunk*. But it wasn't another smirking agent who'd come to tenderize Ben's face.

This time it was Harris.

The CIA director's expression wasn't the gloating smile Ben had expected. Instead, there was a weariness in the dark eyes behind those wire frame glasses. His tie was uncharacteristically loosened, and his sleeves were haphazardly rolled up to the elbow, revealing hairy arms. Ben intuited in a flash what it meant.

"You don't have her," Ben said. He was surprised to hear the degree of relief in his own voice. Harris's men hadn't captured Mack back in Marrakesh. She'd slipped their net and made it out.

"No," Harris admitted, closing and locking the door behind him. "Thanks to you, I don't."

Harris pulled the other chair from under the table, but instead of sitting down, almost as an afterthought, he reached over the table and backhanded Ben across the face. The blow was meant to be more of an insult than an injury, and it worked; Ben burned with fury.

"But," Harris said, "I do have you."

Ben glanced at the two-way mirror. No one who might possibly be watching could stop Harris from doing whatever he pleased with Ben.

"You've wanted to do that for years," Ben said, spitting a gob of bloody saliva onto the floor. "I hope you enjoyed it."

Harris just sat down in his chair and crossed his arms. "You self-righteous prick. You were one of our best. And after all the time and energy I put into you, after all the inroads you made and the assets you cultivated, you just walked away and left us with our dicks in our hands. I had to answer to Congress for you."

"Not every agent enjoys being the Grand Inquisitor as much as you do." Ben's face and head throbbed, pulsing in time with the duller ache of his bruised ribs and abdomen. He sat up straighter and stared at the director with his single open eye; he wasn't about to let Harris see him suffer. "What we were doing was wrong."

"No, you just didn't have the stomach for it. Christ"—Harris wrinkled his face—"everyone has to make compromises in the service of this country. We were trying to stop the next 9/11, and you were losing sleep because some fucking terrorist wasn't read his Miranda rights?"

They stared at each other across the table.

"What did you do with Sergeant Klippman?" Ben asked. He felt responsible for the man; they'd told the Marine pilot he was going on a secret government mission. It had been half true.

"You really pulled him into some deep shit," Harris said with a shake of his head. "Helping fugitives flee the country? He's going down for a long time." He pursed his lips. "Of course, how long depends on you."

"You want me to give you Mack."

"Oh, we're *going* to get her," Harris snarled. "I've sent her picture and information to the FBI, border patrol, and every police department in this country and twenty others. I need her. I need her power. I need to know how it works, how to use it, how to reverse what's happening to our country. Have you seen what's going on out there?" Harris motioned toward the blacked-out window, as though his enraged eyes could see through it, out into the increasing fear and instability of the world beyond. "This is war, asshole. When you helped her escape, that was like passing the plans for the A-bomb to the fucking Führer! So where the *fuck is she*?!"

Harris slammed his palms onto the table.

"How should I know? We were separated in Morocco, remember?"

"You know where she is," Harris said with a nod. "Or at least you know where she's headed—maybe to go hide with the same person who made you those nice passports."

Ben shrugged as best he could with his arms cuffed behind him.

Harris rubbed at his stubbled jaw. "You should know better than anyone that with the right persuasion everyone talks eventually," he said. His voice didn't even have the tone of a threat. It was the simple stating of a fact. "Is that what you're looking for?" Harris leaned across the table. "The right persuasion?"

When Ben said nothing, Harris looked into the two-way mirror and gave a slight nod. A signal.

Ben tried not to react visibly. He wasn't going to give Harris any satisfaction. Whatever information they would eventually get from him—and Harris was right, they'd get it; nobody could hold out under torture forever—Ben was going to make them work for it. He was going to give Mack a fighting chance to make it to Gabe.

He steeled himself for what was to come next. He was done sleeping for the foreseeable future, that much was assured. He could look forward to bright fluorescents, deafening blasts of heavy metal whenever his eyelids drooped, refrigerator-like air-conditioning, and a metal cot with no blanket. And that was just the background, merely the wallpaper of what he was about to experience. The actual interrogations—the stress positions, the freezing firehose showers, the various types and degrees of beatings—those were the main attraction.

The door unlocked again and swung inward. Deputy Director Novak stepped into the room.

"What the fuck are you doing here?" Harris demanded. "You should be back at HQ. I've got this under control."

Novak scratched at his spiky salt-and-pepper hair. "Actually, I don't think you do, sir."

"*Excuse* me?" Harris jumped up from his seat and faced his subordinate. "If you've got a problem with the way I'm conducting my interrogation—"

"You've always been wrong about Zolstra," Novak interrupted. "He's been helping us from the beginning. If it weren't for him leading us to the professor, Heaton, we wouldn't have found out about the existence of the Possessors. We wouldn't be compiling data on Carlton Braithwaite and Constantine Leclerc and their associates. We wouldn't—"

"This is not the time or place to—"

"You're right that we need Mack," Novak cut him off again, as Harris's face reddened in rage. "We need her to perform any of the reconfigured protocols we've been working on to stop all this. And especially," he added, with a glance at Ben, "to work the binding protocol."

"The what?" Harris asked.

The director clearly didn't know what Novak was talking about, but Ben himself was just as surprised to hear those words come out of the deputy director's mouth—until he remembered that text of Gabe's back in Thailand: *Novak says run.* The two of them must have been in closer contact than Ben ever suspected.

But this open defiance—what exactly was Novak's game here? Ben bit his tongue until he figured out how best to play it.

Novak continued, "We're not getting Mack without him." He jerked his head at Ben. "And we both know he's a stubborn bastard who's not giving her up anytime soon, no matter how much you hurt him. In the meantime, where does that leave us? Every hour we fall further into chaos."

Harris glowered at his deputy and spoke through gritted teeth. "I'm well aware of the fucking chaos."

"Then unchain Zolstra from that chair and treat him like a partner instead of a terrorist so we can get to Mack, combine forces, and save this country—shit, this *world*—while there's still time."

"All right, that's enough." Harris pointed to the door, disgusted. "Get back to headquarters if you still want to have a job tomorrow."

Novak didn't budge. "I'm not leaving without Zolstra."

Harris started to laugh—but the sound caught in his throat when he saw the gun in Novak's hand.

"What the fuck are you doing?"

Ben was wondering the same thing. Novak might have been secretly helping Ben before, but *this*—this was the point of no return.

"I'm relieving you of the command of this operation. You're not thinking clearly, and you're putting your personal feelings about Zolstra before the interests of this country."

"You goddamn traitor." The color drained from Harris's face as he realized Novak wasn't playing around. "You'll never make it out of this building."

The door swung open once more. "I think he will," said a woman. Ben recognized Agent Stevens, the blonde Chicagoan in the baseball cap from the safe house where Mack had been held.

"I'm sorry to do this, sir," Stevens said, "but the deputy director is right. We need to act now."

A stunned Harris sputtered in fury as Stevens approached Ben and removed his handcuffs. She helped him to his feet. Ben's every muscle ached, and he stumbled stiffly toward the door.

"You'll stay here and run interference?" Novak confirmed with Stevens, who nodded.

As Ben walked past him, Harris's hand shot out and grabbed him hard around the upper arm. He dug his nails into Ben's skin. "You. Aren't going. Anywhere."

Ben raised his fist but froze when Novak pulled the hammer back on his pistol with an unmistakable click. The gun was pointed at Harris.

"Yes, he is," Novak said. "Let him go."

The director looked at Novak with frank astonishment, releasing his grip on Ben.

"I'm going to nail you to the wall for this," Harris vowed to Novak.

"If I'm wrong, Director, and we can't stop magic—that won't make a bit of difference. There may not even be a wall left standing, much less a government." Novak motioned with his gun toward the chair Ben had just vacated. "Now, with all due respect, have a fucking seat."

34

Mack had never felt so exhausted in her life. This was worse than the consecutive weeks of night shifts at the hospital, more draining than the months of wracking grief over her brother. No experience had made her feel as empty as she now did after using magic continuously for nearly an entire day. There was a hollow canyon inside her that she couldn't imagine ever refilling with energy.

She brought the mug of what had to be her fourth refill of diner coffee up to her mouth. It might as well have been water. Her motions—hand gripping cup, arm raising, wrist turning, coffee entering mouth, swallowing—were purely mechanical; she was as detached from her actions as if she were watching them on television.

Mack had heard Ben's shouted warning back at the hotel in Morocco and had avoided capture by seconds. From then on, for nearly the next twenty-four continuous hours, she'd had to stay single-mindedly focused on remaining invisible and undetectable through a series of international flights and airports.

The hypervigilance alone was depleting, to say nothing of the energy-drain of the magic. She couldn't risk accidentally jostling anybody as she huddled terrified in the back of the bus to the airport. Although the red-eye out of Marrakesh bound for Paris was nearly empty, she'd had to be exceptionally careful—and quick—to sneak down the Jetway and through the closing door. On the full flight from Paris to Baltimore, she'd stood up in the back for the entire nine hours, dodging flight attendants as they reached for coffee and heated up tiny meals that made Mack's empty stomach rumble. She'd watched enviously as one attendant used every trip to the galley to take furtive sips from a flask she had hidden in her small carry-on bag. Mack could smell the booze on her breath as she passed. Whiskey. The proximity to the sweet heat of its golden fire made Mack half-dizzy with wanting—but, although it would have been so easy to steal her own sip, she didn't indulge.

That flight also nearly proved disastrous in another way. Mack must have fallen asleep for a matter of seconds. It interrupted the intention of her spell, and she snapped awake to find that her two sandaled feet and ankles had become visible again. Only the darkness of the cabin had saved her from discovery.

Her whole journey wouldn't have been possible at all if she'd begun it even twelve hours later. Airports around the world had already reduced their schedules by half, canceling tens of thousands of flights, in order to accommodate infrared heat-scanning for invisible stowaways or packages. Those airports that couldn't afford to adopt such measures were simply shutting down. The cost of airline tickets, to *anywhere,* were ten, or even twenty times what they'd been the day before.

The waiter at the diner was saying something to her again. Mack turned her head toward him in slow motion. Her blink was heavy, like the flapping wing of some enormous bird.

"I'm sorry," Mack said. Her voice sounded to her like it was coming from underwater. "What did you say?"

The waiter was annoyed. Mack must have seemed like she'd drunk a whole bottle of NyQuil. "A-ny-thing else?" he repeated slowly, enunciating each syllable. "Or did you want the check?"

The tattooed server evidently couldn't wait the eternity it took Mack to process and respond. He stomped off in a huff and returned to slap the check down on the table in front of her.

It occurred to Mack that it was dangerous for her to be in such a state. The thought came to her distantly but with urgency, like lightning flashing on a far horizon. If she were confronted by a Possessor, or by Merlin—or if one of Harris's men came for her at that moment—she'd be able to put up about as much resistance as a bowl of warm mush.

The thought brought her back to herself . . . but only a little. *Focus, Eila. You made it back to America. What's next?*

Gabe. She had chosen Baltimore because it was close to Annapolis, and she needed to get there and find Ben's friend Gabe. A bus map she had grabbed at the airport showed the stop and the route.

Gabe was an ally; she could trust him. He was good with the spells—his reconfigured revealing spell had been the key to their discovering the note at Braithwaite's. Gabe treated the protocols like lines of code. They'd lost their chance to find the binding spell at Leclerc's—but working together, maybe Mack and Gabe could *make* one? Or at least figure out something to stop the worst people from doing magic? Or . . . ?

Or, Mack thought as she threw a few dollars on the table and dragged herself out of the booth and to the door, *maybe I don't give a shit about saving the world. Maybe I just need to get my fucking life back.*

If Gabe was as good with other documents as he was with passports, he could help her to do just that. Mack could become someone new, a person the government didn't want to make into an eternal science experiment or a nuclear weapon. She'd make sure Gabe gave her new identity the certification that she'd already earned so she could work in a hospital again, helping people and making a difference in their lives. She could run off to somewhere nice and try to start over, to be truly free from all the bullshit of her past, which she wouldn't let define her anymore. The alcohol, the Ray disaster, the fear and self-loathing—with magic or without it, she was done living that cliché.

If there's still a world to make your way in, she thought.

As she pushed through the door and out into the street, a little bell attached to the frame rang. Its bright cheerfulness was a contrast to the downtown scene she found herself in. People darted anxiously through the streets, dodging cars that no longer seemed to be stopping at red lights. Scratch that—the lights themselves were busted out. Half of the stores were locked up tight, and those that were open had armed guards posted at the doors. On one street corner, two teenagers suddenly appeared out of nowhere and made a discreet exchange, then vanished again. Mack was pretty sure she'd just seen her first invisible drug deal.

The dread of random acts of violent magic that Mack had been overhearing as she silently creeped around definitely seemed to be keeping lots of people indoors. Apparently one of them was the president. Mack learned from the news that she hadn't been seen in public since the assassination of the Israeli prime minister, and her location was still undisclosed. Other leaders were staying out of sight, too. But as agency and department heads dropped out of the picture, law enforcement became increasingly confused by how best to deal with magic, and criminals got more brazen—which sent even more spooked leaders underground. It was a vicious cycle.

And why is any of this my problem?

One of the stores Mack passed had a sign that was still well lit: CROWN LIQUORS. Mack was seized with the desire to get well lit herself. Heaton would approve, wouldn't she? The professor drank like a fish, after all, and she was brilliant, funny, kind.

And dead. Dead. Like any hope we had of stopping Merlin.

Mack floated toward the door of the liquor store. The windows were covered in faded ads for specials on Old Milwaukee and Chivas Regal. Mack peeked through the cracks. The stock had been depleted, but there was still enough on the shelves for plenty of good times. Mack felt herself physically cave in, her body slouching forward in acceptance of her spirit's defeat, as she gripped the door handle in her fist.

Carry yourself right, and people will treat you right.

The memory of her mother's words stopped Mack like a cold slap. What was she doing? Was she really going back down this road? Now? When she had more power than she'd ever dreamed of, and people were counting on her? She couldn't give up. She was a helper. A healer.

Wasn't she?

Mack pulled herself out of her stooped posture and let go of the door handle, her trembling fingers releasing one by one. Then she half-ran down the sidewalk, not slowing until she was well onto the next block. That was too damn close. She needed to get on the bus to Gabe's while she still had the willpower.

But before she did that, there was a phone call she both needed to, and really didn't want to, make. In addition to his wallet, Mack had grabbed Ben's burner phone before she fled the hotel room in Morocco, and now she pulled it out and found the number for a contact in Scotland.

Lucas picked up immediately. "Yes? Hello? Mr. Zolstra?"

"No, it's Eila Mack. On Ben's phone."

"God, I'm just glad to talk to anyone." His desperation was evident. "Is Desdemona with you? I've been going crazy not being able to reach her."

Mack took a deep breath. "Lucas, I'm not sure how to say this but, Professor Heaton . . . she didn't make it."

"What do you mean?" he said hesitantly. "Make what?"

"We were at Leclerc's house," Mack began. "And he . . . the evil prick set the place on fire to keep us from getting the binding spell. Ben and I barely made it out alive, and the professor . . ."

"I don't understand what you're telling me." Panic edged into Lucas's voice. "What are you saying to me?"

Do it like a Band-Aid, Mack thought. "Heaton is dead, Lucas. I'm so sorry."

There was a long pause. Then a choked sob. "I can't believe it."

"Neither can I," Mack said truthfully. "I really liked her. She was a good person."

Lucas made a small noise of agreement, then said nothing for such a long time that Mack thought the line had gone dead.

"Are you there?"

"I'm here," he said. "What about the Possessor, Leclerc. Is he dead, too? Is everything useful destroyed?"

"Yeah."

"What about you? Where are you now?"

"Back in the U.S.," Mack said. "Baltimore. Ben was picked up in Marrakesh, I think by the CIA." She shook her head. "Jesus, all this is crazy, isn't it? I'm going to try to find Ben's friend Gabe in Annapolis. Hopefully we can . . . I don't know . . ."

"Are you safe?"

"I . . . I think so."

She glanced around. It was a queasy, uncertain feeling, not knowing if Harris and the government had any idea she was back in the country. Was it risky to even be walking down the street, or getting on a bus? Or was she safely anonymous now, just another young woman on the streets of Baltimore going about her business? Maybe Harris had already found and replaced her with someone more powerful than she was—maybe she was in the clear.

But that wasn't likely.

"Look, I'm . . . I'm sorry again," Mack repeated. "I have to go."

"Be careful."

Mack said she would, and hung up.

Huge buildings—official-looking, concrete, and marble—lined both sides of the street as Mack arrived at the bus stop. She was sweating even though she'd walked most of the way in the shade. She double-checked the number on the post. This was the right place, though given the state of everything, who knew how long it'd be before the bus actually showed? She sat down on the bench.

A kid, who couldn't have been more than twelve, shot by on a bicycle, nearly severing Mack's toes.

"Hey!" she yelled in surprise. "Careful!"

The boy turned around. The little brat was smirking. He sped up and came zooming by Mack again, just as close, his scraggly blond hair waving in the breeze. Mack tucked her feet underneath the bench.

Try it a third time, kiddo, Mack thought, *and you might just end up stuck at the top of that tree over there.* Though she honestly wasn't sure she had the strength to carry out the threat.

But instead of messing with Mack again, the boy decided to jump the curb and cut across the road.

He didn't seem to see the bus bearing down on him.

A woman screamed. Mack was on her feet and saying the words before she knew what she was doing. She sent a wave of intention toward the child that was so strong it picked up not only him and his bike but a parked delivery moped and half the pedestrians on the opposite sidewalk.

The bus, horn blaring, braked hard to a stop directly underneath where the boy was now hovering in the air. The startled boy burst into tears. All around Mack people lifted their phones to capture the moment.

Just the kind of attention she didn't need.

Mack set everyone down and immediately felt achy all over. Her head in particular pounded like the second coming of her worst hangover, and she felt so weak her knees buckled and sent her rushing back down to the bench.

No sooner had she sat than Mack heard the blast of a siren and a flash of red and blue, and a squad car rolled up onto the sidewalk near the bus stop. Two officers got out. *I guess that bus driver is screwed,*

Mack thought. Then one of the cops shouted. His words were so un-expected he had to repeat them—with increased agitation and his gun drawn—before Mack understood what he was saying.

"Do not move! You were seen performing magic in the area and are to come in for questioning. I repeat: do not move!"

Now the female officer had her weapon pointed at Mack, too.

Aw, fuck.

Mack did the first thing that came to mind. She summoned every last ounce of strength she had, whispered the words to make herself invisible, and ran like hell.

35

Ben had barely closed the car door when Novak jammed the accelerator to the floor and peeled away from the suburban safe house. Ben's hunch had been right: they were somewhere outside Washington. Novak was taking them east.

As much as Ben couldn't believe the sudden change in his own fortune, the changed Bill Novak who sat next to him was an even bigger shock. The deputy director was an obliging company man. Seeing Novak pull a gun on Harris in order to free Ben was like watching the family golden retriever turn and sink its teeth into the master's neck.

What Novak had done was irreversible; he, and Agent Stevens, had thrown in their lots with Ben in opposition to the head of their own agency. Whatever happened now, they were in it together. Which meant they had to try to trust one another.

"Where are we going?" Ben asked.

"I'm sure you can put it together."

Novak swerved around a slow station wagon, and Ben sucked in a quick, painful breath as his seat belt pulled against his bruised torso.

Ben peered into the lagging vehicle as they passed. It was stuffed with dented cardboard boxes, assorted bags, bedding, and children's toys. The front widows were the only ones not completely blocked. The top of the car was piled high with suitcases knotted together with bungee cords and twine. A whole family was packed into the front seats—a man was hunched over the wheel, and a woman in the passenger seat balanced two toddlers on her knees.

"People are starting to flee the cities," Novak said by way of explanation, following Ben's look. "There have been home invasions using invisibility, some pretty ugly . . ." He sighed heavily. "The director thinks we can afford to waste time leaning on you. I don't."

"You think I'm going to lead you to Mack," Ben said.

"On this point, at least, I agree with Harris. You know where she's going. If I had to guess, I'd say she's headed for Garcia. So that's where *we're* headed. He's waiting for us."

Ben didn't like hearing the name of his private contact on the deputy director's lips. "How the hell do you know about him?"

Novak threw Ben a look that could almost have passed for a smirk. "I'm a CIA agent."

"Harris doesn't know?"

Novak shook his head. "When my team turned up Garcia as a possible contact for you, I told them there was nothing to it and they dropped it."

The car merged onto Highway 50, heading toward Annapolis, the setting sun in its rearview.

"You've been working against Harris this whole time?"

"I knew you'd get us more intel by being out in the field on your own than you ever could on a leash in Washington. When you led us to Desdemona Heaton and we started looking into her work, I knew it was the right decision."

Ben probed at his still-shut left eye, wincing at its tenderness. Harris's field agents, those two smiling motherfuckers, had enjoyed their work. Ben used his fingers to open the eye, unsticking the blood-caked lid.

"Do you know Heaton is dead?" he asked Novak.

"Yes. We identified her body at the house in Marrakesh. Her and that useless socialite, Leclerc." His tone was matter-of-fact. "It's too bad. She could have been really helpful."

"She was," Ben growled.

"You know what I mean." Novak raced up to the red sedan in front of them in the fast lane, then braked hard and flashed his brights. "Come on, get over!"

The sedan changed lanes, and Novak blew past it.

"The Possessors actually tried to kill Heaton once before," Ben said. "At least, I believe she was the target. This was back in Scotland, when you and Harris were looking for me, arresting my pilot, and impounding my plane—"

"*Stolen* plane," Novak interjected.

"Three cars tried to run us down using magic. One of them crashed and burned after Mack saved all our asses. You must have come across the police filing about the accident, or the coroner's report."

"Nothing happened in that whole fucking country that day that we didn't look at. We scoured that place." Novak squinted, remembering. "But I didn't hear about any fatal accident."

"That's strange," Ben said. "Heaton's assistant, Lucas, told us there was a report, but the identity of the driver was still inconclusive."

"You said a Possessor was involved? They must have buried the whole thing fast."

"Maybe," Ben allowed. But something didn't feel right. Had Lucas lied to them?

Novak shrugged. "There was no record of any wreck, or we'd have found it."

They drove on in silence for a few minutes. Ben saw more cars and trucks that had been turned into makeshift moving vans, loaded hastily and haphazardly with whatever their owners could fit inside or on the roof.

"Just last week I was planning a vacation to Italy," Novak said. "It's like we blinked and the whole world went to shit."

Something in Novak's words struck Ben. It had been over a week since Merlin had uploaded his manifesto along with the first protocol, and four long days since the protocols had burst the web security dam the feds had been so desperately reinforcing, flooding the world with magic. Sure, people were panicking and crime was up, just as might be expected during any major city power outage. But in that time, what large-scale, unprecedented horrors had *really* gone down?

"Actually," Ben said, "I'm a little surprised things aren't worse."

"What are you talking about?" Novak countered. "Since Israel, there have been seven additional assassinations of heads of state, a thousand people dead at that soccer stadium in Belgrade—not to mention the bank robberies and prison escapes too numerous to count—"

"Yeah, it's bad, I get it," Ben acknowledged. "But it's almost just . . . ordinarily bad. I mean, *magic* is out now. Why haven't we seen some maniac release the ebola virus over the skies of Los Angeles? Why hasn't D.C. been nuked?"

They continued to race down the highway. The signs said they were only a few miles out from Annapolis.

"Maybe people aren't as naturally evil as you're making them out to be," Novak offered.

Ben shot him a look.

"Okay, fine," Novak said. "I don't believe that either. But I still don't understand what you're getting at."

"I'm saying . . ."

What was he saying?

"Maybe we're just getting lucky so far," Ben said. "But I'm wondering if there's more to it than luck."

Novak exited the highway and began winding his way toward Gabe's neighborhood of Eastport. The long shadows of dusk crawled over everything.

"What if the reason the worst isn't happening," Ben continued, "is that someone is stopping these things before they happen?"

"What, with magic?"

"Maybe there's a protocol we don't know about that lets people . . . *see* what's going to happen."

Novak snorted. "Are you talking about fortune-telling?"

A week ago Ben would've had himself committed if he'd had the thought: *What if someone out there has a forecasting spell and can see into the future?* But more had changed in a week than anyone could have imagined. Being reasonable in this new world meant trying to anticipate the inconceivable.

"Look," Novak went on, "even if there was such a thing, who would be using it? The only ones who would know about it are Possessors, right? From what we've seen, those bastards aren't exactly altruistic." Novak paused. His fingers drummed on the steering wheel. "Although it would explain Moscow . . ."

"What happened in Moscow?"

As they drove on, Novak informed Ben that Russian authorities had captured a terrorist known as Nezh, a man the Kremlin had long sought in connection with dozens of kidnappings and bombings over at least a decade during the endless scorched-earth war for Chechnya. What had bothered him, Novak said, was the mystery of how, after so many years of Nezh skillfully evading detection, the Russians had managed to catch the insurgent red-handed while arming a dirty bomb on a subway platform.

By the time Novak finished, they were pulling up to Gabriel Garcia's place. The garage opened for them, and Novak eased his hulking black Ford sedan next to Gabe's sleek vintage Camaro. The motorcycle Ben and Mack had ridden there still leaned against the back wall, now partially covered by a tarp.

Mack. The last time he'd seen her flashed through Ben's mind—half-reclined on Ben's hotel bed, her hair still damp from the shower, smiling in an oversize T-shirt. Where was she now? She'd escaped from the CIA, but was she safe? Had she managed to make it back to the States?

Gabe, dressed in a white tank top and baggy athletic shorts, closed the garage door behind them. Ben and Novak got out of the car.

"You look like mad shit, bro," Gabe said to Ben by way of greeting.

"Nice to see you, too."

Gabe turned to the deputy director. "You must be Novak." They shook hands. "No offense, but I kinda thought you'd look like more of a douche bag."

Novak seemed not to know the appropriate response to Gabe's observation. Ben laughed, the action echoing in a wave of pain through his abdomen. Gabe saw it and frowned in concern.

"Come on inside, man." Gabe waved them into the house. "Let's get you cleaned up. You hungry?"

Twenty minutes later Ben was dressed in a fresh set of borrowed clothes, having showered off the stiffness—and the dried blood—of nearly two days of confinement and abuse. He was settling into one of the coffee-stained recliners in Gabe's basement, when Gabe came down the stairs and set a whole pizza onto a large ottoman next to him.

"Careful with that," Gabe said. "It's crazy hot, just out of the oven."

Gabe pulled a battered leather desk chair up to the ottoman, then slid a slice of pizza onto a paper plate. He gave it to Ben, then offered another to Novak.

Novak, already seated, shook his head at Gabe's proffered slice. "While you were in the shower we were talking about your idea," he said instead to Ben. "About the existence of a . . . seeing or forecasting protocol."

"It makes sense to me." Gabe shrugged. "People can be invisible, right? Why not psychic?" Failing to take his own advice, Gabe bit greedily into his slice. He hissed as it burned him.

"I wonder if there's a way we can figure out if it's real," Ben said.

He turned to Novak. "This asshole that they nabbed in the Moscow Metro. Did you see how the arrest went down?"

"No," Novak said. "The surveillance footage was bound to be encrypted, and there was no real reason to bother breaking it."

Ben shifted and looked at Gabe. "Could you do it?"

Gabe cracked his knuckles dramatically, then picked up one of the laptops that cluttered his floor and opened it. "When did this happen, and at which station?"

Novak told him. As Gabe got to work, Ben ate his slice of pizza. Then another, and another. He hadn't realized how ravenous he was; he couldn't remember his last actual meal.

"What are you hoping to find?" Novak asked Ben.

"Evidence that someone went to that Metro station knowing an attack was coming, and waited for the bomber to arrive so they could stop him."

The clacking of Gabe's fingers as they flew over the laptop's keys provided a continual percussive soundtrack to their conversation.

"But it doesn't square," Novak insisted. "If the Possessors can see disasters unfolding in advance, why don't they stop all the other terrible things that are going on from happening?"

"Maybe there aren't many of them who have this ability. Remember that just saying the words of a protocol isn't enough to use it, you have to have a natural aptitude for it." Ben got another flash of Mack's face, the way she'd smiled when he called her the LeBron James of magic. He went on, "It turned out that Leclerc could create this . . . fire wind out of thin air, but that was an ability that even Heaton seemed surprised by. Some abilities are rarer than others. If forecasting is unusual for Possessors, then a person wanting to prevent attacks would have to focus their energy on stopping only the worst ones. They'd have to prioritize."

"Is this your Nezh guy?" Gabe cut in. He turned the laptop screen toward them.

Novak looked at Ben in astonishment. "Shit, your guy's fast. Why isn't he working for us?"

"You couldn't afford me," Gabe answered.

The display was split-screened into two black-and-white images from a pair of subway surveillance cameras. One camera that Gabe had tapped into was positioned above the tracks of a long platform. A train was just pulling into the station, and hundreds of people crowded close to board it.

The other half of the screen showed a closer view of the very end of the platform, apart from the crowd. Visible in the foreground of the image, a mountain of a man was standing against a support column.

The image wasn't crystal clear, but it was good enough for Novak to make the ID: "That's him. If the size hadn't given him away, that mole would have."

Ben looked closer at the suitcase lying open at the man's feet. Then he noticed those feet weren't touching the ground. He was *pinned* to that column.

"Go back a minute or so," Ben said.

Gabe scrubbed the video feeds backward, then let them both play.

A train pulls out of the station. Nezh appears in the wider frame, dragging his suitcase, the crowd parting for him like the Red Sea. He leaves the wide shot and passes into the other camera's tighter frame. He sets the bag at the foot of the column and unzips it, revealing an array of rounded canisters and rectangular bricks. He reaches down toward it—and then is suddenly thrown back hard against the column and held there.

"My God," Novak said.

"Someone *was* waiting for him," Ben said.

In the video, Nezh struggles but can't free himself. The cops arrive and surround him, guns out. But *they* can't free him either. Finally, after another few minutes, the giant crumples to the ground, the protocol's effects evidently having worn off.

Ben directed Gabe to search forward and backward on the videos for any hint of the invisible Good Samaritan who stopped the attack, but after scouring the footage as far out as a half hour on either side of the incident, they had nothing.

"He must have been invisible when he entered the station," Ben concluded. "*Shit*." It was just like Bangkok: more videos leaving another empty void where a person, a clue, should have been.

"You were right, though," Gabe said brightly. "There must be at least one Possessor out there who's working to help people."

"We need to get this guy, or someone like him," Ben said. "If we can't get our hands on the binding protocol, this is the next best thing. With this knowledge we could keep a lot of people safe."

But he wasn't giving up hope that they could still get *both*.

Novak shook his head in awed disbelief. "So there are random do-gooder Possessors wandering around out there, trying to use their magic to hold the world together."

Ben nodded. "All we need to do is find one."

"Sounds good," Gabe said. "Now how the hell are we supposed to do that?"

36

The solution came to Ben with such clarity and simplicity that he actually laughed out loud. Novak and Gabe turned to him, puzzled.

"We don't have to find one of these guys at all," he said. "He'll come to us."

"Why would he do that?" Novak asked.

"Because we're going to set the stage so he won't be able to resist."

Ben stood and began to pace. His muscles were sore—fucking Harris—but it felt good to move.

"The Moscow attack popped up on this guy's . . . radar . . . because the potential destruction from the bomb was massive," Ben said. "What we need to do is plan something *else* that will catch their attention."

Novak leaned back in his chair and folded his arms across his chest. "Oh, really?" His tone dripped with sarcasm. "All we need to do is plant a dirty bomb on the New York subway?"

"Actually, yeah." Gabe answered before Ben could, realization dawning on his face. "That's *exactly* what we do."

"As long as it's big enough," Ben said, "one of these guys'll come."

"Okay," Novak said, still a step behind, "so you're saying we fake a terrorist attack. Everything looks real, we draw one of these mysteri-ous Possessors out of the woodwork, snatch him . . ."

"No." Ben stopped and turned toward Novak. "Nothing can be fake."

"What do you mean?"

"Think about it tactically. What are you failing to consider?"

"Christ." Novak loosened his tie. "All right. I suppose . . . we don't know how this forecasting protocol works. It's possible this Possessor could see even further, to know that he's walking into a trap."

"Maybe," Ben agreed, "but would he really not stop a potential catastrophe because he's worried about spending a little time having to help out the feds?"

"Look, I'm too tired to play this game," Novak snapped. "What am I missing?"

"Tell me this," Ben said. "What would have happened if the Pos-sessor hadn't stopped the bomb in Moscow when he did?"

Novak frowned. "Is this a trick question?"

Ben shook his head.

"Obviously it would have detonated, killing potentially thousands of people."

"Right," Ben said, "and what happens if he fails to stop our dummy nuke?"

Novak's eyes widened. "Not a thing."

Gabe nodded. "Not a damn thing."

"If the threat isn't real," Ben said, "there's never any potential disas-ter to prevent. It's just not going to register."

"What are you saying to me right now?" Novak asked.

"I'm saying it's got to be real."

Novak chewed his lip. "Let me get this straight. You want to put a live nuclear weapon in the middle of New York City?"

Ben shrugged. "What else do you get the city that has everything?"

Now it was Novak's turn to laugh, though his was a hollow bark. He rubbed at his face. "I need a fucking drink."

Gabe stood. "What do you want?"

"Strongest thing you got."

Gabe left the room.

"So your plan is we lure in a Possessor who can forecast," Novak said, "and then we use his abilities to help us predict future disasters?"

Ben grinned. Something was coming back to him now. "That's only part of it," he said. "I think this is how we can get the binding protocol, too."

"What's that have to do with it? I thought that was all lost in the fire."

"One thing Heaton suggested, and that Leclerc confirmed, is that Possessors are organized into sects with leaders, and that those leaders are the ones who have the most power and magical knowledge," Ben explained, pacing again. "Leclerc also let two other things slip. First, that he had a counterpart who was still active in New York City. Another leader. And second, that every leader has access to the binding protocol. It's how they get everyone to stay in their lane. So if Leclerc had it, then the leader in New York has it, too."

"Okay," Novak said, "but what makes you so sure we can get to this person?"

"I'm betting our sect leader *is* our forecaster," Ben said, quickening his pace to match the speed of his thoughts. His blood was thrumming now with the old certainty, the bone-deep intuition a field operative feels when something finally clicks—and all at once he knows who to trust and who's about to betray him, when to get out or when to move in with guns blazing.

"Leclerc told us that there are some rare, high-level abilities that only leaders are allowed to learn and perform," Ben continued. "Since even Heaton didn't seem to have ever heard of forecasting, it must be one of these. And with everything that's been going on, any leader who would choose to stay in New York probably *uses* this forecasting ability regularly to keep the worst from happening. If only to save his own ass."

"So we grab the Possessor, get the binding protocol, then have Mack perform it?"

"That's the idea."

The obvious problem, of course, was that Mack was in the wind.

"What makes you so sure this person's still even anywhere near New York City?"

Ben stopped pacing and stared at Novak. "The fact that the city is still standing."

Novak laced his hands together behind his head. "What you're proposing is . . . it's . . ." he sputtered. "Zolstra, if we're wrong, we'll be responsible for . . ."

"Say it."

"We're going to kill thousands of people," Novak finished. He shook his head. "It's just too big a risk."

"What about the risk if we do nothing? More of Merlin's protocols are released. Many more thousands die. Unchecked magic will destroy everything we care about."

"Who's to say this Possessor even shows up personally?" Novak asked. "What if he just calls the bomb in to the cops and lets the authorities handle it?"

"That's not what happened in Moscow," Ben said. "I bet our guy wants to be the one to stop it. It's too important to leave to others who might screw it up."

Gabe reentered the room, clutching three opened bottles of beer.

Novak eyed the lager with disappointment. "I guess this'll have to do."

As Ben and Gabe took sips of their beers, Novak took a giant swig from his own—the half-frantic kind of pull a man takes when he's gone all in, wagered everything on a single hand, and is waiting to see which way the next card falls.

"We're going to need eyes everywhere so this Possessor can't escape when we show up," Novak said when he came up for air. "Infrared cams, too, if our guy goes invisible on us like in Moscow."

"You have access to the tech," Ben said. "You can task the agents."

"But without the director to authorize . . ."

"Who needs him?" Ben asked with a barely concealed smile. "Isn't he fly-fishing in the Adirondacks, like he does every summer?"

Novak scowled. "You think anyone will buy that, with all the shit going on?"

"What choice do we have?"

Novak took a deep breath and buzzed the air out through his lips. "I can't get us a nuke," he finally said. He set his bottle down on the floor in the midst of a serpentine tangle of cables and wires. He rubbed at his eyes and sighed.

"But there's a contractor we've used before," he went on, "a middle man that could lend us a large conventional device. I'll tell him it's for a top secret training exercise. The military has been developing a new prototype based on the old CBU-72s, but bigger. Way bigger."

Ben knew the older weapon, a thermobaric monster that had been used in Vietnam and Desert Storm. It instantly flooded an area with ethylene oxide and then ignited it. The shock wave it made was massive. Flattened-buildings massive. Even if you happened to escape the physical destruction, you'd still inhale the toxic gas and die. If you somehow avoided that, the pressure wave from the blast created a vacuum that would rupture your eardrums and burst your lungs, a particularly agonizing fate.

In short, it was the perfect lure.

Ben nodded his approval. Novak finished the remainder of his beer in another giant swallow, then stood.

"All right," he said grimly. "Time to pay some visits and make some arrangements." He stopped in the doorway at the foot of the stairs and turned back. The deputy director of the CIA looked haunted. "Do you realize what we're doing, Zolstra? What we've *already* done? Kidnapping, treason, plotting a terrorist attack on an American city. This is—"

Ben crossed to him and put a hand on his shoulder. "This is how we save the world."

"Tell that to Harris."

Novak left the room, the sound of his footsteps receding as he climbed the stairs. Moments later, Ben heard a car start and the garage door open and close again.

He turned to Gabe. "There's something else I wanted to look into while we're waiting for him."

Gabe popped the last bit of pizza crust into his mouth. "Shoot."

"It's about the Possessor who tried to run us down in Scotland. Something's not adding up about it. Novak said there wasn't any record of the crash, but Heaton's assistant, Lucas, said there was. I wonder if you can turn anything up."

Gabe wiggled his fingers. "I'll work my own little magic."

There was a creak on the stairs. Ben reached for his pistol out of habit, remembering with alarm that it had been taken from him. Gabe jumped to his feet.

"Gabe?" a voice called. "Are you here? I think I sort of . . . magically broke your door lock."

Mack?

Ben ran to the doorway.

"Ben?" Mack's mouth dropped open. "Oh, my God, I can't believe you're here!"

She descended the steps carefully, using the railing to steady herself. She looked bone-tired.

"What's wrong?" Ben asked. "Are you okay?"

Mack reached the bottom of the stairs and stood facing him. She scrutinized his battered face. "Better than you, looks like."

Ben smiled. So did she.

He took her in his arms. "It's really good to see you."

"You, too."

The embrace ended, replaced by a loaded silence.

"Well," Gabe finally chuckled, "*this* is awkward, right? I mean, I'm like the third wheel or whatever."

"Shut up, Gabe," Ben and Mack said at once.

"How did you get here?" Ben asked.

"How did *I* get here?" Mack said. "*You* were captured!"

"All right, both of you sit down," Gabe said with a grin. He pointed to Mack. "You go first."

37

It was sweltering, but the weather report said the humid fever was going to burst into a storm later. Hopefully not too soon—a severe downpour would complicate Ben's plan, making it harder to ID the Possessor they were here to trap.

A few people who were still brave, foolish, or drunk enough to try their luck on the Manhattan streets staggered through Union Square, slowing as they passed through the shade of the park's towering trees.

Ben sipped burned coffee from a paper cup and studied the people from the window of a narrow brick apartment building across the street. The entire fourth floor had been purchased by the Agency after 9/11, through intermediaries, as an off-book center for domestic intelligence gathering. A spook's nest in the heart of the city.

Novak had suggested the spot because it was currently gutted and abandoned. The building was undergoing extensive remodeling when magic got out. The workers hadn't been back since.

On the opposite side of the room, Novak stalked through the luxury condo's kitchen area. There were gaping holes where a sink and fridge should have been. On top of a hardwood island in the middle of the kitchen, a bank of security monitors was set up. Cameras were positioned to capture the moving truck that Ben and Novak had parked near the southwest corner of Union Square, as well as the surrounding streets, from every possible angle.

"Nothing?" Ben asked, indicating the monitors.

Novak merely shook his head and resumed pacing.

"Ground team," Novak barked into his headset, "sit rep."

The deputy director began checking in with their hastily assembled renegade squad—the two-person capture team on the ground, the pair of snipers on nearby rooftops with tranq rounds at the ready—for the third time in the last twenty minutes.

It was a shoestring op, but it was the best they could do under the circumstances. A full CIA action would have meant more agents, a host of mandated redundancies and safeguards—and plenty of unwanted attention.

As the situation reports came in, Ben yanked his headset off to rest around his neck. He didn't need to hear four different people say that nothing was going on. That much he could figure out for himself.

Don't you dare get killed, Mack had said to him when they set out from Gabe's at first light, only hours after they'd been reunited. She wanted to come to New York, but Ben had convinced her that it was better to stay with Gabe so the two of them could work on recoding the protocols. Gabe's revealing spell had worked so well that maybe there was more they could do.

The truth was that despite her protests that she was fine, Mack had looked alarmingly weak. The concentration and energy it had taken for her to stay invisible for an entire day so she could slip back into the country undetected was immense. She was regaining her strength, but Ben knew she'd be safer at Gabe's while she got back into fighting shape.

He checked his watch. The bomb's countdown timer would hit zero in twenty-five minutes. If the Possessor was going to make an appearance, he was taking his sweet time.

Unless he wasn't coming. Unless Ben's plan wasn't going to work.

Hours earlier, they'd met with Novak's contact at a rest area outside Philadelphia. He brought the moving truck. As Novak and Ben approached, the man, who was squat, bald, and already sweating from the heat, rolled up the rear door and invited them to climb inside. He quickly pulled the door down behind them. Strapped to the floor of the cargo area was an eight-hundred-pound fuel-air prototype bomb. With its metal shell unpainted, the deadly device looked like a huge hot water heater lying on its side.

"Be careful with this motherfucker," the man said, patting the bomb's casing. "Or you'll have a helluva mess on your hands."

The contact showed them how to operate the bomb's onboard computer and set a countdown timer—and he made sure to draw their attention to the kill command to halt detonation, which Ben wouldn't be using until the last possible moment. Then the man tossed them the keys to the truck and walked into the rest stop to wait.

Later, as Ben inched the truck into the city through the Holland Tunnel, Novak turned to him and said, "If we get caught right now, bringing this thing into Manhattan without authorization, we'll never see the light of day again. You know that, right?"

Now Ben pulled his headset back on, took another sip of coffee, and watched as the two ground agents walked by the parked truck. Novak snatched his own coffee from the counter and came toward Ben.

"Twenty minutes now," Novak said to Ben. "Where's your phantom man, Zolstra?"

Ben hated this part of an op. Everything was over but the waiting. Although the clock was ticking down, Ben's mind stretched the time out like pulled taffy, going over the plan again and again, questioning every decision, worrying that he hadn't accounted for every contingency, hadn't covered every base.

Everything is under control, he told himself. *This is not a net the Possessor can slip.*

The sooner they caught the sect leader and he gave up the binding spell, the sooner they could get Mack to perform it. Unless the guy didn't *have* the protocol . . .

A voice crackled in Ben's earpiece. "Guys, there's . . . uh . . . there's something going on out here."

Novak ran to check the monitors. Ben stood and peered through the window.

On the corner, ten feet from where the moving truck was parked, two uniformed NYPD officers were involved in an altercation with a frantic man. The man was screaming, his hands flailing wildly in the general direction of the truck. The cops were moving closer to him, one on either side, their own hands held up in the universal gesture of *calm your ass down, sir.*

"Is that him?" Novak shouted into his headset. "Is that our guy? Somebody get in close and see what he's saying."

"Snipers," Ben added, "get a bead on him and await the order to fire."

In the continuing scuffle, the man took a swing at the cops, which resulted in his being immediately thrown facedown to the ground. One of the officers kneeled on him as he continued to struggle. The other cop quick-tied the man's hands behind his back.

"Somebody confirm!" Novak yelled again. "*Is it fucking him or not?!*"

Ben watched one of their ground agents, a woman dressed in athletic clothing, jog up the sidewalk toward the officers. She slowed slightly as she passed the cops.

"Not our guy," said the voice in Ben's earpiece. "He must be a local nutball. He reeks. One of the officers even knew his name. Eddie, for what it's worth."

"Jesus Christ," Novak muttered. "They're going to scare off our man."

To Ben's and Novak's relief, the cops soon dragged the deranged man away from the truck and shoved him into their squad car.

Novak looked pointedly at Ben. "Twelve minutes."

The pool of dread in Ben's stomach began to deepen into a sinking pit. His eyes actively scanned everything he could see from his vantage point, but nothing—nothing—was happening with the truck.

From off in the distance came the first rumble of thunder from the approaching storm.

38

A ringing phone snapped Mack out of an unintended sleep. She was lying on a couch. She turned over, sending a scrap of paper fluttering from her chest onto the floor.

The phone was still loudly repeating a surf rock guitar riff in the next room. Gabe's ringtone. Mack sat up, momentarily confused to find a wall in front of her. *Oh, right.* Gabe's couch was wedged into the hallway, so he had more space in the living room to lay out all his electronic odds and ends.

Mack reached down and picked up the fallen paper. It was scrawled with the various new spell combinations she was supposed to be practicing as she regained her strength.

The door at the end of the hall opened. Gabe came inside from the garage. His hands were covered in grease, and smudges of oil were streaked across his bare chest and slight beer paunch.

"Good morning, sunshine," he said.

"Hey."

"I'm going to have that Camaro running soon."

"That's good, because your Explorer is a real P.O.S." Mack rolled the stiffness out of her shoulders. "But don't you have anything more important to do?"

"Probably." Gabe laughed, squeezing by Mack down the narrow hallway. The mingled scents of sweat and gasoline trailed behind him. "But you were busy with the protocols and I got anxious about the operation. When I'm anxious I like to take things apart and put them back together."

Gabe slipped into the other room, then reappeared leaning against the doorway. "Restricted number."

"What if it's Ben?"

He shrugged. "If it's important he'll leave a message."

"Gabe! Answer the—"

"Messing with you!" He slid his thumb across the screen to take the call. "Yo," he said into the phone. "Got it . . . Yeah, she's good . . . Okay, I'll let her know. Hey, I found some info about that crash . . . Sure, after you've got your guy, no problem. Good luck."

Gabe hung up.

"It's all in place," he said. "They're waiting for any sign of the Possessor, but so far, nothing."

"He didn't want to talk to me?" As soon as the words were out of her mouth, Mack regretted them. They were stupid and needy.

"He had to run," Gabe said apologetically. "He's glad you're safe and says to stay put. He'll check back in when they've got him."

Stay put and wait. Pathetic. She was the one with the power! And what was she going to use it for? Ben and Novak were going to get a binding spell and she was going to recite it to eliminate magic. Fine, the world was going to hell because of magic—that much was undeniable—but couldn't she do more than just shut it all down?

The Possessor that Ben was trying to trap was using his power to prevent attacks. Couldn't Mack do something like that? She could use her power to help people.

Oh, that's how it's going to be? her inner critic mocked. *You're going to be a superhero now?*

Well, no. That was ridiculous . . . wasn't it?

Mack felt herself sink into the couch once again. She was the most powerful person the entire U.S. government knew of, and because of that she was being forced to do the one thing no one else was able to do—the very same thing that would completely and utterly rob her of all of her power.

Except they *couldn't* actually force her to do it, not if she didn't want to . . .

Gabe was staring at her with concern. Did he understand the enormity of what she was being asked to do, in a way that Ben just didn't seem to get?

"So you found out who the Possessor was who tried to run us down?" Mack asked.

"I think so. I turned up a coroner's report about a middle-aged man who died that same day." Gabe thumbed through his phone until he found the document. "The family's story was that he'd been electrocuted while 'making home repairs,' but he had a serious neck wound in addition to extensive external third-degree burns. Definitely more consistent with the wreck you described."

"A cover-up, then? Someone paid off the coroner to back their story?"

"That's how it smells to me. The guy was actually pretty famous, at least in Scotland. Weird name. Alexavier something-or-other. A gazillionaire investor philanthropist."

Gabe held out his phone, showing Mack a photo from a British magazine of a sharply dressed man with slick, wavy hair and a gray-flecked beard. Why did he look familiar?

A faint metallic *clang* came from the direction of the garage.

Gabe set his phone on the arm of the couch and shot to his feet.

Mack whispered, "What could that be?"

Instead of responding, Gabe slipped into the kitchen, and quickly returned holding a revolver.

"I'm going to find out," he hissed back.

Mack stood to follow him, but Gabe waved her back down to the couch. "It's probably nothing," he said, though his wary expression showed that he didn't believe it. "But if it is something, let me deal with it. I can buy you time to get away. You're too important to risk."

Gabe moved toward the end of the hallway. He cracked open the door that led into the garage and stepped through, the gun held in both hands in front of him.

A minute ticked into two.

Mack was terrified.

She thought about calling out Gabe's name but stopped herself. The last thing she wanted to do was give herself away.

She stood up and mouthed the words to become invisible. Using her magic again was easier, now that she'd had a chance to rest. She still couldn't do it completely without speaking yet, couldn't only *think* the words, but she was close.

Mack moved toward the garage door. She pressed her ear against it and listened, but couldn't hear a sound. Just as she was about to grasp the doorknob, it began to twist. Someone was turning it from the other side.

The door opened, and into the hallway stepped Lucas Adin.

"*Lucas?*"

Mack was so surprised she nearly dropped her intention to stay invisible—but some instinct told her not to remove the safety of that shield.

"At your service," he said with a slight bow. He wore the same tweed vest and tailored charcoal pants he had on when Mack first saw him back in Heaton's office at Livingston College. "Though you realize I cannot see you."

She backed softly down the hallway, putting the couch between them.

"You told me you were coming here, on the phone from Baltimore," Lucas said. "Don't you remember? I came as soon as I could, to help you."

"But . . . what the hell . . . where's Gabe?"

"He wanted to give us a minute to talk."

That was when Mack started to freak out. Something was very wrong.

"So . . . talk," Mack said, trying to control the tremor in her voice.

Lucas's trim beard framed a tight smile. "Conversation is generally easier if we can see one another."

"I'm good like this."

Lucas was blocking both the garage door and the front door. Mack began backing slowly toward the living room. Gabe's phone was still glowing on the couch, and glancing down at it now, Mack could see why the man in the photo had seemed familiar. He was an older version of the man standing before her.

"What's the matter?" Lucas asked. "I apologize if my entrance was a little—"

He stopped. His head turned toward the phone. His face darkened. "Ah, I see," he said.

Lucas took a step toward Mack.

"You have identified my esteemed father," he continued bitterly. "It seems I'll never stop being the great Alexavier Adin's disappointing son."

Mack felt like she'd been dropped in a bath of ice water.

"Your father was driving the car that tried to kill us," she said, cursing her tiny, constricted voice for betraying her fear.

But if that was true, then Lucas had to have recognized his father's car that night. He must have seen the license plate. He must have known . . .

"Yes, the man in that car was my father," Lucas said simply, "and you killed him. No hard feelings on that front. The old man and I weren't exactly on good terms. In point of fact, he always hated me. He even cut off my magical training. *My birthright*. He said I wasn't fit to be a Possessor. I didn't have the 'moral fiber.' This from a man who tried to kill his own son." Lucas sniffed and cleared his throat. "Make no mistake, it was *me* he was trying to kill on that road, you know, not any of you. Not on purpose, anyway." He laughed coldly. "You were incidental."

Mack's thoughts were a jumble, all competing for her attention at once. She grabbed onto the one that seemed most important: Lucas was a Possessor, and Heaton hadn't had the slightest idea. Was Heaton some assignment of his, a Possessor keeping tabs on her explosive research to make sure she didn't get too close to the truth?

Or had Lucas been using the professor for his own reasons: because of her expertise, her knowledge of the world of the Possessors beyond what he could access through his own family, who had cut him off from magic?

Why would Lucas's father try to kill him, unless he saw Lucas as such a threat that he felt he had no choice?

Unless . . . Lucas was actually *Merlin.*

"Your silence tells me two things," Lucas said, staring directly at Mack as though he could see her. A chill electrified her spine. There was something else, too—some searching *presence* in her head. "First, you figured out who I really am. Good for you."

"And second?" Mack whispered.

He smiled. "You're terrified."

39

Mack snatched Gabe's phone from the arm of the couch, causing it to vanish, and rushed down the hallway into the living room. Still invisible, she dove for a corner and crouched behind a pile of large cardboard boxes that had been used to send Gabe's most recent shipment of new tech.

This is stupid, she thought. *I'm invisible. Why am I hiding?*

—Why indeed, Eila?

Lucas was still in the hallway, but his gentle brogue sounded so close.

—You don't need to hide from me.

He wasn't speaking out loud. The voice was coming from inside her own mind. *No, no, no.*

—I released the protocols, but I am not whatever you seem to fear I am.

As long as he stayed in the hallway, Lucas was still blocking both doors. *Where the fuck is Gabe?* What had Lucas done to him?

—Gabe is fine.

Lucas's thought-voice was calm, reassuring. Mack wanted to listen. She wanted him to continue. *That's* not *what I want,* she chided herself. *He's manipulating you! Fight!*

—You won't believe it, but you are the reason I'm doing all of this.

Lucas's footsteps were approaching from down the hall.

—Not you personally, of course. I didn't know you when I uploaded the first spells. I mean people *like* you. Normal people who have had to go through life with little or nothing, for centuries, because a handful of the rich and powerful decided they were still not quite powerful enough for their liking.

The image of Braithwaite's mutilated body flashed through Mack's mind. *Merlin did that. Lucas did that.* And now he was inside her somehow, weakening her. *Why can't I fight back?*

—Eila, what the Possessors did was not right. That's why I started all this. I'm trying to give the power back to people like you, and to stop the people who would prevent that. That is all I want.

Mack still wasn't fully recovered from her trans-Atlantic trip, and the invisibility spell was already draining her. Lucas's voice was so peaceful, she could almost feel it surrounding her like a warm cocoon. It would be so easy to surrender to it, such a relief . . .

—Please, answer me, would you?

Fuck off! Mack thought. Lucas's creeping presence in her skull seemed to recede. Somehow she'd pushed him away.

In the clear space she'd carved out in her mind, Mack prepared herself to fight. Better yet, to run. After all, Lucas had known about his abilities his whole life. He'd been able to practice and train, at least until his father put a stop to it. Aside from the telepathy or whatever he was doing, he might know other spells Mack didn't know and couldn't defend against. In a contest between her raw, undisciplined talent and Adin's honed skill, she wasn't confident she'd come out ahead.

Or stay alive.

—Except I do not want to kill you. Don't you understand that yet?

Lucas entered the living room at the same moment he reentered her mind. Mack peered over the boxes and saw him. He hadn't even bothered to make himself invisible.

No matter how elegant he looks, he's a murderer, she reminded herself. *More than that, he's responsible for all the havoc in the world right now.*

—I know you found Braithwaite's body. I wish you hadn't seen that. I'm truly sorry I couldn't save Desdemona, either. I never imagined you would find Leclerc so quickly, that you would make it to him before I could.

Before you could kill him, you mean, Mack thought. *Or were you actually hoping he'd kill us?*

—I don't want to hurt you.

Mack had heard that particular line of bullshit before. One of Ray's favorites. *Enough of this. Enough, enough, enough!* She dug deep into herself.

"Get the fuck *out of my head*!" Mack wasn't sure if she screamed it out loud or only in her mind, but it had the intended effect.

Lucas groaned and staggered backward, clutching at the doorframe for balance. Every trace of his slinking presence in her consciousness was gone.

But he was still blocking her only path to the hallway and the doors. She could break a window and leave that way, but then she'd still have Lucas to contend with. Of course, she could always throw *him* through the window first, as she had with Ray . . .

Lucas straightened up and shook his head side to side like he was reeling from a punch.

"You *are* powerful," he said, out loud this time. "And you don't know how glad that makes me." The bastard was smiling. "You can do anything you want to me—I won't fight you." He raised both hands in the air. "But if you let me, I will explain the reason why I came here." He raised his eyebrows, waiting. "Okay, good. You're listening."

Just keep talking, asshole. It only gave Mack more time to figure out how to get away. She wanted to use Gabe's phone to call Ben and warn him about Lucas, but she would have to make the phone visible in order to dial the number, and she couldn't risk revealing herself in the process, not now.

"Have you thought about what happens for you, if you go through with this disgraceful plan to bind up magic? Can you imagine what it will feel like—now that you have had a taste of this power—to be without it?"

Like having my legs cut off, Mack thought, surprised at the intensity of her own reaction. *Worse, like losing my identity.* She couldn't have explained it to Ben or Gabe, or even to Heaton. People without her abilities wouldn't understand. Magic wasn't just something she could *do*; it was her self. She *was* magic: it was the surest she'd been about anything in years.

Lucas nodded sympathetically. "Those who don't have your power don't understand," he said. "But I do."

As Lucas took another step into the room, he opened up the narrowest sliver for Mack to sneak by into the hall.

"I know what people like Ben Zolstra say," he went on. "They say that the world is unstable now, that people are dying."

Lucas stepped farther into the room. Mack tried to settle the shaking in her knees and prepare herself to run.

"But is the whole world really your problem? Haven't people always died? If you take magic out of the world, won't they still die? Is this so-called civilization we have built really worth saving—or is it time to try something new?"

With a small gesture, Lucas slid aside the boxes that Mack had been using for cover. At the same moment, she sprinted for the hallway, passing him by less than two feet.

"You don't have to be their pawn in a game that you can only lose."

Mack looked behind her to see Lucas reaching his hand out to where he believed she still was, palm upturned like he meant to help her to her feet. He hadn't sensed her move.

She crept toward the garage door and inched it open.

"Right now, you are alone and scared, but you could come with me, Eila. I can show you how to use your gifts. I can keep you safe. You don't have to let them take your magic away."

Mack froze. *Don't listen to him,* she told herself. *He's only trying to use you.* But weren't Ben and the government trying to use her, too?

Then Mack saw Gabe's body sprawled facedown on the concrete floor of the garage. A scream escaped her throat.

Lucas's head snapped toward her, and he bounded down the hallway in her direction.

Mack ran. She threw open the front door, fled the house, and took off at a sprint.

40

"Four minutes," Novak said, using the back of his hand to wipe a rivulet of sweat from his forehead.

Ben was sweating, too. The window-unit air conditioner in the unfinished Manhattan condo was old and useless. The room was swollen with humidity.

Ben stepped back from the window. He could hardly see anything down in Union Square. The storm, predicted to hit hours later, had rolled in fast and early, in dark torrents.

It was making everything hell. Both snipers radioed in that they were functionally blind. The agents on the ground had to circle the truck closer and more often than was prudent to keep eyes on it.

Novak was bent over the monitors. "Can anybody out there see any fucking thing?" he demanded desperately from no one in particular.

Novak reached into the pocket of his suit coat, which was tossed over the back of a chair. He pulled out a crumpled pack of cigarettes and, after three tries, lit one with trembling fingers. He drew in a deep drag.

"Haven't seen you smoke in years," Ben said.

"We need to abort," Novak said on his exhale.

"We can't." Ben approached him. "Our guy is on his way. We abort now and he'll know it's a trap. There won't be a next time."

"Yeah," Novak retorted, "and if we accidentally blow up Manhattan there won't be a next time, either."

The rain had one positive aspect. It was coming down so hard that pretty much the only people still outside were their own agents. When the Possessor showed up, he'd be easy enough to spot. Invisibility wouldn't help him, either, not with the infrared cameras. They even had an infrared cam mounted inside the truck, in case there was some teleportation protocol that allowed the Possessor to get in without opening the door.

The minutes ticked down with all the slowness of a grinding glacier. Ben paced the length of the space. Novak checked in with the team, which continued to complain about low visibility. Their voices cracked and popped—their comms were getting wet and beginning to short out. None of this was good.

"These comms are shit," Ben said.

Novak nodded absently.

At two minutes, the rain started coming down harder, practically sideways. Through the rain-washed window, the park below had become a drowned Atlantis, the few people were strange fish, the trees were forests of kelp.

"We're aborting," Novak said, anxiety creasing his features. "This is madness."

Ben stared at Novak, hoping to steel the deputy director's resolve with Ben's own. "Don't forget: if we don't hold until the last second, and we miss our chance to get this guy, the madness only gets worse."

"Or we all die." Novak blew a cloud of smoke into Ben's face.

At a minute out, a figure appeared on one of the monitors, moving across the park. He wasn't there, and then he was, like he'd glitched into existence at that moment.

"*Holy shit,*" Novak said.

"It's him," Ben said, his pulse spiking. "That's our guy."

It was a tall man in a long, old-fashioned raincoat with the lapels turned up. He was stooped over, bent against the downpour, clutching at his chest and drawing deep, shuddering breaths. When he'd recovered, he straightened himself and aimed determinedly toward the truck that held the bomb. He seemed not to notice or care that he was now visible.

Ben spoke into his headset. "All right, listen up. The man in the trenchcoat's who we want. Snipers, stand by. Ground team, move in."

41

Kafele Hajjar had always loved New York, the manic city that wanted to be everything at once and so ended up being nothing but itself. The irrepressible hum of its energy—that's why he'd moved his family to Manhattan from Cairo almost four decades earlier, leaving the staid ancient city for the dizzying rush of the vital metropolis. New York City was not only his home but also, as the most powerful Possessor and now sect leader of the entire East Coast, it was his *territory*. He wasn't about to let some godless terrorist cretins destroy it and kill thousands of people in the process. Not while Allah still granted him breath in his lungs.

Hajjar crossed Union Square, his aging shoulders hunched against rain so thick it was like the rivers of heaven had opened in the sky above him. His destination was the truck parked at the opposite corner—the vehicle that he had good reason to suspect held a giant bomb inside it like a hulking, malignant tumor.

He hurried as much as he was still able: in more ways than one, time was not on his side.

Most descendants of the ancient families had long since stopped believing in anything other than their own enrichment, but it hadn't always been that way. Magic had almost destroyed mankind once, long ago, in time out of mind. The first Possessors had been the ones who stopped the rush toward destruction then. The question was: Were there enough remaining who cared to stop it now?

There weren't many old guard Possessors like himself left, Hajjar knew, who still believed in the original nobility of their calling. Men and women who recognized that this monster that had been unleashed was once again their responsibility to tame. No one else stood a chance of controlling the erupting chaos. He had hoped to convince at least some of the other leaders to join him, but after Leclerc was murdered and his estate went up in flames, the few others who had shown any interest in working together took to the winds.

So Hajjar continued alone as he had since this Merlin character had betrayed them all—running himself ragged, stretched much too thin to stop all but the very worst incidents. Like what would have happened in Moscow. Like what was about to happen here if he didn't disarm this device quickly.

As usual, many of the details were fogged with the haze of precognitive uncertainty, but one thing he had seen with crystal clarity was the devastation that was going to take place if he didn't stop this bomb from going off.

Hajjar moved toward the truck with deliberate briskness, which was as fast a gear as he still had left. His running years were well behind him. He would have to leave the matter to trust. Trust in the instincts he'd honed through the decades, trust in his gift of foresight, trust in providence to see him safely through another catastrophe.

The elderly Possessor brought the words of the revealing spell to his mind once again, then directed his intention outward to find the bomb. He felt the spell radiating from him in concentric circles, like ripples from a stone dropped in water. He waited for the bomb's presence to announce itself again, to blip onto his radar. *There.* It was definitely in the truck, then.

He was maybe fifty feet from the truck's rear when his chest attacked him. He gritted his teeth and held on as his heart seized up on itself in a series of violent palpitations. They were getting more frequent. He breathed deeply until the agony subsided, then kept walking. This was Hajjar's calling now—protecting human life, protecting the fruits of human culture and civilization from obliteration at the hands of the barbarians. He hadn't chosen it; the times had chosen him.

42

The hiss of chopped static came over Ben's earpiece, fragments of different voices cutting in nonsensically.

"*Shit*," Novak said. "Did anyone hear the order to move in? Ground team, come back: do you copy the order?"

Ben went to the window and peered out. He spotted the two park agents. Neither had made a move toward the old Possessor.

"Ground team, *move in on the target*," Ben ordered.

The response was more broken static, and faint voices rendered unintelligible by the thundering rain.

Ben ripped off his headset and flung it to the ground. He ran for the door.

"Tell the snipers to use their tranqs as soon as they get a shot," he shouted to Novak.

Then Ben was out the door and bounding down the stairwell, using the railings to propel himself faster. He sprinted across the marble lobby and burst through the glass front doors.

Immediately soaked from head to foot, Ben ran toward the truck. The rain roared like a waterfall. It was no wonder communication had proven impossible.

Ben tore by the ground team, who, failing to recognize him in the blinding rain, gave chase after him.

Up ahead, the man in the trench coat had reached the truck and used a protocol to raise the rear roll-up door.

Ben was grateful that the rain masked his approach as he splashed his way closer. He was maybe ten feet from the man when the Possessor seemed to sense danger. Just as he turned around, one of the snipers' tranq darts hit the man square in the chest. Ben dove for him, catching him as he tumbled from the truck's rear bumper. Ben lowered the Possessor to the concrete.

"Deal with him!" he shouted at the arriving ground agents as he leaped into the truck.

Water was leaking from the truck's roof. Ben pulled open a panel on the side of the device the way Novak's contact had demonstrated. The small compartment that held the control screen had pooled with water, and the display was flickering irregularly. Only seconds remained on the countdown timer. Ben keyed the kill command into the onscreen keyboard, but the display went black on the last keystroke.

The next moment was the longest of Ben's life.

Then the screen flashed back on. The clock had stopped. The device was deactivated.

Ben looked out from the back of the truck. The two agents were restraining a surprisingly old man. As the tranquilizer flooded the Possessor's system, the fight went out of him and his eyes squeezed shut.

Ben stepped out of the truck and back into the storm. He let the heavy, warm rain wash away all the nervous energy built up over the days of planning and waiting. He allowed himself a deep breath.

His gambit had worked. They had their man.

43

Ben and Novak dismissed the agents, then left Manhattan and the storm behind them. The Big Apple remained blissfully ignorant of how close it had come to annihilation.

They ditched the truck at the rest stop outside Philly, after laying the still-unconscious Possessor across the backseat of Novak's sedan. At a text from Novak, the contractor came out of the rest stop, paper cup of coffee in his hand, and climbed into the cab of the truck without a word. Ben and Novak shared a look of relief when the contractor waved a brisk good-bye and drove the monster bomb away. Novak slid behind the wheel of his car, Ben hopped in the passenger seat, and they set off toward Annapolis.

The Possessor's driver's license ID'd him as Kafele Hajjar. It didn't take Ben much internet searching to learn he'd made a fortune in textiles in Egypt before moving to New York and working as his own importer. He'd kept a low profile for decades, despite steadily increasing his wealth and holdings, not an easy thing to do in the fishbowl of monied Manhattan elites.

As they neared Baltimore, Hajjar started to come around.

"He's waking up," Ben informed Novak.

"Well, knock his ass out again. We're not set up to handle him yet."

The deputy director wasn't wrong. They had no idea what Hajjar was capable of, what other protocols he might be able to perform that they couldn't anticipate or counter. They were going into battle with weak intel against an enemy with unknown capabilities. It *would* be better to wait until they had Hajjar back at Gabe's, bound and gagged, with Mack on hand to fight whatever he might throw their way.

Except . . . he didn't look like he was going to make it that far. His skin was sallow and clammy, and his breath came in slow, heaving gulps. Ben touched his fingers to the man's wrist. The pulse was faint and irregular. He was dying. The heart pills they'd found in the pocket of his raincoat confirmed his dire condition.

"I think we need to talk to him now," Ben said.

"Are you nuts?"

"Look at him."

Novak risked a glance behind him. "He looks a little rough," he admitted.

"He's eighty-four years old, he's got an irregular heartbeat, and he's been heavily sedated," Ben said. "And who knows how much the forecasting protocol took out of him."

"He's still more dangerous than the two of us on our best days," Novak countered. "He can do *magic*."

"Look, if he tries anything, I'll put him right back under."

Ben held up the medkit they'd brought, which contained, among other things, a syringe prefilled with another powerful dose of tranquilizer.

Novak groaned. "Was there ever a time when you weren't—?"

"A pain in the ass? You already asked me that."

Novak pulled them off the highway into a truck stop. He found a remote corner of its vast parking lot and stopped the car.

Hajjar continued to stir. His eyes opened into narrow slits.

Ben's phone rang. Gabe was calling, probably for a mission update.

Ben let it go to voice mail. Hajjar was the priority for now; Ben could inform Gabe of their progress later.

"Mr. Hajjar," Ben said, turning again to face him, "you are in the custody of the United States government. Do you understand me?"

Hajjar moaned. He tried to sit up and examine his surroundings, but his head seemed to swim with the effort, and he fell back onto the seat. Ben reached back and helped him into an upright position.

"Am I a criminal," Hajjar asked with a thick slur, "that you should treat me this way?"

"I apologize about the cold welcome," Ben said. "Especially after your attempt to save New York. But you're very important to us, and we weren't sure you'd want to talk if we asked you nicely."

Hajjar's laugh became a wheezing cough before he asked, "Does the United States government ever ask nicely?"

The man's face was etched deep with the wrinkles and folds of decades. There was a dignity to it.

"Mr. Hajjar, we know you belong to an ancient secret order known as the Possessors of Magic."

Hajjar didn't respond, other than to make a slight, wordless murmur. His bloodshot eyes fluttered with exhaustion. Novak and Ben shared a worried look. They were losing him.

"Speaking is going to be tiring for you," Ben told the Possessor, "so I'm going to take your silences as agreement from now on, okay?"

Ben waited for the man's small nod before continuing. "You are a hero, Mr. Hajjar," he said sincerely, "for what you were trying to do. With the forecasting ability you have, you could have just skipped town and saved yourself, but you chose not to."

"It is merely our responsibility." Hajjar's voice was a fragile spiderweb of a sound. "Our duty."

"You've done this before, then?" Novak asked. "Stopped attacks like this?"

"Many times through the years. New York. London. Beirut." He breathed heavily. "Many more."

"I wish your fellow Possessors shared your sense of duty," Ben said.

When Hajjar stayed silent again, Ben continued, "What we need now is for you to do that duty one more time. We need you to take that responsibility you feel and help us. Help us do, once and for all, what you've been trying to do for decades. To stop magic from destroying the world you want to save."

The Possessor fell into a coughing fit, which worsened each time he tried to catch his breath. It was agonizing to watch. When he finally collapsed back onto the seat with an exhausted whimper, he spat out a series of angry swear words in Arabic.

"Do you want to continue in Arabic?" Ben asked the man in his own language.

"English is fine for talking," the man said with a slight shake of his head, "but Arabic, better for curses."

"Who are you cursing?" Ben asked.

Hajjar tried again to laugh, and again it broke and cracked in his throat. "You," he said. "Me. The whole world." He sighed. "I know what you want. You want the finishing words. Yes?"

Ben and Novak exchanged a charged look. This was it.

"Yes."

Novak took out his phone and began recording the old man, waiting for the recitation of the binding protocol.

Hajjar looked pained. "You do not realize what you ask me to do."

"We understand this isn't easy for you," Ben said. "But it's the only way. You know better than anyone that the world is not ready for magic. Not our world. Not like this."

Hajjar brought two quivering fingers to his lips. "Cigarette?" he asked.

Novak's face questioned Ben.

"Why the hell not?" Ben said. "We're not his doctors."

Novak set his phone down to fish out a smoke and light it for Hajjar, who mumbled his thanks.

"These words will be no help," Hajjar croaked, smoke curling from his mouth. "I cannot use them. Even when I was strong, I would not have had enough power. Now . . ." He trailed off.

Now, Ben finished in his mind, *you're minutes from being a warm corpse.*

"We have someone we think can do it," Ben said.

"What you ask of me is a betrayal of everything . . . of everything . . ." Hajjar seemed to drift off, becoming disoriented.

Ben was about to speak and try to bring him back to the point, but Hajjar went on, "And yet we have already betrayed ourselves. Allah knows, our end has been coming for a long time . . ."

Hajjar closed his eyes. He continued to speak, but his words lost any sense, devolving into a series of fractured nonsense syllables. Was the man too old and frail to be of any use to them?

That's when Ben realized what he was hearing.

Hajjar continued to intone: " . . . *ou-dri-ach, dei-ah, jie-bah, ou-kun-mish-tu . . .*"

"Are you getting this?" Ben whispered. He could feel it now, that same uncanny sensation he got when Mack recited her own incantations. "He's giving it to us."

Novak brought his phone closer to the old Possessor's face, capturing Hajjar's utterances as he continued to deliver the lengthy recitation.

After another minute, Hajjar went silent. He raised the cigarette to his lips, inhaled deeply, and let out a long, shuddering exhale.

"Thank you," Ben said.

The Possessor said nothing. His glazed eyes didn't seem to see Ben anymore.

Ben took out his phone. "I'm going to tell the others."

He called Gabe. "We got it," Ben said as soon as the line connected. "We got the—"

"Lucas is Merlin." It was Mack's voice, breathless and tight with fear. "I think Gabe might be dead. *Lucas is here and he's chasing—*"

The call cut out.

Ben dropped his phone. "Drive," he ordered Novak. "Gabe's. Right now."

"What is it?" Novak asked, throwing the car into gear. "What happened?"

Ben's only response was the one word now stuck on repeat in his mind like a sounding alarm.

"Mack."

44

The street Mack was running down dead-ended at the water.
Shit.

She'd dropped Gabe's phone as she ran, but she knew Ben had heard her before they lost contact. Hopefully he was coming—and she'd still be alive when he arrived.

At the marina, there were a few tourist establishments—a café, a bar and grill, a seafood place. All were empty and shuttered up though it was nearly dinner time. Even in this little seaside city, people were afraid to be outside.

There was a police car close by, though, with two officers in it.

Mack abandoned her cover of invisibility and ran toward the car, waving her arms. *Recognize me,* she willed them. *I'm a wanted criminal, right? Come out and get me.* If she could get the cops involved, if they called for backup, they just might keep Lucas busy while Mack got away.

If she was lucky they'd even shoot the motherfucker.

Her magic crackled inside her. *Use me,* it called. She didn't listen. Lucas was too powerful for her, too experienced. Better to run.

The police officers hadn't spotted Mack yet.

She became aware of Lucas's presence, his calm thought-voice worming into her mind.

—The government is going to put you back in a cage.

"You're psychotic!" she screamed, banishing Lucas from her head again.

She reached the cop car and started pounding on the trunk and windows. The startled officers opened their doors.

"You sound like my father!" Lucas shouted aloud.

His father. The thing that had driven Lucas to become Merlin, Mack realized, wasn't some egalitarian wish for a fairer world. That was just self-justification. Really, he was after the ultimate revenge: if his father didn't think Lucas deserved to know magic, he'd stick it to the old man by sharing magic with everyone on the planet. The ultimate *fuck you* to Dad.

The cops scrambled to their feet. They drew their weapons but seemed unsure where to point them—at the crazy lady who'd pounded on their car, or the screaming man coming toward her?

Lucas, less than a hundred feet away now, paid them no attention. "They're going to hand you the binding spell and order you to recite it!" he yelled, slowing from a run to a fast walk. "And it will be *your* decision, Eila Mack! If you do it, it will be you *alone* who kills magic and dooms humanity to a half-existence, when we were meant for so much more!"

The officers leveled their guns at Lucas. The female cop shouted, "Freeze!"

"That will be your legacy!" Lucas continued, still ignoring the police, stalking closer. "Can you live with that?"

He was too close. Mack was going to have to do something.

"Fuck you!" she shouted.

"*Wrong answer!*"

They both unleashed their magic at once. Lucas used his to render himself invisible, while at the same moment Mack used hers to pick

Lucas up and send him flying toward the water. She heard a grunt, followed by a splash as he landed in the harbor.

"You've gotta help me!" Mack said, turning to the officers. "He's fucking insane, and he's *powerful*." She pointed toward where Lucas had gone into the water. "You need to call for backup."

She looked over her shoulder toward the docks. Nothing yet, but she knew Lucas wouldn't be down for long.

"We'll decide what needs to happen here," the male officer said. Mack noticed with a jolt that his gun was now pointed at her. "Put your hands up, slowly, and identify yourself. If you try to use any more magic, we will have to shoot."

Down the harborside path, where Lucas had gone in the water, the twilight was refracted through a disturbance in the air, shining out in little prismatic rainbows. As Mack watched, the anomaly grew in size until it stood as tall as a man.

Lucas had crawled ashore and water was dripping from his still-invisible body.

"Please just—"

Mack pointed toward Lucas's shimmering form.

"Don't you move!" the man shouted at her. Mack obeyed. The cop was jumpy, and she wasn't trying to be another statistic. "Don't fucking move!"

Screw this. She mouthed the words to make herself invisible, and at the same time dropped into a crouch. One of the cops fired a round just over her head. The blast was deafening.

Mack scrambled around to put the patrol car between herself and Lucas. All at once, she felt a scratching against the skin on her arms, her legs. She knew it was *him*, trying to reveal her. She looked down at her forearms. They had become bizarrely mottled—spots of brown skin appeared, floating disconnected in the air above the asphalt street below.

Mack dug deep inside herself and willed her own invisibility spell to become stronger. It was like stoking a fire by blowing on the hot coals, and it worked. The visible parts of her arms disappeared once again. Maybe she *was* more powerful than that murderous Possessor.

She craned her neck up to peek through the bottom of the cruiser's windows. Behind the officers, in the dusky light, Lucas's ghostly outline was advancing on the car.

The woman saw him first. "MacDonald," she said, elbowing her partner. "There he is."

They trained their guns on the bizarre figure.

"*Freeze!*" the man shouted. Mack heard the fear in his voice. "Not another step!"

The response was sudden and shocking in its violence. Lucas, with incredible magical strength, lifted MacDonald into the air and threw him toward the police cruiser headfirst. The officer flew into the car and halfway out the other side, his head shattering both the driver's-side and passenger windows.

Mack dropped back into a tight crouch to avoid the flying glass, then looked up. The cop's split-open head and one tangled arm extended above her through a jagged hole in the window. Blood gushed from his wounds onto the street.

Mack took a deep breath, then dashed up the waterfront. Behind her, the female cop was still screaming at Lucas, but her words were coming out jumbled and incoherent with terror.

There was a snapping sound and the woman's screaming stopped short. The officers were dead.

As Mack ran, she noticed a pain above her left shoulder where it met her neck. She touched the area with her hand, and it came back wet with blood. A lot of it. The window glass had cut her.

She raced past hundreds of boats moored at the marina on her left. On the right was another section of mostly empty stores that once must have thronged with tourists. She whipped around to see if there was any sign of Lucas. There wasn't, yet, but the motion made her woozy. Though she was still invisible, she'd left a line of blood droplets behind her, the substance having turned crimson as it left her body and hit the ground.

Oh, God. He could follow it right to me like a trail of bread crumbs.

She had to get off the street. Mack ran slower now, her stamina waning as she continued to use magic—and as the blood continued to flow out of her.

She stumbled past a convenience store, amazingly still open. The clerk was out for a smoke. The young man stared at Mack, open-mouthed, cigarette dangling from his lower lip.

"Are . . . are you okay?" he sputtered.

With a jolt, Mack realized she'd lost the strength to stay invisible.

Shit. Shit. If Lucas found her like this she was dead.

Mack ignored the kid and pushed forward. Where the hell could she hide? She looked around, fighting panic.

One of the boats. Lucas couldn't possibly look through every single one.

She pressed her hand down hard on her wound to staunch the flowing blood. She ran toward the water, passing the marina's boat-fueling station with its large cylindrical tanks, and up onto the dock. She climbed onto a small sailboat and squeezed under the tarp that covered it. She huddled there, waiting. She tried to listen for Lucas, but her pulse was suddenly way too loud. Even her breath was a thundering wind.

After a minute or so, she risked pulling back the tarp and taking a look for Lucas.

She didn't see him—he must have still been invisible—but she *felt* him out there, in a way she couldn't explain. He felt close. Could he feel her, too?

She slid back down into the boat, her panic immediate and overpowering. Her whole body was like one thumping heart. Her fear mixed itself with rage, and her mind became a red storm, churning in time to her throbbing shoulder. Tears of frustration and pain rolled down her face. Her shallow breathing quickened.

You're powerful, Mack tried to tell herself. *Don't forget that.*

But she wasn't, not now. She was exhausted. Her tongue was thick and useless, as if pinned down. She couldn't form the magic words, couldn't even mouth them.

Focus, for God's sake. You don't need *to say them. Lucas doesn't need to.*

She called to mind her intention to reveal Lucas, and tried to fix it in place while she mentally introduced the associated incantation. But she couldn't hold them in tandem. The pulsing red cloud of her anger and fear either covered her intention, or obscured the words.

That's not good enough. Lucas was an unrepentant killer, and Mack bet—she *knew*—that she was more powerful than he was. She wasn't going to be another one of his victims. She had to pull herself together and fight.

She tried again, closing her eyes and entering the chamber of her mind, shutting everything else off from her awareness. The outside world dropped away. This boat, this city, this danger: gone. She summoned her power.

Mack concentrated only on the words, willing the angular sounds of them to cycle in her mind—again, and again, and again. Having set them cycling, she found she could just let them be, and they'd continue on their own, humming along on a loop in a corner of her mind like a tiny perpetual motion machine. Now she could introduce her intention.

She drew energy into herself, like breathing through her skin, waiting until the tingling of unexpressed magic was so strong her bones ached with it, until its lightning crackled in her mind. Then her eyes snapped open, and she peeked out over the edge of the boat once again. With every ounce of her intention and will she concentrated the magical torrent on Lucas.

It worked. His body shimmered for a moment, then became fully visible. He whipped around in confusion, searching for her. He had stopped near the end of the trail of Mack's blood droplets and didn't know where to go next. He turned toward the docks, his eyes scanning wildly for her, but it was nearly dark now, and there were so many boats bobbing in the waves—she wasn't invisible, he just couldn't find her.

Lucas roared in anger.

Mack tried to hit him again, to throw him as hard as possible against the nearest building. But when Mack sent her intention toward him, he countered it with a defensive spell of his own. It wasn't like in the movies, where some sparking purple lightning flowed out of Mack's hands and slammed into a bolt of snapping green energy that Lucas was shooting out. Magic couldn't be *seen* like that; but it could definitely be felt. Mack experienced his resistance as a wrenching knot in her stomach.

Get away, every instinct told her. *Just run. Run and live.*

She almost did. But then she remembered Braithwaite's battered body—and Gabe's, facedown on the garage floor. If Mack left now, Lucas would keep hurting and killing people, exposing more protocols, stalking Possessors and anyone else who tried to control the anarchy of unbridled magic. Mack was stronger than he was. She could stop him. Other people couldn't, but she could.

She got out of the sailboat and lowered herself onto the dock. She walked toward the shore.

I'm not afraid of you. She directed the thought toward Lucas like a bullet. She wouldn't hide behind invisibility this time. *I'm not a fucking coward and I'm not afraid.*

Lucas flinched, turned, and saw her. A look of disbelief spread across his face, replaced quickly by a wolfish smile.

Mack stepped off the dock and onto the asphalt. She stopped. She and Lucas squared off, facing each other from across a hundred feet of empty waterfront.

Lucas shouted to her, "I know I've done some things that you don't approve of, and I can't take them back."

Mack took a step toward him, then another.

"I don't regret what I've done," he continued, "and deep down, you know I'm right, Eila. It's a shame you won't let yourself admit it."

"You can stop talking." Mack didn't break her stride. "Nobody's listening."

"I think you are. I think you know that magic should be free." Lucas shook his head. "And they're trying to make you kill it."

"Maybe. But I'm gonna kill you first."

A deafening, low-pitched horn pierced the air, from a ship somewhere out in the harbor. It was just enough of a distraction that Mack's focus wavered for a split second.

Something hit her hard and fast from behind, knocking the wind out of her and sending her to her knees. A length of wrought iron fencing, torn out of its foundation from where it had run along the water, had slammed into her. Before Mack could react, the metal wrapped itself around her from head to toe. It began to contract inward from all sides.

Mack couldn't catch her breath. Lucas forced the iron bars to curl in tighter, pinning her arms down. She groaned as the unyielding bars dug into her skin and crushed her. Lucas stood with his arms outstretched, a victorious smirk on his face.

Mack closed her eyes and tried to shut out the agony she felt as the metal continued to constrict her body tighter and tighter, as the last desperate reserve of oxygen was squeezed from her lungs.

She accessed the corner of her mind where the engine for telekinesis still ran hot. She willed it into a higher gear, injecting into it all her anger and panic. She fed it with more and more magical energy—pulled from the air, from the earth beneath her, from the atoms of the iron bars themselves. *Everything* became fuel. When her mind was a single-pointed, white-hot generator, Mack channeled the spell by directing it outward toward the metal fence around her.

The iron screeched as it stretched away from Mack, expanding to the breaking point until it finally burst. Mack filled her empty lungs with a huge breath, as fragments of twisted metal clattered to the ground around her. She stared at her enemy.

This time it was Lucas who turned and ran.

Mack zeroed in on a tree nearby, then mentally took hold of it. With a grunt of effort, she tore it from the ground. For a moment she held it there with her mind, suspended in the air, as giant clumps of earth dropped from its roots onto the ground.

She upturned the tree so that its roots pointed skyward, then hurled it toward Lucas, bringing it straight down on top of him as he ran. There was a loud snapping of branches as the tree top was driven hard into the pavement.

Lucas was still alive. Mack could just make him out through the canopy of leaves, pinned down in a half-crouch beneath a tangle of branches. In the near-darkness, she couldn't see the extent of his injuries.

Suddenly Lucas's hand shot out, and a long broken branch came flying like an arrow toward Mack's head. She waved it aside and moved toward the tree. Another branch emerged from the thicket of canopy. It flew at her, sharp on the end like a spear. Again, Mack's hand swept the projectile easily off its course.

"I'm stronger than you," she said, feeling triumphant.

And she believed it. Until Lucas's next branch struck its real target: the largest gas tank of the boat fueling station behind her.

The tremendous explosion knocked Mack off her feet, spun her around, and flung her onto the asphalt. Her skull cracked against the ground, and her vision swam with bright, flashing dots. She tried to raise her head, but the wave of dizziness and nausea that crashed over her made her lie flat again.

A chorus of sirens wailed in the night, getting closer. Mack rolled onto her side.

From where she lay on the ground, she watched Lucas crawl out from beneath the tree and stumble in her direction. She tried to concentrate. Where was the magic in her mind? Why couldn't she access it? Her head spun, and her ears rang from the concussive blast of the explosion.

An image of Nathaniel flashed before her mind's eye, smiling in his cap and gown, strutting across the auditorium stage on graduation day. Then she saw Heaton, the old professor's eyes wide with glee as she took in Leclerc's vast library—the realization of a life's pursuit of magical knowledge . . .

Focus! Lucas was closer now. He was limping, and his face was scratched and bloody, but he knew she was incapacitated. *Come on, goddammit!*

Mack dug deeper. There it was, her magic—that humming generator. Now for the intention . . .

But Lucas was on top of her. His knees pinned her arms to the ground as his hands clamped around her throat. Mack's mind went blank with terror. She was going to die.

Somewhere nearby a gun fired.

Lucas screamed and jolted upright, his back arching. His face contorted in a grimace of pain.

There was another shot, even closer.

Lucas's body shook again. For a moment, his grip on Mack's throat grew tighter. Darkness edged her vision. Lucas's wrathful face was the last thing she would ever see.

Then Lucas's own eyes clouded, and he fell to the side, his hands finally releasing Mack's neck.

She drew a gasping breath and looked in the direction the shots had come from, just in time to see Ben toss his pistol aside and run the last dozen feet to her. He dropped onto the ground next to Mack.

"You made it." Her voice was barely a croak.

Ben put his arm around her and pulled her close. Mack closed her eyes and squeezed him with the tiny bit of strength she had left, until everything went black.

45

B en watched Mack enter the conference room of Langley's magic HQ. She moved slowly, injured and still unsteady from the previous night's battle. Ben's feelings of gratitude and admiration for her were as intense as any he'd ever experienced. Single-handedly, Mack had taken on an exceptionally dangerous psychopath. Ben didn't want to think about what would have happened if he hadn't arrived when he did.

He had gone to the hospital with her after the showdown that left Lucas dead and Mack badly depleted. By the time the doctors were finished and he was allowed to see her again, she was fast asleep.

When Novak approached and informed Ben that Gabe, too, had been brought into the ER—unconscious, with a severe head wound, but alive and expected to recover—Ben could hardly believe the relief he felt. His asset, his *friend,* had also survived the encounter with an angry young man who'd called himself Merlin.

Ben spent the night in a chair by Mack's bed, but sleep didn't come for him. Though Merlin had been eliminated, the mission wasn't finished.

Novak had wanted Mack to perform the binding spell the very second they'd found her there, bleeding and half-mad from exhaustion on the ground next to the smoldering ruins of an exploded boathouse. Ben wouldn't allow it. He understood the urgency—every hour they waited was another hour when the chaos of free magic reigned in the world—but a spell as monumental as that? For all they knew, it would kill her. They agreed to wait until morning.

There was another reason for haste: the situation with Harris was unraveling fast. It had been over a full day since they had left him at the safe house with Agent Stevens. People were beginning to ask why the director wasn't responding to calls, texts, or emails. The sooner Mack performed the binding spell, the sooner Ben and Novak could show Harris they'd been right to team up, and let the director go.

Novak was confident that Harris would keep quiet about his temporary imprisonment—provided they completed the mission and gave the director all the credit for its success. The only thing Harris loved more than punishing bad guys was *himself,* Novak assured Ben. As long as the director was lauded as the hero who saved the world from its spiral into pandemonium, he'd leave them alone. Besides, being bested by a group of rogue subordinates would stain his carefully cultivated reputation. *Fine,* Ben thought, *let the asshole have his glory.* Ben was an intelligence operative; the last thing he'd ever been interested in was public recognition.

Mack flashed a quick smile at Ben as she joined him in the empty conference room. Her head was bandaged, and thick gauze covered the wound near her shoulder. Her face and arms were a topographical map of cuts, scrapes, and bruises. Yet somehow she was still radiant, her brown eyes bright and present.

Ben smiled back, shaking his head in wonder. He stood and went to her.

"You didn't have to get up," Mack said.

He ran his hand across the side of her loosely braided hair. Up close, the extent of Mack's wounds was more pronounced. Ben winced to see them.

"He did a number on you."

She shrugged. "It doesn't matter now. I'm still here."

"And all of this is almost over."

Mack smiled thinly, then slid into one of the leather chairs around the table.

Novak blew into the room, flanked by Agent Walters and the young Agent Thompson, whom Ben remembered from his feeble demonstration at the White House briefing. That felt like years ago, though just over a week had passed. Everyone but Novak sat. His performance was about to begin.

"Well," Novak said, looking from Ben to Mack, "here we are. You two have broken dozens of national and international laws, and—just so we're all *crystal* clear—I have every right to lock you both in a black box so deep underground that neither of you would ever see the light of day again."

Ben tried not to smile. Novak was really laying it on thick for the other agents.

"But the president would rather I didn't do that. As a matter of fact"—his look changed to one of grudging respect—"I'm not inclined to do so myself, either." He smiled. "Now let's finish this fucking mission, shall we?"

Novak produced his cell phone and set it on the table in front them.

"We believe," he continued, "that these words are, in fact, the binding protocol that we've been looking for. But so far no one here has been able to make it work—"

"Yeah, yeah, I know," Mack said. "That's where I come in."

Novak leaned over and tapped his phone to play the audio.

Kafele Hajjar's voice came rasping through the device's speakers.

"*Ou-dri-ach, dei-ah, jie-bah, ou-kun-mish-tu . . .*"

Hajjar was dead. Ben found the old Possessor's body when they returned to Novak's car after the showdown on the waterfront, his heart finally having succumbed to its chronic disease. Hajjar's sole living relative, an estranged daughter with her own family in Connecticut, had been notified that her father died a hero. His body was being returned to her. The voice that reached Ben and the others now, reciting the ancient incantation, came from beyond the grave.

The syllables of the timeless words tumbled and rolled over one another, sounding less and less like human utterance as Hajjar repeated them. For some reason Ben was reminded of the cascading fall of rocks at a landslide.

" . . . *ab-beh, mu-un-ah-guhl, kah-la-ah-mu* . . ."

Hajjar continued his solemn intonation for another minute, repeating the same sequence of words several times. When he finally stopped, Thompson reached into a folder he'd brought and slid a sheet of paper over to Mack.

"This is a transliteration of the sounds into English letters," he told her. "It might help."

When Mack didn't respond, Novak restarted the audio. Once again, Hajjar's haunting pronouncements filled the room. About halfway through, Mack abruptly stood up and left.

"Where is she going?" Walters demanded.

"I'm on it," Ben said, standing.

He found her in the hallway, leaning against the wall with her arms folded.

"I can't do it," Mack said as Ben approached her. "It's not right."

"I know this is difficult . . ."

"It's not 'difficult,'" she said indignantly. "It's *wrong*. And we don't have to do it. We're just not . . . thinking hard enough. There's got to be a different way."

Except there isn't, Ben thought. He bit his tongue.

"Look," Mack went on, "Lucas said something to me last night. He said that, if I do this, I'll be the one who kills magic, and . . ." She closed her eyes, as if trying to remember the exact words. ". . . and 'dooms humanity to a half-existence.'" Mack looked imploringly at Ben. "That's on *me,* do you understand?"

Ben nodded. "I think I do, a little bit. It's a huge responsibility. And you're right. Magic could be wonderful. It isn't right that the Possessors kept it to themselves for so long. If regular people in the past had access to this kind of power, we might be living in a very different world. Probably a better one."

"You don't really believe that, though. All you can see is its potential for evil. That's why you want to end it."

Ben shook his head. "You didn't get to meet him, but this Possessor, Hajjar—the one who gave us the protocol—he was a good man. He traveled all over the world, trying to stop the worst attacks before they happened. He was old and in bad health. But he kept going. He made that sacrifice."

Mack sighed. "What's your point, Ben? That I'm not self-sacrificial enough?"

"No, my point is . . . we didn't have to press Hajjar to give us the binding protocol. We didn't threaten him or hurt him. He just gave it up, because he knew the time had come. The world we live in is already crazy, dangerous, divided—and then Lucas releases *magic* into it?" Ben stared at her, willing her to understand. "Hajjar knew he couldn't stop all the terrible things that were going to happen. He knew they would only get worse. He didn't want that on his conscience."

Ben took Mack's hand in his own. "Hajjar knew that for the first time ever, we actually have the chance to close Pandora's box. He wanted us to take it."

Mack covered her face with her hands and groaned.

"You're not dooming humanity," Ben said softly, "you're preserving it."

Mack lowered her arms. "But . . . what about me?"

"What do you mean?"

"What do I *mean*?" Her voice rose in frustration. "I mean I'm *powerful*, Ben. I am strong and capable beyond my wildest dreams. You're asking me to give all that up and go back to being a nobody. Don't you get that?"

Ben looked into Mack's pleading eyes. "You're right," he said. "You are powerful. But your power isn't magic. Your power is *you*, it's the person that you are."

"I want to believe you. You're saying all the right words. But I'm *not* powerful. If I do this, what happens to me?" Mack's chin dropped to her chest and her voice went soft. "Before I discovered magic, I thought about taking a drink almost every minute of the day. But now so much of the craving is gone. It's like magic is . . . filling this space inside me, this need, that I used to fill with alcohol. What happens when it's gone?" She looked up at Ben, stricken. "What do I do then?"

You come and live with me, Ben wanted to say. *We leave the world behind, fill the family farmhouse with kids, and grow old together.*

He said none of it. That life would have been a lie for both of them. They each wanted more.

"Lucas asked if you could live with yourself if you do this," Ben finally said. "But that's the wrong question. The right question is, can you live with yourself if you *don't*?"

Mack looked away and took a deep breath. Without another word, she turned and walked back into the rooms of the command center.

Ben followed her into the conference room. He sat; she didn't. She took Thompson's sheet of paper from the table.

"Should I play the audio again?" Thompson asked.

Mack shook her head. "I got it."

She cleared her throat, and began.

"*Ou-dri-ach, dei-ah, jie-bah, ou-kun-mish-tu . . .*"

Mack's voice, like Hajjar's before, quickly became low and uninflected as she recited the ancient words. There was a dryness in them, like wind-blown sand.

"... *ab-beh, mu-un-ah-guhl, kah-la-ah-mu* ..."

Mack's eyelids fluttered, then closed, but she continued to speak the words. The incantation had somehow moved inside her. Her arms opened and began, involuntarily it seemed, to spread wide.

She repeated, "*Ou-dri-ach, dei-ah, jie-bah, ou-kun-mish-tu* ..."

The overhead lights flickered. Ben went cold, like all the heat in his body had been sapped away at once by an unseen force. Ben glanced at Novak and his agents, who were also shivering, their frozen faces a mix of confusion and terror.

Ben turned back to Mack. She had left the ground and was floating a foot off the floor, arms outstretched, head thrown back.

A frigid wind picked up, sweeping through the conference room. The chill bit at Ben's skin. Tendrils of fast-growing frost crawled across the surface of the glass dividing wall.

Mack's lips had stopped moving, yet Ben could somehow still hear the words repeating, darkly casting their primeval spell.

In the flickering light, Ben noted with horror that Mack no longer looked like herself. The structure of her face had changed, *was* changing, her features shifting, rearranging—her eye and nose shape, cheekbones, forehead, all undulating grotesquely. At the same time her hair, too, was changing color, becoming shorter, longer, straighter, curlier.

What the fuck was happening?

The wind grew hot. Thick, almost viscous blasts of superheated air burned at Ben and the others. No one dared move.

The frost melted. The glass wall spidered with cracks, then shattered.

The lights went out.

Mack screamed—a sound so full of pain and anguish that Ben shuddered to hear it.

The darkness and silence that followed seemed to last forever.

When the lights pinged back on, Mack lay flat on her back on the floor, unmoving.

"Oh, my God," Walters said. "Is she all right?"

Ben ran to Mack and kneeled next to her. "Mack? *Mack?*"

No no no.

Walters was already calling the paramedics.

Ben bent over Mack and took her in his arms like he had the night before, pressing her to his chest. The spell had killed her. It had been too much to ask her to take on in her weakened state. He felt for a pulse on her neck . . . waited . . . waited . . .

"*Come on.*"

Finally, a heartbeat. Faint, but there. Then, an eternity later, another. Ben tightened his hold—as though he, who had proven so hopeless at doing magic, might now have the power to channel life back into Mack.

"*Please* come back," he begged.

Novak, Walters, and Thompson stood over them, the looks on their faces fixed somewhere between shock and disbelief.

Mack took in a shuddering breath. She curled into the fetal position and started shaking and coughing violently.

"It's okay," Ben said, putting a hand on her back. "You're okay."

She's alive. Joy—pure, exuberant joy—coursed through Ben. He helped Mack sit up when she was ready and offered her a bottle of water. She downed half of it in seconds.

"How do you feel?" Ben asked.

"Like someone tore my guts out with a pitchfork," Mack rasped. She lifted herself into a chair.

Novak cleared his throat, opened his mouth, tried to speak and couldn't. His face was still bleached white with fear, though color was slowly returning to his cheeks. He looked to Walters, who only shook his head like he was trying to chase away a bad dream.

"So," Mack asked Ben faintly, "did it work or not?"

Thompson's skin was still puckered with goose bumps, despite also being covered in a sheen of sweat. "I can . . . uh . . . try to do something . . . ?" he offered.

Ben nodded for him to go ahead.

Thompson leaned forward and squinted at Novak's phone. He recited the protocol for levitation. When nothing happened, he did it again.

Thompson shook his head and fell back into a chair. "I . . . I can't. I can't feel anything anymore."

Ben and Mack shared a look. They'd finished the mission. Together.

Novak finally found his voice. "I'll be damned," he said. "It actually worked."

As it dawned on the members of the CIA team that it was over, that the mission which had consumed their days and nights had really ended, they slowly emerged from beneath the unsettling pall the ancient spell had cast over the room. Though wariness lingered in their eyes—betraying the fear that one last unearthly trick might still be in store—tentative smiles gave way to pats on the back and handshakes.

"If you'll excuse me," Novak said, "I need to call the president."

On his way out the door, he stopped and took Mack's hand. "That was remarkable."

Mack barely acknowledged him. Novak and the others left the room. A moment later, a cheer went up from the rest of the agents in the command center next door as the news was relayed: they'd done it.

46

Ben stayed behind with Mack, who remained seated, with her gaze fixed on the floor.

He sat in the chair next to her. "Are you okay?"

"I don't know," she said. "I feel like I need to sleep for a thousand years."

Ben bent over in his chair and looked up into her downcast eyes.

"Listen," he began, "maybe this is as good a time as any to say something I've been wanting to say for a while."

She held up a hand. "Don't say anything."

"Please, I'm a man," Ben said, forcing a grin. "If I don't talk about my feelings they'll just pile on top of me until I need to go blow something up."

A hint of a smile appeared on Mack's face. That was enough. He pressed on.

"I just wanted to say that . . . I left the CIA because . . ." Ben let out a deep breath. This wasn't easy. He touched his brother's ring. *A little help here, John?*

"It was for a lot of reasons, I guess," he finally said. "But a big one was I wanted to do everything my own way, you know? I stopped being able to trust anybody. This mission started out the same way.

I thought everyone around me was an unnecessary distraction just slowing me down. I thought I could do this alone. But . . . I couldn't."

Ben reached out and held Mack's hand.

"I couldn't do it alone," he repeated more forcefully. "I needed Gabe and Klippman. I wouldn't have gotten *anywhere* without Professor Heaton. Without Hajjar . . . I mean, shit," he laughed. "I even ended up needing Novak, the whole CIA, and a truck bomb to find one old Possessor."

He squeezed Mack's hand.

"But most of all what I needed was *you*, Eila," he said. "We couldn't have gotten Lucas if you hadn't held on and fought him so hard. We couldn't have used the binding spell."

Ben ran his hand up Mack's arm and lightly held her bruised face.

"I needed you more than I ever thought I'd need anyone," he said. "I still do."

He leaned in closer, seeking an answer for his unasked question. *Do you need me, too?*

Mack raised her head. She brought her fingers to Ben's stubbled jaw. She kissed him. It was soft yet urgent, and fleeting. A moment later she stood and stepped away from the table. Ben's hand fell from her face. Something about the gesture made his stomach plummet right along with it.

"Eila—"

Mack silenced him with another kiss. This one was tight-lipped. A dismissal.

When she pulled away, she couldn't look at him. "Thank you for everything. But my life . . . I'm not in a place . . ."

"What are you going to do?" Ben asked.

"I spoke to a friend earlier this morning, a woman I used to work with at the hospital in Cincinnati. She's going to let me crash with her for a while until I get back on my feet."

"Can I call you?"

Mack smiled sadly. "I don't have a phone, remember? I don't really have . . . anything."

Ben tore the corner from a piece of paper on the table and scribbled on it. "Well, here's my number. Use it anytime. For anything."

Mack took the paper, holding Ben's hand for just a moment longer than was necessary. Then she walked out of the conference room, gliding through the crowd of celebrating agents almost as though she were invisible.

Agent Walters leaned into the room. "Where does she think she's going? She needs to be thoroughly debriefed. We have to write up a full—"

"Let her go," Ben said. "She's been through a lot. We'll follow up soon."

Mack slipped through the main door and was gone.

This isn't over, Ben told himself. *She just needs to figure some things out.* He didn't totally disbelieve it.

In the meantime, he had his own decision to make. That morning, Novak had been making noises about bringing Ben back into the fold as the head of a field office in the Middle East. There was an opening in Beirut that was his if he wanted it. He would answer directly to Novak.

Ben thought of his family's farm in Vermont, of storm-damaged barns and rutted dirt roads, of his mother sipping a beer on the front porch . . .

Novak peeked his head back into the conference room where Ben now stood, alone.

"Let's go, Zolstra," he said. "The president's waiting for us."

EPILOGUE

The numbers on the pump climbed steadily higher as Mack's truck filled with gas. She'd bought the used pickup with her first paycheck back at the hospital. It was a rusty old beater of a thing, and she was sure it would cause her any number of headaches in the months and years to come—if it even made it that long. But Mack loved it. It was hers.

Libby was staring at her through the back window, her wet little nose pressed against the glass. The brown-and-white puppy yipped in excitement when Mack looked at her. Adopting Libby had been an impulse, but it was the best decision Mack had made in years. Luckily, Mack's friend Karen already had her own dog, and she didn't mind another creature running around the house.

For now, Mack and Libby spent the nights curled up together on Karen's guest bed, but they'd have their own place soon. Two more paychecks. Maybe she'd give Ben a call then, just to say hi, see how he was doing. It had been over a month since the morning she'd performed the binding spell.

The pump handle jerked in Mack's hand as the tank topped off. She hung up the handle and screwed the tank cap on. She looked up at the blue sky of the cool September Saturday. Libby barked her impatience; the puppy was going to love her first trip into the woods.

Mack opened the door to the cab and prepared to hop in but stopped when she heard a loud screeching of tires. A brown sedan zoomed off the road and slammed to a hard stop in front of the gas station.

The driver was alone, and he jumped determinedly out of the vehicle. He wore work boots, dirty jeans, and a jean jacket. His blond hair was pulled back in a tight ponytail. He eyed Mack through jittery, red eyes but quickly seemed to decide she wasn't worth bothering with. He reached through his back window and grabbed a shotgun, then entered the gas station. He blasted a shell into the ceiling.

Through the windows, Mack watched the few customers in the minimart as they either hit the deck or tried to flee. The man used the butt of the gun to viciously swat down a teenager headed for the door.

It was all happening so fast that Mack barely had time to process what she was seeing. The man pumped the shotgun and waved it in the face of the clerk behind the counter. Near the back of the store, a little girl with her hair in tight rows of braids peeked out from behind a shelf, her face haunted with fear. As the girl tried to see what the bad man was up to, her hand knocked a can of peanuts from the shelf.

The can hit the ground. The crazed gunman wheeled around, shotgun pointed in front of him. His finger was on the trigger.

No! Mack reached her hands out toward the man. *Oh, God, no!*

The gun didn't fire. The man was no longer holding it. Instead, the weapon rocketed from his grip, skittering across the floor, just out of his reach. One of the customers, a heavyset man in his forties, used the opportunity to tackle the gunman and knock him to the ground. Another customer and the clerk joined in to hold the flailing man down.

The adult customers were still too busy wrestling with the assailant to notice Mack, but the little girl wasn't. She tottered to the window in her pink church dress, bright barrettes in her braids. The girl looked out at Mack with her mouth agape. Mack held a finger to her lips. *Shhh.* The girl smiled.

Mack winked at her, then scrambled into her truck and drove off. The miles rolled out behind her.

I still have it. No one else does . . . but I do.

Heaton had been right that magic was a kind of natural force. How stupid that they thought they could ever get rid of it entirely. It would have been as impossible as abolishing gravity.

A few days after the binding at Langley, Mack had tried to perform the telekinesis spell, just to see if it would work. When it *did*, that's when she understood the reality of what she had done: she hadn't bound up all magic and eliminated it from the world. She had taken the world's magic . . . and bound it to *herself.*

Mack had become the sole Possessor of Magic.

Her heart thrilled with that knowledge, even as her mind still burned with questions. What did this mean for her life? For the world? Today was the first time she'd used her secret power in public. Would she do it again?

In the passenger seat, Libby yipped and wagged her tail happily.

"Your mommy's really powerful," Mack singsonged, reaching over to scratch the puppy's velvet ears. "What do you think about that?"

Libby barked delightedly. Mack laughed.

She knew she would have to make some hard decisions about how she wanted to use this gift, but they could wait. She needed time to think, and Saturdays were not made for thinking.

She clicked on the radio. A sad, old love song brought Ben back into her mind. Yeah, she'd give him a call soon. Why not?

The song finished and the next one began. A remix of another oldie-but-goodie. Mack cranked up the volume and sang along at the top of her lungs:

"Well, you don't know what we can find. Why don't you come with me, little girl, on a magic carpet ride?"